Nathan Baylet

Passion
or
Pancakes

Book 1 in Nathan Baylet's Marina Rom-Com Series

NATHAN BAYLET

ISBN 978-1-959920-00-7 (paperback)
ISBN 978-1-959920-01-4 (ebook)

Editor : Erin Brown
Proofreading : Sara Fargo
Book cover creation : Nick Castle
Typesetting : Sabrina Milazzo
Map : Candace Rose Rardon

www.nathanbaylet.com

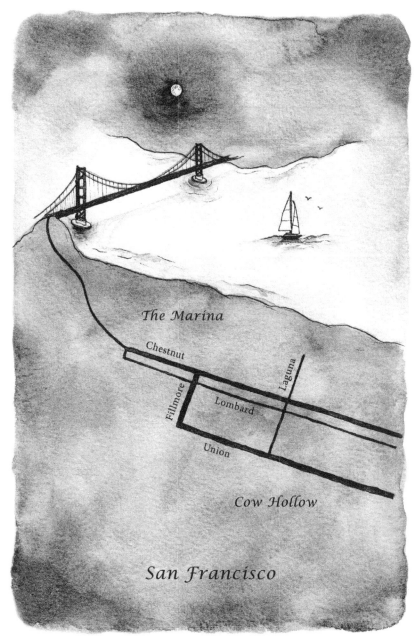

The Marina

Chestnut

Fillmore

Lombard

Laguna

Union

Cow Hollow

San Francisco

Map illustration by Candace Rose Rardon.

Author's Notes:

This novel is intended to be a prequel to the other upcoming romantic, fun novels in my Marina Rom-Com Series.

The first draft of this novel was shorter, 99% dialogue, and from all the characters' different points of view. I thank my super-wise editor Erin Brown for challenging me to make this novel simpler, fuller, and awesomer!

Thanks to family, friends, Erin Brown, Sara Fargo, Nick Castle, Candace Rose Rardon, Sabrina Milazzo, Bryan Wasetis for their help, advice, and talent on this project, and thanks to Reedsy (for connecting me with so many helpful, talented contributors).

Thanks to Silver Cloud for letting me set chapter 8 in their amazing karaoke bar/restaurant.

I had oodles of fun living in the Cow Hollow / Marina district of San Francisco. I hope you have a hoot too experiencing it's hoopla through these pages.

Each character in this nutty novel is a unique, fictional individual and is not intended to represent any group or community.

Super thanks to Sara Fargo for her brilliant narration of the audiobook of Passion or Pancakes – available at audible.com.

Thanks to you for reading my first novel!

Nathan Baylet

June 22, 2013
Saturday night
San Francisco

Chapter 1

KRIS DANCED her bathrobed body around the steamy bathroom to P!NK's "So What," rockin' her spirit into hot tingles for tonight's barhopping extravaganza! Swinging her long hair! Singing into her hairbrush! Flinging her arms – *clang* – knocking down her hanging plant.

"Holy dingle balls! I'm sorry, baby."

Scooping up Frank the Ficus, Kris marched his floppy leaves into the apartment's cozy, second floor living room, past Bren's head buried in a book.

"Everything going okay in there?" Bren asked without looking up.

"Suuuupertastic." Kris parked Frank in their sink with a clunk and danced back.

"We don't put plants in the kitchen sink," Bren reminded.

Kris rolled her eyes and body around, sticking her tongue out at Bren.

"I hear you sticking your tongue out at me."

Kris laughed. She picked up Frank and gently carried him across the hardwood floor of their earthy-tan place made happy with colorful furniture and their year-'round plastic Christmas tree prettied with penis key-chains. She swung open their wooden backdoor and found Frank a safer home next to Sunny the Sunflower and Fern the Fern in her glorious collection of plants foresting the big patio under the maroon twilight sky. "This is Frank everyone," she announced. "He likes weekly watering, dance music and watching me take showers, the little perv. Now make him feel welcome or I'll kick your potted asses."

She sensed all her lovelies warmly welcome Frank in their secret, silent plant language and she smiled big at this affectionate family she had created, feeling the flow of oxytocin release from her head's hypothalamus and fill her bod with gooey closeness. Good times.

Cool wood was under her bare feet, fresh ocean air in her lungs, but boring, brown three-story buildings surrounded her and blocked the sunset and moonrise. She looked up to the big balcony above and fantasized about Madeline switching apartments with her and Bren so they could move up to the top apartment and get more sunlight for her leafy babies, and every night watch the sun slip down behind the distant Golden Gate Bridge with bowl-sized margaritas, and awe at the blue bay fading into a glitter of gliding, lit sailboats. Though she'd need an ass-ton of more clients to afford that view. Still more of climbing up life's ladder to do. But not tonight.

"Have a good night, my sweeties. I love you all. And if I throw up on you later don't take it personal." Kris marched back into the warm apartment, locked the door, and danced back toward her bathroom party while Bren still sat like a boring librarian at their round, wooden kitchen table. "Hey, book-nerd, get your butt up and come hang with me."

"Hey, slowpoke, hurry up and let's go."

Kris grabbed Bren's book. "Come over here and get it before I accidentally wrinkle a page."

Bren's eyes flew wide.

Kris laughed and danced back into Club Bathroom to Britney Spears's "Outrageous." Brit's sexy beat triggered memories of dancing with grungy dudes to this song at smoky, South SF parties ten years ago – nervous, naïve, but finally free of her crazy-restrictive parents. Holy ass fuzz, *ten* years. Where'd the time go? And what ever happened to her torn up sneakers? She looked over at her pile of spendy shoes by the front door, below all her marathon certificates and fitness trophies, by the fridge plastered with pictures of friends, fun times, and hotter dudes than her early SF days. Only a little space was left for more pics. She tensed. *Gonna need another fridge.*

Bren clacked into view.

Kris knew Bren could never rationalize another fridge, or another picture-plastered bathroom mirror, or pictures on walls without frames. What next then? Bulletin boards? Mobiles? Ooo, maybe they could hang picture mobiles from the ceiling and –

Bren plucked her book back. "Oh my fricking gosh, enough dawdling."

3

Kris smiled big and bumped hips to her bestie's black mini-dress. "I'm not dawdling. I'm dancing."

"Stop dancing and get ready."

"Stop reading and hang out with me." Kris snatched back the book and tossed it onto Bren's crazy-clean side of the bathroom counter.

Bren leaned against the doorframe, her perfect pink nails *tap-tap-tapping* the wood. "I like reading romance before going out; it gets me in the mood to go out."

"Talking with you and dancing gets me in the mood to go out," Kris said.

"Get in the mood to hurry," Bren said as she leaned toward their mirror, eyeing her semi-long locks. Then she pointed at Clark the Clock. "It's almost nine. I don't wanna celebrate seven years as roommates in our bathroom."

"And celebrate the Giants finally beating the Marlins."

"Those two things are probably equal for you."

"Of course not. The Giants winning is the cherry on top of our sundae."

"Sunday is when you'll finally be ready," Bren said. "I'll be eating breakfast when you finally bounce out and say, 'Let's go.'"

"Hmm, breakfast sounds good."

"That's what you got from that?"

"I want pancakes," Kris said.

"That's your unhealthy food for this week?"

"Yep."

"We just ate poached salmon and the zucchini foo foo thing."

4

"My dancing burned it off," Kris said, dropping the brush for her blush as she spotted Bren's sexy book cover of a woman's legs wrapped around a suited man. "You're reading *Wallbanger* again??"

"I love *Wallbanger*. The wit, the fun, the passion."

"Forget books," Kris said. "We'll go get real guys and real life passion."

"Real life guys are never as good as in books."

"No guy could live up to your fictional expectations," Kris said, smearing on her blush.

Bren smiled. "And your expectations are too low."

"They are on Saturday night," Kris said. "But I have a feeling tonight we're gonna find passion."

"You think so?"

"If not we'll go get pancakes."

"Hot stuff either way."

Kris laughed. "Totally."

Justin Timberlake started singing, "Dick In A Box."

Kris's smile wilted.

Bren's hands scrambled toward Kris's phone and changed the song to some jazz crap.

Too late. Heartache filled Kris's chest.

"No no no," Bren said. "It's been almost 3 months. You are *over* that jackass."

Kris sniffled. "David used to put his dick in a box for me."

Bren nodded. "And what a delight to find that box left on my bed."

5

"Yeah, sorry about that." Kris chuckled.

"There's the smile I love," Bren said, clutching onto Kris's arms. "Remember, you're ten feet tall."

Kris straightened. "I am."

"And you're gonna find a new guy who won't walk around here in his tighty-whities."

Kris grinned, feeling sadness slowly sink back down, like Godzilla going back in the deep.

Bren let go. "But we can only find you a new guy if you get out of this stupid bathroom."

Kris smiled again. Cheesy saxophone tooted, as she marched to Tommy the Toilet.

Bren sighed. "Let's go.

"I gotta go before we go."

"Go quickly or we're not getting passion *or* pancakes."

"I'm going as quick as it goes."

"I'm getting that dick song off your playlist," Bren said.

"And get this elevator jazz outta here."

Bren boogied her booty to it. "No. It'll motivate *you* to get outta here."

"Bitch."

"Bug-eater."

Kris laughed. "Cricket powder is great protein."

"It's frickin' gross."

Kris looked at her friend and smiled. Bren's little black party dress was so cute. The back's mesh cutout showcased her taut shoulder blades. *Excellent.* The new fitness routine she had Bren on was totally toning up her favorite client, further sculpting her from pretty good to head-turning *wow*, and it was a kick to see Bren going out more and slowly getting comfy with showing a little more skin. Her tight, sleeveless clubwear looked fun and flirty, yet stylish and smart, and this saxophone crap was *maddening*. Kris saw Bren's reminder note on the wall: "Please flush."

Flush.

Kris bumped Bren's bod outta the way and blasted Jessie J's "Domino." *So much better.* Fun, sexy beat, beside her sweet friend. Bren and Jessie J were goddamn angels.

Bren leaned against their doorframe. "Today I read that there's only like 2,000 yellow-crested cockatoos left in the world."

"What?"

"It's a really pretty parrot, and it's super endangered."

Kris shook her head. "Bunny, it's Saturday night. Time for fun. If you don't talk about dying cockapoos —"

"Cockatoos."

"Cockatoos, or how the economic recovery is raising rents, then I won't talk about how muscular activity stimulates hypertrophy and capillarization. No deep stuff."

Bren rolled her eyes. "Then what shall we talk about?"

"I don't know. How are my cheeks?"

Bren grinned. "Like two pretty pillows."

Kris smiled. "Cheeks are an underrated part of the face."

"How so?"

"You hear songs about eyes and lips, but never cheeks."

7

"Not the face ones," Bren said.

"My cheeks are sorta looking softer."

"Your face ones?"

"'Cause of my secret combination of kale, green tea, and daily orgasms."

"Your orgasms aren't so secret."

Kris grinned, then sighed. "Gotta keep looking smooth."

"Careful. Too smooth and men will slide right off of you."

"Is that why I can't keep a man?"

Bren laughed. "It *is* actually. You're so awesome they can't hang onto you."

"Ah, sweetie, you're awesome to say that."

"It's true."

"I'm not looking for a guy to hang," Kris said. "Now I just wanna bang."

Bren laughed. "That's the spirit."

"Seems like forever since we hit the bars together," Kris said.

Bren nodded. "My conference, your grandparents visiting."

"Grammy said she loved visiting big-city San Francisco," Kris said, still amazed that someone from her family finally flew out from Ohio to see her. She still felt the fun of showing her grandparents her spacious apartment, charming neighborhood, cool friends, and her awesome life here, and the fun of proving to them that she wasn't the "disappointment" her mom and dad had labeled her, and amazed that her grandparents *had* sorta sided with her. Kris smudged on some lip gloss. "Grammy liked SF so much that she said she'd tell my parents they should fly out here."

"To the land of 'unholy hedonism?'" Bren said.

"I know, right?" Kris looked around the bathroom. "Where the hell is my perfume?"

Bren's stylish flats *tap-tap-tapped* the floor.

Kris barefooted to her bedroom. "I'll find it."

"I'm very hopeful."

Kris flipped on her ceiling light and tripped through skirts and shorts and shoes to her wood dresser, pulling drawers, lifting dirty plates. "Oh, there's my phone bill."

"Lordy."

"Hey, if my folks actually come visit, you should take the pressure off me by flying your mom down too."

"Yikes," Bren said. "I'm pretty sure meeting my Tinder-obsessed mom would *really* make them fear for your soul."

"You think?" Kris emptied a drawer onto her bed.

Bren grimaced. "My mom wouldn't know which boyfriend to bring," Bren said. "She might bring them *all.*"

"Our folks are definitely different."

"Like apples and orgies."

Huh, Kris thought, grinning at another perk to being single again. "I've never done an orgy."

"What?"

"I should experience an orgy at least once."

"Please don't experience it here."

"I don't wanna miss out on *anything* in life. There's still so many things I haven't done yet."

"You've done lots."

Kris rummaged through boxes of fitness textbooks and boxers of ex-boyfriends. She *had* done lots, she thought. No longer that innocent runaway, but still in noooo hurry for a minivan, kids, or mom-jeans, still aching to *LIVE!* "Aren't you group-curious?"

"Orgies aren't on my to-do list."

Kris looked under her lamp, her laptop, her handcuffs handcuffed to her bedpost. "There it is." She held up a fashion magazine, twerked in celebration, then stepped over her bicycle and back to the bathroom.

Bren clicked off her bedroom light.

Kris danced while thumbing through the magazine, found the latest celebrity perfume ad, and rubbed the sample scent all over her neck then flung the mag onto her menagerie of makeup.

Bren shook her head.

Kris smiled. "Have you done most of what you wanted in *your* twenty-eight years?"

"I'm ahead of schedule," Bren said, while pacing. "From burger flipper to corner corporate office. Now I just need to travel the world, get Ryan Gosling to build me a house, and get you out of our door tonight."

"What's the difference between a swinger's party and an orgy?" Kris asked.

"I wouldn't know."

"I bet you've read about them in all your millions of romance books."

"I think a swinger's party is like *my* shoes: all paired up together neatly, and an orgy is like *your* shoes: all piled in a mish-mash mess."

"You always explain things so well." Kris took a look at her finished face in the mirror. It was a pretty okay face, maybe not as head-turning as the glam-izons of glitzy Cow Hollow and the Marina, she thought, but remembered she could kick their asses. She grinned seeing Bren's reminder note with the smiley-face that said: "Please put makeup away." Kris rolled her eyes, pulled out her drawer, and dragged all her mish-mash mess of beauty stuff down into it with a clatter and shoved it sorta shut.

Bren shook her head again. "Ready?"

Rihanna's "Don't Stop The Music" came on. Kris O-faced and cranked up Rihanna, remembering her and Bren dancing to the song in '07, the Halloween night they did ten bars and two guys from that band. Perfect song to start their night. Kris grabbed her bestie's hands and flung them around wildly with hers to the loud bathroom beats so Bren would focus on fun and stop being such an on-schedule pain in the ass. Bren finally took her eyes off the clock and began smiling, moving, grooving, swinging her hips and head, tossing hair, throwing arms in the air.

"Yeah!" Kris roared.

But then Bren's eyes looked at the time again. She broke away, and stopped the music.

Silence.

11

"*Hey*," Kris said.

"Let's go do this with *guys*," Bren said.

"Is that why you're so extra eager to go out tonight? You're feeling a sex drought too?"

"I want us to have lots of fun hours celebrating ... our ... roommate ... anniversary ..."

Bren looked out of breath.

Kris yanked open Bren's drawer and, thanks to all of Bren's freakishly well-labeled trays, she easily found Bren's inhaler and popped it in her hand.

Bren inhaled a hit, and slowly breathed back to normal. "Thank ... you."

Kris rubbed her friend's arm. "You all right?"

Bren nodded and breeeeathed. "I'm ... good."

"Come here, sweetie." She wrapped her arms around Bren and rubbed her back so that relaxing oxytocin would flow and calm her. "Remember," Kris said. "*You're* ten feet tall."

Bren laughed. "Not even close."

Kris laughed and saw Bren's reminder note by their bathroom door: "Please remember, I remind because I love." Kris's heart felt a lot less ache, but her mind worried. "I haven't seen you take an inhaler hit in a while."

"I know," Bren exhaled. "Work lately. Super stressing."

"Don't stress."

"I'd be a lot less stressed if you were ready."

"I *am* ready." Kris jumped out of their hug and flung off her bathrobe, revealing her already-on shirt and skirt.

Bren smiled big, then winced at Kris's polka dot top and green leather skirt combo, literally bit her tongue, then zoomed toward their front door. "Let's go."

"Let's PoP!" Kris shouted.

"PoP?"

"P.O.P. Get passion or pancakes."

"PoP's a thing now?"

"PoP's a thing."

"Very well. Let's PoP."

"Yeah!" Kris cheered, as she slipped into her tan ankle boots, ready to jump back into the singles scene vagina first. "Let's go celebrate our roommate anniversary with the funnest Saturday night ever!"

"Okay."

Kris turned. "I just need to eat another dinner before we go."

"Uuuugh," Bren groaned. "How have I lived with you for *seven frickin' years?*"

Chapter 1

MARK STOOD in his Sheryl Crow concert t-shirt, jeans, and dress socks in front of his 72-inch TV, staring at his video-game. Stretched. Flexed. Hand through his short hair. Focused on the pitch. SWING! And missed the ball completely.

"Dang."

Well, at least his arms were getting a nice workout. He glanced at the glass of bourbon he hadn't yet earned tonight, then paused the game and rested his controller on his spotless couch and moped his socks through his apartment's big, warm-brown living room. He past Chet who was kicking back at the shiny wood kitchen table in jeans and a button-up shirt re-re-fixing his hair in his phone camera.

Uh oh. Looks like Chet really did want them to go to a bar tonight.

Mark grabbed a beer coaster and placed it under Chet's sticky soda can.

"Dude, have you hit the ball once tonight?" Chet asked without looking up.

Mark smiled. And now he had a heckler in the stands. *Hmm, was getting a roommate such a brilliant idea?* "My swing is off, but

14

you know, game's not over yet," Mark's deep voice said as he sat his relaxed fit jeans down on his long green bench, discouraged but still hopeful, then watched Chet spill soda all over his mahogany table, again.

"Whoops. My bad."

Mark shook his head. "Well, at least making my table sticky will help the plates not fall off in an earthquake."

Chet rolled his eyes. "I know, I know. It's my second spill since I moved in."

Mark smirked. "Three strikes and you're out."

"No way will you kick me out," Chet said. "I'm the funnest roommate ever."

"Most of my roommates have been girlfriends," Mark said. "So I don't foresee you reaching the level of 'funnest.' You definitely are the messiest." Mark watched Chet grab the $40 oven mitts to mop up the soda. "Dude, paper towels."

Chet rolled his eyes then used the paper towels as he looked at Mark's TV, then back at Mark, then at the baseball dugout bench Mark was sitting on. "Are you actually sitting on your bench because you struck out at your videogame?"

Mark smiled. "Yeah. That's how you play baseball."

"Wow, man. Your are deep in it."

"It's an important ritual thing," Mark said. "The uncomfortable bench motivates me to get back up and get on base."

Chet grinned and put Mark's shoes next him. "And I'm the uncomfortable roommate motivating you to get back out in the bars tonight and get on base with a girl."

Mark sighed, then leaned back on his bench, not ready for that game.

Chet put on his left brown dress shoe. "Why doesn't baseball have cheerleaders?"

What? "Baseball doesn't need cheerleaders to get fans excited," Mark said.

"It'd be more exciting with cheerleaders. Everything would," Chet said, putting on his right dress shoe. "How much more kick ass would life be if everything had cheerleaders? Golf, bowling, tying my shoe. In fact, I wish I could have cheerleaders around me all day hopping and hooraying all my daily deeds. 'Chet, Chet, tie that shoes, way to go, we'll bounce for you.' Bouncy, bouncy, and a sexy cartwheel. That'd be aaaawesome." Chet laughed.

Mark grinned. Okay, heckling aside, having a roommate to make him laugh was better than living alone. "Would your cheerleaders pay your deposit to live here, because I pretty sure you haven't."

"I swear I get paid next week."

Mark sat up. "Chet, Chet, I hope you pay, so you can, continue to stay."

Chet smiled.

"I'm not doing a cartwheel," Mark said.

Chet chuckled.

Mark stood up. "I am, though, going to finally hit the dang ball this time, I hope."

"No," Chet said. "It's time to go out."

"It's the top of the fourth inning." Mark said. "I can't quit in the middle of a game."

"I've got a better game. It's called: Go Get Laid."

Mark winced once again, and stepped over his shoes. He walked his socks and his tall, muscled body across the beige carpeted floor of his spacious place dignified with fine wood furnishings and past his spendy stainless steel bowl full of garters caught at friends' weddings.

He noticed the darkness and city lights out his glass backdoor. Over his big empty patio, a purple twilight sky hovered above the hundreds of elegantly restored 1920s three-story houses scattered around the charming Marina neighborhood below his balcony, his view bejeweled with nightlights spread out gloriously from the distant Golden Gate Bridge on the left, all the way to Russian Hill on the right, where a full moon was just starting to rise over the hill's houses like a waking eye in the sky. And forward, beyond all the little buildings, the whole North Bay glittered with gliding, lit sailboats. Such a cool sight. But what was a great view without being able to share it with someone?

"Ooh, dude. My soda spilled on your briefcase."

Share it with a girlfriend, more than with a nutty roommate. But that would mean having to actually go out and meet a new woman that would probably end in another breakup. He sighed. Then Mark bee-lined back to his game.

"Why do you have pictures of mountains and stuff on your fridge," Chet asked.

"Those are the rock climbs I did."

"You rock climb?"

"Yeah," Mark said, picking up his controller. "I probably should have asked you this before you moved in today, but what are your hobbies, besides spilling soda?"

"Well," Chet said, patting on cologne. "I've become excellent at body painting bikinis. You wouldn't believe how many girls are excited to try it. They love it. It's like erotic fashion. But the real fun is washing it off." Chet winked.

Mark smirked. *Who was this guy he let move into his place?* "That's an unusual hobby."

"Oh, I'm a fascinating dude. You're gonna love living with me."

"Yeah, I can't wait until one of your painted bikini women sits on my couch," Mark said, as he stepped up to his invisible home plate on his carpet to the roar of the artificial crowd, remembering the sonic glory of the real crowds cheering his name at packed college games, imagining the major league life that could have been. SWING! Missed again. "Dang." His eyes landed on his framed law degree and trophies and wall decorated with pics of past college baseball, beer-swigging friends, his parents dressed up as cardboard robots, and that bleak blank space where Jill's picture once was.

Her perfume still lingered on his throw pillows. The unread political thriller she gave him gathered dust on his shelf. She was probably over him by now. Or was her heart still healing on a Saturday night too? He straightened tall. *Nope, not gonna think about her.* He focused on the next pitch, not knowing what was gonna come at him, a pretty but disappointing curve-ball, an outside zinger he'd try to steer good, or ... a rare perfect pitch? SWING! Miss. *Dang.* Another try. Another miss. This was getting frickin' ridiculous. He looked again at the blank space where Jill's picture once was, and sighed. Who would be the next face in that space?

Chet's face poked up.

Not the face he had in mind.

"That was a horrible pitch," Chet said. "Why'd you swing at that?"

"I always swing," Mark said.

"Why?"

"That's my style."

"You need to swing your flesh bat in the bars." Chet said, waving his soda can around. "We need to get you back out there before it's too late."

"Late for what?"

"I read that giraffes grew long necks from trying to reach their own genitals."

Mark paused his game. "What?"

Chet nodded. "Human's are next. And every night you don't get laid your urges grow stronger and your neck grows longer, and by next year you'll look like a bobbleheaded giraffe-man."

Mark stared at Chet. "And I thought the pain in my neck was you always talking."

Chet grinned. "Nope. It's nature finding a way. But there's a better way with bar girls. So let's get you back in the wild."

"Why? It sounds like in a year I'll be self sufficient," Mark said as he resumed his game.

"Come on, man."

"Chet, if you wanna go out, then go out."

"You gotta go with me. We've only known each other for seven hours. We need to bond as roommates."

"We can bond here, over baseball."

"No baseball," Chet said. "I went to the game with you today. That's enough."

"I recorded *The Bachelor*. I'm down for rewatching it."

"Ugh," Chet groaned. "No baseball. No *Bachelor*. It's time for bars. I need to use your handsomeness."

"My handsomenss?" SWING! Missed. "Dang."

"In Nowhere, New Mexico, I was sexy eye-candy," Chet said. "But here in pretty-people-land I'm like sexy eye-asparagus."

"You're what?"

"I can't compete against all these mega-handsome Marina dudes without really pouring on my charm and funny. It's a lot easier with a draw like you."

"A draw?"

"Your movie star looks will draw in single ladies like hot bees to honey," Chet said. "You'll get a girl and I get her friend."

"Thanks for the compliment, but can't you get some other dude to be your 'draw?'"

"I need *you*. You're the handsomest guy I know. I need you to help me get girls instead of jerkin' your joystick and guzzling this Pap-a-Dap bourbon."

"I don't guzzle. If I earn it by rounding the bases, I only drink a careful pour once a week because it's $3,000 a bottle."

"Are you kidding me?"

"It's a thank you gift from a player for negotiating his contract."

"*Man*," Chet exclaimed. "I wish I got spendy swag from my ad clients. A copywriter's lucky to get the last piece of cake at the office birthday party. Can I try your Pap-a-Dap?"

"You sure? It's not carbonated."

Chet plopped down his soda on the shiny wooden coffee table. "Dude. I gotta know what *three grand* tastes like."

Mark grinned, moved Chet's sticky soda can onto a coaster, and handed Chet his glass of golden Pap.

Chet looked so happy.

"Sip it. Don't chug it."

Chet chugged it ... paused ... and O-faced. Chet's eyes sparkled as if blown by an angel. "I never knew. I bet it'd taste even better if I hadn't just brushed my teeth."

Mark smiled. "Oh jeez." Mark took back his glass.

Chet was all smiles. "I love your swanky world. But it needs girls. Let's go meet some."

Mark exhaled. "I'm not ready."

"Just throw on a dress shirt."

"I meant I'm not ready to, you know, flirt."

"Get your shirt and I'll get you to flirt. We'll go to the bars. We'll drink. We'll laugh. You'll forget your ex-girlfriend and feel happy again and wanna flirt with some hotties."

"Maybe next week."

"No. Tonight."

"I wanna round the bases."

"That's what your mom said."

"Whooooa."

Chet laughed.

"No shading my mom," Mark calmly warned.

"I'm just trying to pull your focus from your video game and get you back in the *real* game. But, dude, look at that picture, your mom is a babe. Is she gonna visit anytime soon?"

Mark moved in front of his parents' picture. "How would you like me flirting with *your* mom?"

"Oh man, I would bust a gut seeing you flirt with my police officer mom. She'd rough ya and cuff ya."

Mark smirked. "Maybe I'd like that."

Chet laughed. "Wow. Then let's go find you a rough and tumble girl." Chet reached for the controller but Mark's moves were too *fast*, easily keeping it away from Chet's cartoonish swings, then returned for the next pitch.

Chet reached into the recycle bin and began tossing empty water bottles at Mark.

Mark just played his game.

Thunk ...

Calmly.

Thunk ...

Amused.

Thunk ...

Unmoved.

Chet gruffed.

Mark chuckled.

Chet used his body to block Mark's TV, waving his arms.

Mark just laughed.

"It's time to go out."

"Not tonight."

"Yes tonight."

"I don't want to."

"Why not?"

"Because."

"'Cause why?"

"Just because."

"'Cause why?"

"Just because."

"WHY DON'T YOU WANNA GO OUT?!"

"... I've got an ingrown hair."

"An ingrown hair?"

"An ingrown hair."

"Where?"

"Down there."

"An ingrown hair down *there?*"

"Down there."

"Dude?"

"Yeah."

"What's an ingrown hair?"

Mark felt warm with embarrassment. "My dermatologist said an ingrown hair is a hair that can't grow *out* of the skin so it grows *under* the skin, irritates the skin, and causes a big, red bump."

"Ew," Chet said.

"I know. That's why I can't go out tonight."

"Why not?"

"Because I'm Rudolph the Red Balled Reindeer."

"That'd be a weird way to guide the sleigh."

"It'd be weird to barhop with my ball so bright."

"So just tell a girl it's a birthmark."

"I don't lie."

"Then tell her it's an ingrown hair."

"She might not believe me and think my big red bump is super gonorrhea and tell all her friends."

"How'd you get an ingrown hair?"

"... I shaved."

"You shaved?"

"I shaved."

"Where?"

"Down there?"

"You shaved down *there?*"

"Down there."

"Dude?"

"Yeah."

"*Why?*"

"I'm nervous to get back in the dating scene. I thought I'd try something new to bolster my confidence. But my bald balls backfired."

"And now you got a clown nose on your nads."

"I know."

"This is why you should listen to me," Chet said. "I would have told you to *trim*. You should never shave, you neaten, just enough so a girl sees you're willing to make an effort for her, but that you're not willing to totally compromise your whole self for her, and she likes that. She likes seeing that you're not a push over. Trimmed ball hair says: 'I'm a considerate man, but not a pushover.'"

"Dang."

"Oh well, let's go."

"I can't go out with my balls on the bench."

"You can still wingman me."

"I'll be too self-conscious."

"You're fine."

"I'll feel false, like my being at the bar says that I'm fully functional, but I'm not. I'll feel deceitful. I'm not deceitful."

"Your baseball heroes, if they had an in-grown hair would they cower in the dugout? No. They'd get out there and play anyway."

"But they play with their pants *on*."

"It's time to go!"

"Then go out," Mark said, not wanting to be alone, but really not wanting Chet bugging him all night to go out. "Go out with your friends."

"I don't have any friends."

Mark paused.

Chet stood silent, breathing.

Wow. Chet was being real.

"I don't have any friends, dude," Chet said again. "No single friends, not anymore. They've all moved away, one by one. No one's from San Francisco and no one stays. I'm the only dude left of my SF posse. And all my other peeps are in relationships. I gotta make new single friends all over again. That's why I moved in with you, man. You're my new single friend. Congratulations."

Mark felt honored, yet burdened with being a wingman.

"I'll do dating apps on weeknights," Chet said. "But Saturday night is for fishing in bars, and I don't wanna keep going out on Saturday nights alone. Alone sucks. It's more fun with a friend. I need you, dude," Chet said.

Mark sighed. *Dang.* "All right," he said. "I'll go out."

Chet smiled ear-to-ear. "Really?"

"Yeah," Mark said. "A lot of my friends have also moved away. And I could use a new friend too."

Chet jumped up and down and did a cartwheel.

Mark feared for his vintage guitar.

"See? Wasn't that cartwheel great," Chet cheered.

Mark laughed. "That was something I never need to see again. Now chill. I'll go, but I'm gonna negotiate."

Chet perked up.

"I'll go out, but I'm *not* hooking up," Mark said. "I'm going just so that you're not 'alone.'"

"My guilt trip worked?"

Mark smirked. "Yeah."

"Sweet." Chet rushed towards the front door.

Mark reluctantly got his shoes on, without cheerleaders, to take another swing at life, discouraged but still hopeful. "All right. Let's go."

"Let's Pap."

"Pap?"

"Let's make this night as great as Pap-a-Dap bourbon."

"All right. We'll Pap," Mark said.

"Though craziness would have to happen to be as great as Pap," Chet said. "So bring on the crazy."

Nervous to trek back into the dating scene with gnarly nads, Mark veered to his bathroom. "I just need to baby powder my thighs."

"What?"

"Without hair, my balls stick to my legs."

Chet winced. "And the crazy begins."

Chapter 2

KRIS AND BREN finally stepped out their apartment door and onto the carpeted square landing at the top of the narrow-walled staircase as Madeline twirled through the front door to their building twenty maroon carpeted stairs below them. Her graying hair dyed blonde swung around to reveal her bright eyes and smile.

"Ooooh, helloooo girls!" Madeline sang up sweetly. "You both look beeee-yoo-teeful."

"Thank you."

"You two will break some hearts tonight."

"That's the plan," Bren called down, checking her watch.

Kris noticed the man, the latest man, Madeline was enticing home with her. "And what's *your* plan, Maddy?" Kris asked with a hubba-hubba tone.

Madeline smiled big and proud as she and her new prize ascended the cream-walled stairway towards the only other apartment in the building, the third-story penthouse with the stunning panoramic view of the Golden Gate Bridge and the whole bay that men she fancied "simply must see." "Girls, this is ..."

28

"Lamar," the sexy-exotic man said to their intrigued yet unsurprised faces.

"*Lamarrrrrrr*," Madeline purred.

"Hi," Kris and Bren greeted him with a mix of awkward and impressed.

"A pleasure to meet you ladies," had-to-be-early-thirties Lamar politely cooed to them.

Kris saw Madeline waste no time getting Lamar away from two "beeee-yoo-teeful" young ladies, scooting him through her apartment doorway to go up many more stairs into her private den. She then leaned back out. "At Le Plaisant he served me and the book-club girls dinner, but he's only serving *me* desserrrrt," she said with a wink. "Have fun tonight, girls."

"Bon appétit," Bren said.

"Boner appétit," Kris said.

"Happy boners to you too," Madeline said with a flourishing wave. "Gotta live it up while we can!"

Door swooshed shut. Sound of eager high heels throbbing up her stairs.

Kris and Bren smiled at each other.

"No dust on her," Kris admired. "How does she do it?"

"She's got charm, will, and Vagisil."

Kris laughed. "Let's go enjoy our non-tube-lube years while we can."

Kris's Gucci ankle boots followed Bren's eager Prada flats down their many carpeted stairs and out their front door next to the coffee café on the first floor. They entered the alive-feeling chilly air with bare arms and legs, Kris in her polka dots and short leather skirt, and Bren in her cute/sexy black mini dress with cut off sleeves, shoes clacking into the after-dark splendor of San Francisco's colorful Cow Hollow.

Walking east, the golden Moon before them looked like a big lemon drop, reminding Kris that she was hungry since Bren wouldn't let her eat again before they left. Now, with food on her brain, their Saturday night neighborhood looked delicious with all the different-shaped two and three story buildings squished together along both sides of cute Union Street looking like Victorian gingerbread houses with neon frosting from the gobs of bright bars and trendy restaurants blasting yummy blue, red, and gold forever in both directions. Kris clacked left with Bren through their Cow Hollow candy land, past a high end boutique with a lemon custard colored cami, past floofy pear-green trees sprinkled with starry icicle lights like powdered sugar, and past a yummy group of guys with mouth-watering muscles as she and Bren eagerly stepped their favorite shoes down their favorite street toward their favorite first-stop-bar.

"While you were in the shower Carl texted me and asked me out," Bren said.

"Who?"

"The financial advisor I dated for a week last year, the one who talked endlessly about his Ferrari."

"Yikes. You tell him to go play with his stick shift?"

"No, no," Bren said. "I just non-committingly texted him back: Cocktailing with Kris Sat night. Maybe catch you at the bars. And he texted back: that's such a marina girl thing to say."

Kris laughed. "So true."

"Except we live in Cow Hollow," Bren said. "I'm a Cow Hollow girl."

"Cow Hollow and Marina are pretty much the same neighborhoods. They're both yuppy-uptopias."

"Yes, they're right next to each other, but if I'm gonna be labeled I want accuracy," Bren said.

"'Cow Hollow girl' is too many syllables. 'Marina girl' has a ring to it."

RING-RING

Bren's phone had a ring to it. "Speaking of Marina girl. Holly sent us a text." Bren read their friend's text out loud. "We're at Monoghan's bar with Kyra and Tom. Tom and Collin are drinking Tom Collins', ha ha. See you soon. Then two emojis and a picture of her drink." Bren showed Kris her phone's pic of Holly's scrumptious-looking blue cocktail.

"Could you call a cocktail pic a 'cock pic?'" Kris asked.

"Doesn't have a ring to it."

"A cock ring?"

"I don't know what that is."

"I don't know either."

"Really?"

"We should ask a guy tonight what that is."

"How will you segue to *that?*"

"I don't need a segue," Kris said.

"That'll be a fun non-sequitur: 'I like your shirt. What's a cock ring?'"

"Exactly. Keep guys on their toes. I'm a non-segue girl," Kris pronounced herself. "You know, I've never ridden a Segway."

"You just segued to Segways."

"So I'm a sometimes-segue girl."

"I've never ridden a Segway either."

"We should ride Segways tonight too."

"How?"

Grrrrrrrowl.

"Shush, Stacy."

Bren grinned. "You know, when you look down to talk to your stomach it looks like you're talking to your hoochie, in public."

"Well," Kris said. "If Stacy the Stomach would stop growling in public then I wouldn't have to look like I'm talking to my hoochie."

"You burn through food so fast."

"I know. I just fed you two hours ago, Stacy," Kris griped at her stomach. "Shush. I'll give you booze in minute."

"Yeah, you'll be a wonderful mother one day," Bren said.

"I'll be the most *amazing* mom ever, a million years from now. Right now I love being a single, party-loving Marina girl."

"You should be called a 'Marina *woman*,'" Bren pointed out.

"Still too many syllables."

Grrrrrrrowl.

"Shush, Stacy! She's never satisfied. I wish there was magic food that satisfied me forever."

"I wish your food would magically not invade my side of the fridge," Bren said.

"It's not."

"It is."

"It's not."

"Your kale. Your tofu. Your bottled condiments."

"That's my new guilty-pleasure butter," Kris said excitedly. "You gotta try my butter."

"No thanks."

"It's great."

"I'll never eat it."

"Why not?"

"It's in a squeeze bottle."

"Bren, it's efficient. You like efficient."

"I like my butter."

"But my butter's fun squeeeeze-bottle butter."

"I like my butter in the tub."

"In the bathtub?"

"No, the butter I buy is in a 15 ounce tub."

"My bottle-butter is better than tub-butter."

"Tub butter's better because closing the lid has that satisfying *click*."

"Ooooh my God," Kris said. "You're a crazy *click* chick."

"I'm a *click* chick?"

"You're a total *click* chick. You tell me to shush so you can hear the *click* of your water bottle cap twisting."

"I do like that," Bren said.

"You like *clicks*."

"*Clicks* feel good."

"I like *crashes*," Kris said.

"That says a lot about you."

"But I also love calmness."

"You're very complex."

"I am complex," Kris said. "As complex as my mismatching clothes."

Bren smiled.

Kris smiled back at her. "I saw you gasp at my leather skirt and un-matching polka dot blouse and I know you wanted me to change, but you wanted to leave, and it's gonna drive you crazy all night that I don't match."

Bren laughed as they walked.

"I know you so well."

"And I bet you mismatched on purpose just to bug me."

Kris laughed back at her. "I wore these 'cause they're comfy and sexy and that's how I feel and you should dress how you feel, not 'cause it matches."

"You just broke the fashion industry."

"I'm revolutionizing it."

"Your non-matching *is* vexing me," Bren said. "I'm changing the subject."

"You're announcing it?"

"Yes."

"Hey everyone, she's changing the subject!!" Kris hollered to the neon neighborhood. Drunk partiers outside all the bars

"whoooooooo"ed back wildly for no reason. Kris laughed.
"That's how you announce something."
"But now you've built my subject change into *something*."
"Yep," Kris said. "Now your subject has to be *fantastic*."
"Your ex-boyfriend."
"I don't like that subject."
"But you like crashes and we're about to crash into him."
"*Yikes! Serious?*"
"At the restaurant outside. In front of us. With a girl."
"What *girl?*"
"*That* girl."

Holy tooshy-twerks. Kris spied David, "Dick In A Box" David, dashing David, sitting outside the pasta place where she used to squeeze him under the table. Now he was sitting with a new squeeze, wearing one of his sexy button-up business shirts that she used to love *ripping open* as buttons flew and his chest was bared for her lips and hands. He must have bought a hundred shirts while they dated for those four hot months. Now her hands began to sweat just seeing him again sitting at a little round table, eating pasta ... with a beautiful woman?

"Not a fantastic subject change," Kris exhaled, staring at David's date, a skinny beauty wearing a blue top and skirt that matched and over-laughing at his every whispered word as they canoodled over noodles in public. Then Kris saw David see her, saw him panic but politely wave at her. Kris *HAD* to see who this tartlet was and marched right over to her former love, remembering his lame excuse for breaking up on April Fool's Day, that she had "too much energy."

"Hey" stuff.

"Good to see you" stuff.

"How you been?" stuff.

Awkward introduction to his date, Lisa, stuff.

Then Kris saw the sparkly ring on Lisa's finger.

HOLY SHIT STUFF!

"Are you fucking engaged?" Kris non-segued.

"Uh oh," Bren said.

David handsomely smiled ear-to-ear. "We *are* engaged," his husky voice replied. "As of last night."

World stopped!

Mouth dropped!

Mind popped!

"Were you banging her while we were dating?"

He rolled his eyes "No, Kris. Don't fly off the handle."

"I'm not flying."

"You're flying."

"I'm just asking what-the-fuck?"

He shoved meat in his mouth. "Lisa and I only met a month ago."

"At a Giants' game," little Lisa said, squeezing David's big bicep.

Kris gaped. "You met her at a Giants' game a month ago? A game I bought tickets for, and said you could use?"

David nodded. "We thank you." He smiled at Lisa.

Lisa kissy-kissed his new mustache.

Kris ... was actually at a loss for words. A million mixed feelings zoomed down a million different roads. *Surprise* he'd moved on, *embarrassment* that she hadn't, *anger* that he wasn't weepy without her. All her heartachey weeks getting over David, not wanting him but still missing him, without knowing he was as happy as a hard-on with some new girl. She felt stupid and confused and replaced and jealous and hungry and pissed off that she actually friggin' cared about any of this!

Wild silence.

Grrrrrrrowl.

"SHUT UP, STACY!"

"Ooookay," Bren said. "We're gonna go before Kris seems strange."

David nodded.

Lisa sat wide-eyed.

Kris stared big-eyed at the stupid-huge engagement ring! How could David want *that* girl instead of *her*. She felt Bren's kind hands steer her shoulders away from the weirded out couple, away from the past, and towards somewhere other than here.

"Congratulations to you both," Bren said to them.

"Okay," David said.

Kris's silent open mouth followed her Bren-guided body away from Lisa and David and down the sidewalk, into the darkness.

Emotions surging, Kris struggled to be more like Bren and get a friggin' grip. She sweated hot with shock, yet felt strangely cool with relief that David was no longer an option. Now she could *really* move on from him. But everything had changed. Their whole power dynamic had *changed*. They were no longer equally single. Narrow-minded, full-of-himself, really-sweet-sometimes, fun-be-with, made-her-feel-loved, then-made-her-feel-like-crap-when-he-insulted-her-energy David, had won the game of love. Even though there was no game, there was, 'cause everything's a game. Not that she needed love, not that she wanted love, but she would *not* be defeated. Kris felt *anger* rising like a volcano building up to blow, like a bomb tick-tick-ticking as she clack-clack-clacked farther and farther away from victorious David – "15 OUNCES?!!" she screeched.

"What?" Bren asked, still steering Kris down the neon-lit sidewalk.

"How do you know your butter tub is 15 ounces?"

"I know things."

"You know weird things. Normal people don't know those things."

Bren grinned.

"Oh you like that?"

"I'm smiling at you being silly."

"I'm not silly," Kris insisted. "You like knowing not-normal things so you can feel superior."

Bren's face fell. "Not 'superior.' Just ..."

"Better."

"No, not better."

"Why is she better than me?"

"Who? Lisa?"

"*Leeee-sa*. Did you see *her* butter?"

"Her butter?"

"Her better butter."

"Her better butter?"

"Her better butter better than *my* butter."

"What?" Bren asked.

"Buttering her bread? Did you see her?"

"Probably not the way you did."

"She buttered her bread right in front of me, soooo proudly in a '*my butter is better than your butter so I GOT him and you didn't, nah nah nah nah, and I eat carbs during dinner*' way."

"I didn't see *that*."

"I wish I had my squeeze-bottle butter so I could squeeeeeeeze it all over that buttering bitch. HERE'S SOME FUCKING BUTTER!"

"Breeeeathe," Bren said.

"Fucking bitch cunt whore slut twat cock-sucking ass-licking ass-douching skank ho man-stealing bitch."

"You said 'bitch' twice."

"Good. She's a two-timing bitch."

"She didn't two-time. She just dated him after you. He moved on, and you should totally move on too, without looking back."

Kris looked back, but Bren steered her back around and kept her walking away.

Bren gave Kris's shoulders a squeeze. "You only dated David for four months."

"That's a long time for me. A Kris-month is like a year to non-Kris people, 'cause my heart goes all in."

"Yes, I know," Bren consoled her. "And I was so proud of you for actually doing a relationship instead of just hooking up and doing week-long romances. But you've also had two and a half Kris-months and two hookups to get over David. Now you're free to find a much classier guy to have a relationship with that might even go *five* months."

"Screw that," Kris said. "I'm done with deep relationships. It hurts way too much. Besides, I don't wanna get married and have babies and stuff right now. I'm staying single and safe."

"Okay."

"You know, I could have said 'no' if he had proposed to me. Or we could've had a long engagement."

"Since when do you want to be engaged?" Bren said.

"I ... I wanted to be *wanted*," Kris said, her voice cracking. "Why wasn't I wanted? Why is *she* so much better that he proposes to her after only a month?" Kris breathed, and walked, and looked up into the night sky, seeing darkness, and no answers, and trusted Bren's hands to keep her from smacking into a parking meter. Kris eyed smiling couples walking by holding hands, and even two kissing in the red neon outside a bar. She felt both safe and alone.

"Maybe they just *clicked*," Bren said.

Kris full stopped at the corner. Realization. Maybe that was it, why her and David's relationship didn't work. Maybe what she and David had together hadn't really been love. Maybe she had never really loved. Then what the hell had they experienced? "Maybe David and I weren't a butter-tub lid. We didn't *click*."

Bren shrugged.

"Maybe David and I were just a squeeze-bottle. Easier, but not as real."

"You guys were real."

"Do you really think we were real?"

"Sure. It's just that maybe you guys squeezed your relationship bottle dry until you got that air fart sound."

Kris laughed loud. "You explain things so well." Kris hugged her hard.

"Don't squeeze me too tight or *I'll* make a fart sound."

Kris laughed again, feeling at least loved by Bren, and smiled at her angel. But then her angel gasped and suddenly lowered her face into Kris's cleavage. *Wow,* Kris didn't realize Bren loved her *that* much. "Um ... bunny ... what'cha doing down there?"

"Hiding from Abe."

"Abe?"

"Abe. My ex," Bren said, as she hid in Kris's cleavage.

"Abe the Asshole?"

"Yes," Bren mumbled. "He and his friends are walking toward us, behind you." Boobs muffled Bren's words.

"The asshole who used to flirt with other girls right in front of you?"

"Yes. I don't wanna deal with him."

Kris started to turn around but felt Bren yank her body back.

"Keep your back to them and they won't notice me," Bren instructed.

"Uh, I think a woman with her face to another woman's chest will definitely be noticed by guys."

"They can't see me," Bren said and slowly pivoted Kris's shielding body like a non-seeing periscope as Abe and his preppy posse passed behind her.

Kris sighed at Bren's hiding from confrontation. She should be standing tall and strong, not cowering her face in books and now breasts.

"Bren?" Abe's voice asked.

Plan failed. Good, Kris thought. Time for Bren to literally stand up for herself, ten feet tall-ish.

Bren turned around. "Ooooh ... hi, Abe."

"He noticed," Kris announced.

"I noticed he noticed."

Kris noticed his popped collar and rolled her eyes.

Abe's friends all grinned, looking like they got a group discount at J Crew.

Abe scratched his stylish stubble. "What are you doing?"

"Oh," Bren said. "I'm, just, um ... Kris's shirt button hole ... had a loose thread and um I – I – I couldn't get it off with my fingers so I had to get it with my teeth."

"Good one," Kris whispered down to her.

Abe smiled really big. "With your face in her boobs I thought you'd gone lez."

Bren cringed.

"Ooooh, there's that Abe sense of humor I remember," Bren said, as she slowly stood up.

He grinned and chewed gum. "Did you finish reading that big book, *Infinite Jest*?"

"I did," Bren said. "Did you finish reading that choose-your-own-adventure book?"

He grinned. "Still working on it." Then stepped closer. "You're lookin' mega sexy tonight, Bren."

"Uh, thank you."

"You wanna hook up later?" he asked, plain-faced.

Bren stood silent.

Uh oh. Kris hoped like hell that Abe's familiar sweet cologne didn't tempt Bren to backslide back to his bullcrap.

"Um, I'm seeing someone," Bren lied.

Good choice, Kris thought.

"If you're dating Kris I'd be totally cool with being the meat in a Bren-Kris sandwich."

Kris bit her tongue.

Abe popped his gum.

"Gosh, that's a sweet offer," Bren said with a thin smile. "But no thank you."

"Just puttin' it out there."

"Does 'puttin' it out there' ever work with women?"

Abe then smiled big. "Enough times to keep putting it out there."

"Well, good luck with that," Bren said. "Bye."

Abe stepped even closer.

Uh oh. Kris's memory flashed back to all the times Abe referred to sex as "borrowing Bren's vaj."

Abe smirked. "You know, if you ever wanna give me another try –"

"FUCK OFF!" Kris roared.

Abe jumped back.

"Bren's too good for you, you smug-for-no-reason, tiny-dick putter-downer! Leave my friend alone and go to respect-school before you screw up another girl's life with your bullshit!"

Abe stood unblinking and open mouthed, as if he'd swallowed his gum.

"Now go fuck yourself! And if you ever come near my friend again I'll *MAKE* you fuck yourself!"

Abe's friends yanked him away and pulled him down the street, hopefully to go catch a clue.

A heavy silence seemed to fill the whole neighborhood.

Kris huffed ... feeling better.

Bren grinned. "How exactly would you make him fuck himself?"

Kris laughed. "I don't know. But he clearly didn't wanna find out."

"That'd be a sight."

"You'll see it if he bothers you again."

"I don't think he will."

"Because I stood up to him," Kris said right to her friend's eyes. "You should've shooed him away yourself."

"I shooed politely."

"Screw polite."

"Don't screw polite."

"You need to screw polite."

Bren rolled her eyes. "*What is going on tonight?*"

"It's night of the living exes," Kris joked.

"We have to start sleeping with guys outside of this neighborhood or *every* Saturday night will be a bump-into."

"It already is, sweetie."

Bren exhaled. "Let's get drinks."

Grrrrrrrrowl.

"And get food."

"And meet new guys we'll eventually hate running into."

Kris smiled. "That's such a Marina girl thing to say."

Chapter 2

MARK AND CHET finally stepped out of Mark's apartment and onto the brown hardwood landing at the top of the wide-walled staircase just as Vicki and Charles came canoodling into the building and started up the twenty wood stairs, happily swinging post-dinner take-home boxes.

"Hey," Mark said.

Vicki looked up. "Oh heeeey."

Charles kept his eyes on Vicki, holding her close as they wobbled up the stairs.

"Where'd you two lovebirds eat tonight?" Mark asked.

"Fancy Fish Café," Vicki sang out as they bumbled up to the landing and stopped with her husband, Charles, cuddling her from behind. Vicki flung her hair aside and gave Mark stern eyes. "Look here, Mr. Mark, we miss going out to dinner with you, with you *and* Jill."

"Oh, I'm sorry," Mark said. "I'm sure Jill would love to see you if you call her."

"No no no no. *You're* the one we like to hang out with. But we can't double date with you if you don't have a girlfriend."

"I'd love a girlfriend," Mark said. "Maybe tonight I'll meet my

46

next ex." He chuckled. "Vicki, this is my roommate, Chet. He moved in today."

"You got a roommate?"

Mark nodded. "I hate living alone. Chet these are our neighbors Vicki and Charles."

"A pleasure to meet you," Chet said to her with a wink.

What a charmer.

"Helloooo," Vicki sang as she leaned back into her husband's embrace, smiling.

Charles then kissed Vicki's hair and cheeks shamelessly as usual.

"Well, Chet is pulling me back out to the bars, and maybe –"

"No 'maybe,'" Vicki said as she waggled her purple fingernail at Mark. "This time you gotta find a *keeper*. I can't invest months of my life again with a girl you're just gonna break up with. I want a *lifer*."

As Vicki's take-home box flung around in her pointer hand as she spoke, Mark realized that given his track record, he probably wouldn't be able to fulfill that lifer-dream for his nice neighbors, nor for himself.

Charles nuzzled in Vicki's hair.

"Don't go out tonight to just find a one-night stand," she ordered. "Bring home a keeper."

"The guy was caged for a year," Chet piped up. "Let him swing his thing."

"Swing it into a keeper."

Charles began kissing the back of her neck.

"And this time swing your thing into a girl that doesn't click her fork on her teeth."

Charles cupped Vicki's buttock as he kissed her neck.

"And one that doesn't mind our pot smoking."

Charles moaned.

Vicki purred.

Mark bit his lip trying not to laugh.

Chet started to laugh.

"I'll try to make everyone happy," Mark negotiated.

Charles's hands cupped her breasts.

"Ooookay then. You two enjoy your Saturday night."

"Oh we will," Vicki said, spinning around and jumping into Charles's arms as they both succumbed to passion right there on the landing.

"Um," Mark said. "We're gonna go."

Vicki and Charles kissed wildly.

"Happy hemping," Mark said.

"Happy humping," Chet said.

"*Ooooh yes!*" Vicki swooned.

Mark clomped his shiny, black dress shoes down the wood stairs and away from the ooh-la-la that also awkwardly reminded him that he hadn't had sex in four months, but he found himself alone at the front door. He looked up and saw Chet still on the landing, happily watching the about-to-bone couple. "Chet."

Chet snapped out of it and slowly walked his brown sort-of-dress-shoes down the stairs, still staring up at Vicki tearing Charles's shirt off.

Mark opened the front door and pulled Chet out with him, away from the wild woops of pleasure as tumbling take-out boxes whammed the door behind them.

Wow.

Mark and Chet laughed beside the busy bistro restaurant by their front door as Mark felt the alive-feeling chilly air in his thin green dress shirt and jeans and saw the carnival of San Francisco's cool Marina district all around.

Walking east toward the golden Moon, wishing he was still upstairs playing his game or guitar, as he saw their Saturday night neighborhood looking like a jazz club, with the mix of modern and old timey two and three story buildings sharing both sides of classy Chestnut Street like steadfast bass and youthful piano making magic in the night, with bright lights from well-worn whisky bars jammin' beside slick sportswear shops, and venues groovin' like that for blocks both east and west. But Mark and Chet turned right and walked across Chestnut Street, and then swung another right, now walking toward the disappeared sun, past the Marina's night party mix of neon colors, ocean air spiced with restaurant smells, and streetlight lit green trimmed trees swaying with the breeze. All this jubilation reminded Mark's spirit of the fun he used to have being out and about, and he began thinking that just maybe tonight he could feel some of that fun again, as Chet and he sported their stylin' shoes down their stylin' street toward a stylin' night out.

"Charles and Vicki met three years ago," Mark said. "They've been married for two and they're still crazy for each other."

"They sure seemed crazy," Chet said.

Mark smiled. "They're so in love that they don't care who sees them all over each other. I wanna find that kind of love."

"Vicki's the kind of horny girl I wanna find," Chet said. "We'll find one for you too."

Mark beheld the colorful dazzle of the Marina night for the millionth time as they walked, and he sighed. Maybe *he* was crazy, still looking for long-lasting love in these magical-looking but so-far-love-unyielding bars. Maybe he should begrudgingly do the not-as-romantic online dating thing, try a different neighborhood, or maybe he'd never find a Vicky-Charles love.

Dang. That would suck.

"Hey, Chet," Mark said. "Do you believe in ... soulmates?"

"Is your shirt the same color as mine?" Chet asked.

"What?"

"Our shirts."

"I'm asking about soulmates."

"I'm talking about shirts."

Mark rolled his eyes. "Our shirts aren't the same color. Yours is blue. Mine's green."

"But at night they look the same color. We look like twins."

"No one will mistake us as twins," Mark remarked. "I'm taller."

"I meant we look dressed the same, like twins."

"We all look like twins," Mark said. "*Every* Marina guy is dressed the same: spendy button-down dress shirt, jeans, spendy dress shoes."

"Do you think that happened naturally or did a Marina meeting declare that's what all Marina guys should wear?" Chet asked.

"I don't remember a meeting."

"That's probably like asking: at what point in history did humans decide all pictures should be rectangles?"

Mark was confused. "What other shape would pictures be?"

"Anything."

"You are a weird wingman," Mark said.

"Now that I've pointed it out you're gonna notice that all pictures are rectangles. And then you'll notice *everything* is rectangles: buildings, walls, doors, magazines, computers, phones, and you'll realize all this time the powers that be have been cornering you into a limited life of rectangles."

"Chet, your mind is wacky."

"I think outside the box. Literally."

"Says the guy wearing the same outfit as me."

"I could wear a clown suit, but it would hinder me getting laid."

"Not by another clown."

"That would be a bad dating app: Hinder," Chet said.

"A water bottle isn't rectangle. It's got curves."

"Speaking of curves," Chet said.

"Heeeey, Chet," a girl walking by with her friends said.

"Heeeey, Deana," Chet said as she hugged him. "How are you, beautiful? You look amazing tonight." Chet chit-chatted then wished her well, then he and Mark walked on through the bright white light from the huge glass front of the Apple Store then back into night.

"How do you know her?"

"We banged," Chet said.

"Really?"

"She's cool. She's into wine and studying to be a sommy-something."

"A sommelier?"

"I guess."

"That's impressive."

"What's impressive is she can put her feet behind her head."

"That's quite a visual."

"She curls her toes when she org –"

"TMI, man."

"I could introduce you to her."

"Is she a hopeless romantic like me?" Mark said, lifting his leg as he walked, then put it back down.

"What the hell are you doing?"

"Just adjusting."

"Adjusting what?"

"I told you," Mark said. "Without hair, my balls stick to my legs."

"Yikes, that's not romantic."

"I tried to be romantic by trimming."

"I thought you baby powdered your thighs."

"I didn't have any baby powder. I forgot that Jill took it when she left."

"Well, don't lift your leg in front of girls."

"Heeeey, Chet," another girl walking by with her friends said.

"Heeeey, Lorna," Chet said as she hugged him. "How are you, beautiful? You look amazing tonight." Chet chit-chatted then wished her well, then he and Mark walked on past the classy remodeled movie theater.

"And how do you know her?"

"We met at the gym," Chet said.

"Oh."

"And then we banged."

"Of course."

"She's so cool. She's a web developer who's into glow sticking?"

"What's that?"

"She twirls glow sticks. It's really cool."

"And now I'm waiting for you to say something lewd."

"She twirled *my* stick."

"There it is," Mark said.

"I'm not always lewd."

"Says the guy who always says something lewd."

"I'm just trying to make you laugh. I know that's why you let me move in," Chet said. "You're a brokenhearted mope and my story about having sex on the girl's floor heater that branded grill marks on my ass made you bust a gut."

"Yeah, our dermatologists must love our weird wounds."

"And now you get to enjoy my 'lewd' humor daily."

"And your 5A.M. yoga."

"Yep."

"And your insane collection of bikini mags by the toilet."

"You like those, huh?"

"I'm being sarcastic."

"Oh," Chet said. "Well *I* have to enjoy your constant video gaming and your bamboo shampoo."

"Bamboo shampoo?"

"Bamboo shampoo."

"Oh, bamboo shampoo."

"The bamboo shampoo in our shower."

"You don't like bamboo shampoo?"

"The bottle's HUGE!"

"It's bulk."

"It takes up half the shower."

"Not half."

"It's like showering with a fire hydrant."

"That would be an odd place for one."

"You gotta move your bamboo shampoo."

"I'm not moving my bamboo shampoo."

"Why won't you move your bamboo shampoo?"

"I like it."

"Well I like my bikini mags."

"Clearly."

"And I like my yoga."

"Great." Mark said. Being out of his apartment did feel good, outside in the fresh night air, among the Marina's fun neon lights and the reminding-him-of-good-times smell of booze as they passed each bar crowded with happy sounding chatter, sort of glad that Chet coaxed him out on the town. Though it felt weird to be out and about without Jill, to be single, noticing all these Marina women again, wondering if one of them could be 'the one.'

How does one know which one is 'the one?' Seriously, how do you know?

"Heeeey, Chet," another girl walking by with her friends said.

"Heeeey, Awna," Chet said as she hugged him. "How are you, beautiful? You look amazing tonight." Chet chit-chatted then wished her well, as he and Mark walked on through the golden glow from the big Delarosa restaurant with happy people eating outside and –

"Hey, wait," Awna said.

They stopped.

Awna, a very smiley young woman in a very short black skirt and gold top that revealed her very sexy midriff and billowing cleavage came clacking after them and came right up to Mark.

He tried to gentlemanly keep his eyes on her eyes and not on the tops of her beautiful tan breasts.

"I recognize you," she said to him.

"Me?"

"You're Mark."

"I am."

"You used to date Jill."

Mark's heart fluttered. "I did date Jill."

"But now you don't."

Mark's heart sank. "But now I don't."

"So now you're single."

"I am."

"Cool."

"I guess."

"I'm Awna."

"Anna?"

"Awna. Like sauna."

"Awna."

"Yeah."

Was Awna 'the one?'

She stuck out her hand.

He kindly shook it. It felt lovely. He politely released it. He felt back in the game, though still nervous. Awna seemed really nice and Mark's mind started picturing Chet moving out and Awna moving in and Christmases together, and their wedding, and –

"My boyfriend and I saw Jill last night at *Circa*," Awna said.

Boyfriend? Dang. "So you know Jill?"

"Oh yeah. She's friends with Kim who's friends with Ruby who's friends with Roxy who's friends with Chantal."

"Small world."

"Small neighborhood," she said. "You're looking very tall and muscular tonight, Mark," Awna said. "And I love your shoes."

"Thank you," Mark said.

"What size are they?"

"Fourteen."

"Excellent."

"Thank you?" Mark said.

56

Why was his shoe size excellent?

"Awna's cool," Chet said. "She's an interior designer who used to be a gymnast. A *flexible* gymnast."

A flexible visual was now in Mark's head. "And she has a boyfriend."

"Both your shirts look the same," Awna said, looking at them. "Like twins."

Chet funny-glared at Mark.

Mark rolled his eyes.

"But you look great," Awna said.

"Thank you. So do you."

"I mean you look cheerful even though Jill's moved on with Jack."

World stopped.

Mouth dropped.

Mind popped.

"*What?*" Mark said.

"It's great to see that you're back in the nightlife and moving on too."

"Jill's with Jack?" Mark asked.

"Yeah."

"Stockbroker Jack?"

"Yeah."

"Oh."

"You didn't know?"

"I didn't know jack about Jack."

"Oh. Well, now you know."

57

"I do."

"Is that cool?"

"Oh, of course. Um, that's great if she's happy."

"She's happy."

"I'm happy she's happy." Mark ached, smacked by a meteor of truth: Jill was gone from him, with someone new, surprised that she had moved on quicker than he had, and that she was no longer an option. He stood thunderstruck, lost, alone, overwhelmed, sweaty, and sticky, and lifted his leg to unstick.

"What are you doing with your leg?" Awna startled.

Mark froze.

Awna stared.

Chet laughed. "Oh jeez, dude."

Mark put his leg back down.

"Mark has a condition. When he sees a beautiful girl like yourself his leg involuntarily spasms. You should take it as a compliment."

Awna looked weirded out.

Mark felt weirded out about Jill and embarrassed in front of Awna, and bewildered of what to do now except be embarrassed and go regroup. "Nice meeting you, Awna," Mark said.

"Uh huh," she said with a raised eyebrow.

Mark quickly turned away and his unstuck legs walked his size fourteen shoes back into the night.

Mark struggled to negotiate all of his emotions for a common solution but finding none, he slightly envied Chet's choice to not get deeply involved in love and just be happy with quick and simple romances. Surprised that Jill had moved on, what a big change, and yet he wasn't surprised since it had been four months after their break up. Now he could *really* move on from her. But her truly gone-ness officially solidified another failure. Like a pattern he couldn't change. Nothing had changed. Why did his relationships keep failing? All his ex-girlfriends always seemed so happy with him during their time together, but in the end they all turned out to be incompatible for the long-term. Why? Was he doing something wrong? Or was life just as random as asteroids? Or was he destined to be alone? He didn't wanna be alone at home. So here he was heading toward another singles bar, fretting and sweating and sticky-legging as he walked closer and closer toward beginning another relationship failure.

"Bamboo shampoo," Mark said.

"Bamboo shampoo?"

"Bamboo shampoo."

"What about the bamboo shampoo?" Chet asked as they walked.

"The bamboo shampoo is Jill's."

"Jill's?"

"Jill's."

"But you and Jill broke up."

"Yes."

"So why's Jill's bamboo shampoo still in our shower?"

"I like to smell her bamboo shampoo and remember her."

"Duuuude."

"What?"

"Eeeew."

"What?"

"I don't want you thinking about your ex in our shower that I use right after you."

"All I do is sniff."

"Sniff and get stiff."

"No. I sniff and reminisce."

"I don't want you to sniff and get stiff from her bamboo shampoo and spend an hour in our shower."

"I don't want you looking at your sexy bikini mags on our toilet."

"Why not?"

"Because *your* bamboo might get stiff and touch the seat."

"Oh jeez."

"That's ew. Especially when your bamboo's been all over the Marina."

"Not all over."

"Heeeey, Chet."

"Heeeey, Darcy."

"Case in point."

"My *wrapped* bamboo."

Mark calmly stopped at the corner of Chestnut and Pierce, and looked up into the night. He saw a few stars that the city's bright lights let through, the lucky few. He exhaled. "I was keeping her bamboo shampoo in case she came back, but now ... *dang.*"

Chet stepped up and fist-bumped Mark's big shoulder. "Well ..." Chet said. "Let's get you laid."

Mark looked back down at Chet. "That's all you got?"

Chet shrugged. "It's all I got."

Mark grinned. "Well, I appreciate your sentiment."

"I'm here for ya, dude. But you gotta toss out her shampoo, and her purple Loofah."

"Actually, the purple Loofah's mine," Mark said.

"Oh, then I shouldn't have used it on my – anyway."

Mark grinned through the ache of lost love ... and went on with life. "I'll toss her shampoo if you remove your mags."

"Oh, we're negotiating again?"

"It's what I do."

"So bye bye to bamboo shampoo if I move my mags?"

"Yes."

"Can I flirt with your hot mom?"

"No."

"Oh all right, deal."

They shook hands.

"I told you we look like twins; even Awna thought so," Chet said. "I need a new shirt."

"Heeeey, Chet," *another* girl walking by with her boyfriend said.

"Heeeey, Melony," Chet said as she hugged him. "How are you, beautiful? You look amazing tonight." Chet chit-chatted then wished her well, then –

"Hey, man," Mark said to Melony's boyfriend, noticing his nice gray dress shirt with red pinstripes. "You look about my friend's size. Will you trade your striped shirt with my friend's blue shirt?"

"My shirt?"

"Yeah. Chet's and my shirts look so similar we look like dorks. Would you trade shirts with my friend?"

"Seriously?"

"Yeah," Mark negotiated, sensing the guy's reluctance as he pulled out his wallet and took out a card. "Here, take this gift card to the Apple Store a client gave me. It's still got over five hundred dollars on it."

"What are you doing, man?" Chet asked.

"You we're being a good friend to me," Mark said. "So I'm thanking you."

"You could give *me* the $500 gift card."

"You wanted us to have different shirts."

"$500? Hell yeah, I'll do it," her boyfriend said.

"He'll do it. See? Problem solved," Mark said.

Chet laughed and changed shirts with the guy on the sidewalk while women gawked. Some whistled at Chet's naked chest, and he grandly bowed and dressed.

They thanked Melony's boyfriend and, wearing different shirts, now walked on across Pierce Street's streetlight-lit goldenness and onto a new sidewalk.

Chet fist-bumped Mark's other shoulder. "Way to think outside the box, man."

Mark smiled. "So ... back to my question about soulmates."

Chet rolled his eyes.

Chapter 3

KRIS HOPED booze would clobber the memory of that damn engagement ring so it wouldn't F-up the rest of her Saturday night. And she really hoped she didn't die of starvation before she could stuff Stacy with a burger. Squished between an upscale boutique and a high-end beauty spa, Back Scratch Bar looked like a greasy burger between two fine wines, the perfect low-key starter bar to kick it off before hitting the major-league venues. In the orange neon, hot door guy handed back their I.D.s with a flirty smile that gave Kris a needed grin that got her blood pumping and party-mode flipped back on.

Inside, the tiki-meets-sports bar's fun vibe helped lift her spirits too with Bowie's "Blue Jean" rockin', lots of talkin' people packing the pretty-gritty place, yet with space, not too crowded, casual and cool. Low-lit, low ceiling, and a long stretch from the colorful Christmas lights decorating the front windows, and along the tan, tropical grass over the bar, all the way to the scratched pool tables in the back. A non-Cow Hollow-ish bar in Cow Hollow. No Grey Goose served here and no people in $400 shoes. Just sneakers sticking to the beer-spilled floor. Worn wood tables, ball games on the four TVs, and new Hello

Kitty string lights hung over the booze-stained bar for probably no reason other than the owner saw them on sale.

Kris quickly scanned the crowd for more ex-boyfriends or past hookups, but the coast seemed clear, a safe haven from most of their upscale exes, where she and Bren could ease into the nightlife like a warm-up walk before a wild work-out, just talk and drink casual without having to do the uptown schmoozey scene just yet. And maybe make-out with some random hot dude.

Their two favorite center barstools sat empty. *Odd.*

Kris smiled. "Tonight I wanna drink, dance, and bang."

"That's the sequel to *Eat, Pray, Love,*" Bren said.

"That's a book I *would* read."

"You won't hear your stomach growl in here; the music's loud."

"No, but I can feel Stacy's emptiness."

"We'll get her filled up."

"Speaking of getting filled up. Here comes the perfect Back Scratch back scratcher."

Barry the bartender and his muscles strode towards them with his cute spikey hair and a dreamy smile that he aimed sweetly at them, but far more at Bren. Kris watched her bestie shy a giddy grin back at his smile and his large chest stretching tight his Springsteen t-shirt. Kris knew just how she'd mount him if Bren wasn't so smitten with him.

"'Hello Again,'" Barry greeted them with big smile and extended his palms.

Wow. There was at least one gentleman around tonight. "You reserved these seats for us," Kris asked?

His smile lit up his face. "I was hoping my two favorite liquor likers would stop by."

Holy damn. "You're hella awesome. Bren, isn't Barry the best?"

Bren sheepishly smiled. "I also called ahead that we'd stop by."

"Of course you did," Kris said. "Is that why you were so eager to get us out the door tonight?"

Bren smiled.

"How are you gorgeous ladies doing tonight?"

Kris slammed her palms on the bar and smiled. "We're in desperate need of fun."

"We got lots of fun here," Barry said, spreading his thick arms wide.

Bren licked her lips.

"Tonight we're looking to hookup," Kris said loud and proud.

"Cripes, don't *announce* that," Bren said.

"We'll either get passion or pancakes."

"Well, I wouldn't bet on pancakes," Barry complimented. "You both look amazing."

"Keep your compliments coming," Kris said, loving all the positivity she could get right now. "Isn't Bren looking *super* amazing?"

Barry's eyes danced all over Bren. "She absolutely does."

Bren blushed. "I'm changing the subject."

"She's changing the subject!" Kris yelled.

"Lordy jeez."

People looked.

Barry laughed.

Bren wiped her sweaty forehead. "Do you, um, have happy hour prices for us regulars?"

"For *you* lovely ladies I do." He winked. "Bren, do you have more book recommendations for me?"

"I don't think so," she half-flirted.

"Why not?"

"You never read what I recommend."

Barry leaned a little closer. "But I like hearing you talk about all the books you're reading," he said, grinning. "When you talk about books you get so excited. I like hearing you excited."

Bren bit her bottom lip.

"Oh pleeeease don't get her talking about books," Kris cut in. "She'll babble for an hour and I need a drink *now*."

"And we need fun music."

"Well you're both in luck. Tonight is '80s night. We're serving up songs from the '80s and all-decades-drinks."

"I want –"

"A bourbon and Coke in a martini glass," Barry guessed Kris's fave drink correctly with a smile. "And Bren would love a Lemondrop."

Bren smiled.

"I also need a burger, *stat*," Kris ordered. "No bun, well-done, and a side of veggies."

"Are you 'Hungry Like The Wolf'?"

Kris and Bren looked confused.

"It's an '80s song."

"Ah," they said.

Kris perked up. "I've heard of the 'Macarena.'"

"That's '90s," Bren corrected.

"I didn't say it was '80s."

Barry laughed. "You were just saying it for fun?"

"I was non-segue-ing-ing."

"She does that."

"She's a 'Wild Thing?'"

"What?"

"'Relax' my 'California Girls' I'll get your drinks as fast as a 'Little Red Corvette' so you can feel 'Just Like Heaven.'"

Kris and Bren confused-grinned.

'80s played.

Smell of perfume and booze.

Barry went to find bottles.

"Bren and Barry sittin' in a tree," Kris teased.

Bren shook her head. "It can't happen."

"It totally could."

"If I dated Barry and broke up then you and I could never hang out here again," Bren reasoned. "And you might try to make him fuck himself."

Kris laughed. "I didn't mean date him, I meant do a 'Madeline' and take home the server."

"I'm thirty-four years too young for that."

"You'd be practicing."

"Not with Barry."

"'Cause he's a bartender?"

"No, I like hot bartenders," Bren clarified.

"So?"

"Barry's not a reader."

"Oh, get over that."

"I need a book lover."

"He doesn't need to read Ball Sack to boink you."

"Balzac."

"Whatever."

"Guys who read are better lovers."

"'Cause they use their bookworms?"

"That was a good one."

"Thanks."

"Book lovers take their time," Bren said, grinning.

"But you like efficiency."

"Not in bed," Bren explained. "In bed I want to savor every sensation, and readers are attentive to detail. They love to feel and appreciate a good romp between the covers, readers are romantic, and sensual, and slowly build to a climax."

"Oh my."

"Oh yes."

"What if he's a speed reader?"

"Then we wouldn't read together again."

"I bet Barry reads drink recipes."

"Hmm. How fast?"

"'Abracadabra,'" Barry sang as he served their yummy-looking yellow and caramel cocktails. Bren's drink sported four big umbrellas, Barry clearly remembering Bren's fear of people's talk-spit. What a gent. Then his manly hands turned both of the napkins their glasses were on so that their drinks faced his favorite customers just right.

"Why do you do that extra drink-turn thing?" Kris teased.

He grinned. "Details matter."

"You hear that, Bren?" Kris said. "Barry does details."

Bren pinked pretty and looked down.

"What? Even detailed he's still not good enough for you?" Kris persisted. "Barry, could you read a few books so Bren will let you bang her?"

Bren's cheeks went raspberry.

He grinned at Bren. "Is my non-book reading what's keeping us off the 'Freeway Of Love?'" Barry asked.

"The what?" Bren asked.

He smiled. "I might not read much, but I can show you that 'Heaven Is A Place On Earth.'"

Bren smirked.

Barry winked at Bren then tended to his flock of other thirsty seagulls while Cyndi Lauper sang.

"To girls just wanting to have fun," Kris toasted.

"Heck yeah."

They raised their glasses.

"Hey, tonight's Cyndi Lauper's birthday," Bren said.

"How do you know this?"

"I know things."

"To Cyndi."

They raised their glasses again.

Bren sipped.

Kris slurped from her martini glass. The sweet Coke and thick carmel-ly bourbon tasted like fun Saturday night. "Oh my God, so good." She soooo needed this fun right now. She could feel the bourbon dissolving her memory of David already.

Oh yeah. Go bourbon go!

She floated into happiness, and ached for her burger as she watched Bren swallow Barry's sweetness and smile.

Then Bren looked at her phone and read out loud. "Also, on this day, in 1851 a fire burned down San Francisco City Hall, in 1847 the first ring donut was invented, and June 22 is also No Panty Day."

"Today is No Panty Day?"

"For those celebrating it."

"Are you celebrating No Panty Day?"

"I couldn't totally commit," Bren whispered. "So I'm rockin' a thong."

"Half-assing it?"

"Cheeking it."

"Would a song about thongs be about cheeks?"

"If you need it to be."

"We need to hear thexy thongs to thelebrate our Thaturday night."

"Thalude!"

They raised glasses again to the fun of Cyndi's, Whitney's, and Blondie's beats giving them "Rapture" to forget exes and work and focus on fun talk about the Giants' chances for the World

Series again and what books Bren wanted to read next. Kris felt lighter, drink in hand, laughing with her friend, focusing on her single life, her free life, and also her to-hell-with-David sex life by totally not subtly staring over Bren's shoulder at the two hot bad boys shooting pool in the way back of the bar. A good banging would definitely help shake that ring out of her head.

BLEE-DEE sound.

Bren read Holly's next text aloud: "Now we're at Delarosa with Bob and Steve, they're showing me pics of their new cute AF beagle! I think I see Emma Stone eating here (or her look-a-like). I'm drinking a Sidecar, deeeelish! C U soon. Do I have anything in my teeth? Then four emojis and a picture of Holly smiling big and teethy." Bren texted back where they were, what decade they were in, that her teeth were spotless, and pix of their sweet drinks, then showed Kris Holly's selfie.

"Ooooh." Kris said. "Holly's hair looks really pretty tonight."

"It does."

"Does my hair look pretty tonight," Kris asked.

"It does."

"As pretty as *Leeeesa's?*"

Bren rolled her eyes.

"David was sitting differently. Not slouchy."

"Probably because you didn't have your hand in his pants."

"He sat taller, as if he'd upgraded to boxer briefs. How come being with me didn't make him wanna wear boxer briefs?"

"What are you doing, Kris? You sound as insecure as Holly."

"Am I not boxer brief worthy?"

Bren sighed. "I'm changing the ... anyway. Tomorrow I'm gonna wear the yellow sundress you got me for my birthday."

Kris slurped and sighed. "Me and David had fun ... until he sucked."

Bren nodded. "Let's talk about something else."

"Josie found a good guy," Kris continued not talking about something else.

"Josie?" Bren asked. "Your client who dresses up for Renaissance fairs?"

"Her boyfriend likes Renaissance fairs too. He also likes buying pianos and pushing them off cliffs, which keeps things interesting. And they laugh a lot."

"Crazy people do." Bren sipped.

"Darcy found a good one. Ashley found a good one. How do we always end up with buffoons?"

Bren shook her head. "Just lucky I guess."

"*Leeeesa's* not gonna do daily kegels. He's gonna miss that."

"Lordy."

Damn. The bourbon wasn't clobbering all the memories. "I'm not tipsy yet. I wanna be tipsy."

"I think you're getting there."

"Are you tipsy yet?"

"I wish."

"How long does it take you to feel tipsy?"

"I've never timed it," Bren said.

"Hey, there should be an app for that."

"A tipsy app?"

"Yeah."

"The police have one."

"Theirs comes with penalties."

"True," Bren said.

"My phone should sense my drink's alcohol content and tell me how long before I get tipsy."

"I like that idea."

"Yeah?"

"It'd be like a taxicab: your buzz will arrive in two minutes."

"Exactly."

'80s music played.

"I'm doing kegels right now."

"Thanks for sharing." Bren grinned.

Kris drank, starting to feel warmer and looser. Then she tensed seeing Bren's cocktail glass near the edge of the bar. She shivered and quickly pushed Bren's glass further onto the bar, breathed, and felt much better.

"You still can't handle a glass near an edge?" Bren snarked.

"No," Kris said. "And I can't handle all this change."

"What change?"

"David. All our friends moving 'cause rents are rising. Dying Cockapoos."

"Cockatoos."

"Cockatoos."

"I thought you didn't want to talk deep tonight."

Kris drank another swallow. "I found paradise here, paradise from my crazy parents. And now it's all changing. Even

73

the Metro Movie Theatre down the street is getting turned into a gym, with trainers, that are gonna compete with my fitness business."

"You train housewives in their homes. The gym is for people *going* to the trainer. It won't bother your niche business."

"What if my clients like going to this new gym more than training with me?"

"They won't," Bren assured her. "They love being trained by you."

"That's true. They do."

"You're fun and inspiring. You inspire *me* to keep fit."

"Yeah, you're looking good."

Bren shrugged. "My butt still needs some change."

"You look great."

Bren shrugged. "Jane Austen once said –"

Kris tapped Bren's leg. "Those guys shooting pool keep staring at us."

Bren smirked. "And now we're back to non-deep talk."

"Ooo, listen!" Kris shouted, pointing up to the music speakers. "I love this song."

"'Love Awesome,'" Barry said, passing by.

"Thanks," Bren cooed.

Kris sighed, felt feely, and sniffed. "I love this city. I don't want it to change. I don't want anything to change."

Bren rubbed Kris's shoulder and sipped her Lemondrop. "Change can be good."

Kris scoffed. Then wiped her eyes and sniffed.

"I think your tipsy-buzz has arrived. You're getting uber-emotional," Bren said as she reached into her purse then handed Kris a tissue.

Kris *honked* her nose into the tissue. Then she looked around for where to put it. Then hid it down into her drink.

"Oh gosh, please don't forget you put that in there and drink it."

"Ooooh, I won't."

Barry brought Kris's sizzling burger with a smile and theatrically presented it down before her wide eyes and did his details by turning her meal toward her perfectly, making her feel special and cared for by a guy, and making her smile again, and *hungry*.

Grrrrrrrrowl.

"Shhh, Stacy. I'm about to feed you." Kris smiled at Barry.

Bren smiled at Kris's smile.

"Oh my God. Barry, my second dinner is so beautiful that if Bren doesn't bang you, I totally will."

Bren went simply red.

"All right, you can have my junk, but my 'Heart And Soul' belong to Bren," Barry said and smiled.

Bren smiled.

"Wow," Kris said. "We might have to take you home with us."

Barry *really* smiled. "Just 'Wake Me Up Before You Go Go.'"

"Whack you off before you what?"

Barry laughed before bailing on their bizarre love triangle as those guys playing pool sauntered over.

Kris saw the muscly one approach her. *Mmm.* He didn't look like a buffoon. Maybe her and Bren's luck was turning around.

"You're hotter than your burger," he said, low and slow.

Maybe their luck wasn't totally turning yet. Kris and Bren shared a look.

Bren tapped his shoulder. "You literally compared my friend to a piece of meat."

Kris laughed.

The dude smirked, and reeked of cologne and beer.

Kris loved that Bren was defending her. If only Bren could stand up for herself. "So you think I'm hot?" Kris flirted back, eager for a David-forgetting bang.

"I think you're Sizzlin', baby," the guy said.

Kris smiled. "I'm glad you came over. A burger and boys, the service here is five-stars!"

He laughed, big and toothy.

She licked her bourbon-flavored lips, feeling warmer. "I'm Kris."

"I'm Ron."

"'Da-Doo-Ron-Ron?'"

"I think that's '60s," Bren corrected Kris. "*And* '70s."

Ron clearly da-didn't understand, but he looked agreeable to anything that would get him laid.

Excellent.

His decent-sized hand shook Kris's.

Decent hand, decent feet. Saturday night's looking much better.

"I'm Ian," the other guy said.

Kris watched sorta-muscled, sorta-mulleted Ian eagerly shake Bren's hand, clearly choosing her for whatever weird fantasies were behind his weird expression.

"I'm Jen, Jen Itaylia," Bren told them.

Kris bit her lips to keep from laughing at Bren's test for smarts and humor, but neither dude understood Bren's name game.

Bren gave her the secret side-eye look of "time to politely reject these guys."

But these guys were good distractions from ex-boyfriends and change, and fun with them felt like punching back at heartache. Though the guys' eyes did drift around to peek at other girls, and they clearly weren't the sharpest tools in the shed, they were handsome, and fun, and just what she needed. They knew all about pool and cars and retail sales and Kris standardly coaxed business cards from them to get their full names so she could Google them, and grinned at Bren rolling her eyes when they thought Virginia Woolf was a wolf in Virginia.

Ron put his beer pint down by the edge of the bar.

Yikes. Kris slid it further in. "A glass by the edge makes me jittery."

Ron rambled more about how he once drunkenly caught a fish with his bare hands, drank, then put his beer glass back by the edge of the bar again.

Ugh. Ron clearly didn't hear her, or didn't care that a glass by the edge made her feel uncomfortable. *Maybe it really was time to ditch these dudes.*

The Go Go's "Vacation" blasted!

"Oh!" Kris shouted. "I love this thilly thong!"

"You wanna dance?" Ron quickly offered.

"Hell yeah!" Kris jumped up. "Bren wants to dance too!"

Bren did a "*What?*"

Before Ian could ask Bren to dance Kris grabbed her hand. "'Come On Eileen.'"

"Hey, *I* know that one."

Kris laughed and pulled Bren wildly to the dance floor. And they danced. Bren swayed. Kris flailed. Purses swung. The guys quickly joined them with their overbite, crotch-thrusting dance moves. Bren rolled her eyes about this to Kris, but Kris loved dancing and boogied and woogied her body and limbs, losing herself in the *SONIC GLORY*, taking a "Vacation" from all her exes: the duds, her loves, her heartbreaks, and all her dating wackiness, and focusing only on tonight and the music and this new Mr. Right Now as he twirled her, then impressively dipped her and brought her back up. *Wow.*

She saw Ian see their fancy dancing and then dip Bren, and drop her!

Oh damn! Kris ran over to Bren and helped her up.

"Whoops," Ian said. "Guess I gotta practice my dips, heh heh."

"Smooth move," a guy said to Ian.

"Oh, fuck you," Ian said to the guy.

"What'd you say?"

"I said 'fuck you.'"

The guy pushed Ian.

Ian swung at the guy.

The two guys threw fists!

Oh damn. Ian was an ass. Kris pulled Bren away, toward the restrooms.

"Hey, Kris," Ron hollered to her over the music. "If you're going to the bathroom to look me up online, you should know, I did *not* kill those people."

What?

The '80s were over!

Kris grabbed Bren to leave the dance floor, as the bar fight got bigger, and a dude fell into Kris. Kris pushed him away. He fell against a girl. The girl pushed him back at Kris. Kris jumped out of the way. "Hey, fuck you," Kris said to the girl.

"What'd you say?"

"I said 'fuck you.'"

The girl pushed Kris.

Kris swung at the girl, but Bren grabbed Kris's arm and pulled her back to their stools.

"Calm yourself down," Bren said.

Kris exhaled and drank from her cocktail, then saw her nose-tissue in the glass. *Gag.* But swallowed snot-bourbon.

Bren watched and *gagged.*

The bar became a fist-swinging madhouse!

So much for a low-key starter bar. "Sorry," Kris shouted.

Barry grinned. "Let the 'Good Times Roll.'"

This *did* help her take her mind off things.

Bren tossed Barry a smile and $40 on the bar, and yanked Kris out the door and back into the twenty-first century!

Chapter 3

MARK TRIED not to wonder what Jill was doing with her new boyfriend tonight. And, he chose not to care. He was moving on. Again. He exhaled the night's chill and re-focused on the lines out the door of The Tipsy Pig and Campus Bar that they passed, and on all the sexy-dressed, new potential girlfriends eyeing him as Chet stopped his shoes at the line for the Mingles Bar. It was a rectangle. But the bare-shoulders of the ladies in line were beautifully round, and had to be freezing in this ocean-side air. The barely over twenty-one doorman barely checked Mark's ID. *Ouch.* Was he really back in the singles scene again at age twenty-nine? Admission back into the bar scene felt like an admission of failure. Yet, back into the scene he strode, hoping for an easy-going evening, with a muscled up grin and nothing riding on his next dating choice but the entire future of his love life.

Forget earning alcohol tonight. Gonna need it to get through this night.

Once again he saw the inside of this familiar go-to bar that looked like someone had put every decade's pop culture in a blender with the top off and let it splatter everywhere. Olivia

80

Newton-John sang "Xanadu" as Mark looked around at the front half of a 1950s Chevy attached to the wall, tie dye shirts, disco balls, '80s movie posters, Nirvana video on the TV, and Britney Spears and Beyoncé cardboard cutouts. The mix used to seem kitchy-cool to him but now it seemed as if all along the owners had been desperately trying to please every demographic by being both fun *and* elegant, but jarringly, like the coffee house set of *Friends* also trying to be dark and Victorian, with happy colorful couches and Tiffany lamps clashing with gothic chandeliers and Dracula red walls. The shiny oak floor and stylish leather booths by cute stuffed animals bejeweled randomly around. The place looked as confused as Mark felt about his life; maybe it was the perfect place for him to be he wondered while wandering with Chet through the shoulder-bumping crowd all sporting different colored drinks, to the beat of ironically spun classic rock, through the jumbled scents of beer and incense, passing the crappy dartboard beside the framed Monet, as they squeezed up to the classy brass bar decorated with superhero bobble heads and sat on different colored stools.

"Girls are checking you out, man," Chet said. "And they're checking me out more than usual 'cause I'm hanging with you. I knew that you as my wingman would be boss. We're gonna do this a lot."

A lot?

Mark sighed and looked around for Miss Right with Chet eyeing for Miss Tonight. Several singles were in sight, no awkward exes. But, the scene seemed slightly different. Suddenly Mark realized the other reason he hadn't been eager to get back into singles bars: they had changed. He noticed baby faces, a new concert t-shirt of an unfamiliar singer, and some guys wearing sneakers. *Sneakers? In a Marina bar? On a Saturday night? What the ... oh.* Surrounded by the now younger, cool crowd, Mark reminded himself that he was only twenty-nine, but he felt like the oldest single there. He thought of all the only-two-year contracts he negotiated for baseball players in their late twenties, their career as a player considered almost over. *Dang.* Now *he* felt like a dinosaur.

Twenty-five-year-old Chet wouldn't understand and wouldn't want to hear his insecurities. And Mark sure didn't want to think about them. So, time to get back in the game. He straightened up tall. "Tonight I wanna feel happy again."

"That's the spirit," Chet encouraged. "This place is packed with hotties for ya. Just don't do your sticky leg lift here."

"I'll try to be more subtle." Mark practiced being subtle.

"You're gonna have a different pants problem in a second."

"Why?"

Chet grinned and nodded toward one of the attractive women shaking drinks and body parts behind the bar. "That's Bonnie," Chet said. "Bonnie's awesome. She likes delivering food to the elderly."

"Oh that's cool."

"She also loves a pinky in her tookus."

Mark smirked. "TMI, dude."

Chet chuckled.

Was there any woman in the Marina that Chet hadn't slept with, and what would they think about Chet's oversharing?

Bonnie the bartender pranced over to them as if with fairy wings, her curly hair bouncing, long legs tempting, and her pink-tank-top-stretching breasts arriving before she did. Chet's tongue almost rolled out onto the bar, clearly up for another go with Bonnie if she gave him the green light. Instead she gave them both her baby blues.

"Heeeey, Chet," she said with smile.

"Heeeey, Bonnie," Chet said as she air-kissed him. "How are you, beautiful? You look amazing tonight."

She swayed super happy-dappy to Beyoncé's "Single Ladies."

"You look smiley and thirsty," she said.

Chet winked. "You look ready to quench my thirst."

"With aaaall kinds of specials."

"Tell me all about your specials."

"Juicy Lucy. Bahama Mama. Fuzzy Ass."

"No ass fuzz for me."

"A Hurly-Burly? A Brass Funky? A Purple Helmeted Warrior?"

"You know what I want."

"Yeah, but I don't have my paddle with me," she said.

"Ooooh." Mark laughed. "Waaaay TMI."

"No, no, I meant a Scotch, or better yet, do you have any Pap-a-Dap? Mark's buying."

"I'm not buying Pap," Mark said.

"Uuuugh, Scotch and bourbon are borrrring," Bonnie said. "I like making fun drinky-drinks. Let me make you guys fun drinks."

"Like what?" Chet asked her.

"A Golden Shower?"

"Nope."

"A Big Johnson?"

"I've already got one of those."

Bonnie bit her lips like she had a different opinion.

Mark bit his lips to not laugh. Then saw her bat her blues over to him.

"What about you, wingy-wingman? Would you like a Flaming Anus?"

"That doesn't sound comfortable."

"A Jack and Jill."

"Definitely not."

"A Red Ball?"

Mark winced. "What's *your* favorite drink, Bonnie?"

Bonnie smiled big. "Wow, a guy who actually cares what *I* like. You're a super sweetie."

Chet raised eyebrows.

Bonnie clapped her hands. "I'll make you what I like and *surprise* you!"

Mark smiled. "That sounds fun."

"And I'll surprise you too, Chetty."

Bonnie bounced away.

Mark grinned. "Chetty?"

Chet winced. "Dude, check out Bonnie's Venus dimples. The two dimples above her booty."

"They're called Venus dimples?"

"Bonnie's are so hot."

Hmm. Kind of fun looking at women again as a single guy.

"They're very nice."

"Did Jill ever have any wild stuff? Unusual piercings, secret tattoos, vajazzlings?"

Mark smirked. "That stuff's private, man."

"Your ex is gone. Spill."

"Nope. That stuff stays locked."

"You're no fun."

"I'm all kinds of fun, with boundaries, like not wanting to be paddled."

"Don't knock it 'til you try it," Chet said.

Bonnie poured and mixed like a wild circus performer.

Hmm. Bonnie might be a fun girlfriend.

Mark imagined living with her, without Chet. He could cook them dinner. She could mix them drinks. They could talk about feeding the elderly and how she learned to spin a bottle like that. "Hey, 'Chetty,' what are Bonnie's other hobbies?"

"I don't know," Chet said. "If she's cowgirling on me later tonight I'll ask her."

"Or I could ask her now," Mark said.

"Dude. Do you wanna bang Bonnie?"

"She might an interesting girlfriend."

"Girlfriend?"

"Yeah."

"Dude, you don't want another girlfriend. That's crazy."

"No it's not."

Bonny pranced back. With a super big smile she presented two multi-little-umbrella parties in two glasses to two confused faces.

"*Surprised?*"

Two heads nodded.

Her florescent pink nailed hands turned both of the napkins their glasses were on so that their drinks faced her open-mouthed customers just right.

"What's my big drink called?" Mark dared to ask.

"It's a Galactic Fucker Upper."

"... Oh." Mark smiled politely.

"It's my fave," Bonnie giggled to Mark.

"Golly," he said. "Thank you."

"You'll love it!"

"I can't wait. And what is Chetty's drink?"

Chetty rolled his eyes.

"Chetty," she cheered. "I *invented* a drink just for you."

"Oh?"

"It's Paddle Me Punch."

"Oh ..."

Mark laughed, hard.

Bonnie's smile seemed completely sincere.

Classic.

Mark handed their awesome bartender two $20 bills. "Keep

the change, Bonnie. And thank you so much. You've truly brightened up my night."

"Yaaaay!" she sang.

"Bonnie," Mark said. "Just out of curiosity, what are some of your hobbies?"

"I like to Netflix and chill."

"Oh?"

"And I've started making art out of bacon. I made a whoooole bouquet of roses out of bacon. It was beautiful, until my snake ate it."

"Snake?"

"And Chet painted a bikini on me. That was fun."

Chet smiled.

Mark grinned. "Do you think you'd like rock climbing, or hiking?"

Bonnie O-faced. "You mean ... leave the city?"

"Yeah."

"Oh I never leave the city. All the fun stuff's here."

"There's fun in nature."

"Not my fun."

Dang. "Well," Mark said. "Your drinks sure are fun."

Bonnie smiled big. "Thanks. Enjooooy." She boogied her booty away to fun up some other boring-drinker's night.

Well ... maybe he could make a relationship with Bonnie work, Mark thought. He could go hiking with friends while she stayed home making bacon bouquets, and he could massage her Venus dimples while her snake laid eggs around his condo ... maybe.

Chet pulled the clown-car of umbrellas out of his punch.

Mark smirked. "Hey, Chetty, you got a drink named after you."

"Grrrrreat," Chet sarcasmed.

Mark raised his Galactic F-er Upper. "Here's to the start of our roommating."

Chet raised his Paddle punch. "Here's to No Panty Day," Chet said.

"No Panty Day? That's a thing?"

"A glorious thing."

They drank.

Wow. Mark never needed to eat sugar again.

Chet's face scrunched up as he put his glass on the bar. "So who do you guess is doing No Panty Day in here?"

"You gonna take a poll?"

"That's brilliant. I'll take a poll, for my pole, to get some pull."

"And probably get pulled outta here for not being polite."

"We'll ask politely."

The Spice Girls really, really wanted something over the speakers.

Mark drank more Galactic sugar, kind of enjoying something new. "So you sleep with all these women once, never call them again, and they all still like you?"

"They do."

"How?"

"'Cause I'm brilliant in the bedroom."

"And modest."

"And I'm not a jackass," Chet said. "I don't false advertise. I'm straight up with them on what I'm about."

"What are you about?"

"A fun night."

"You don't want more than that?"

Chet looked around. "Nope."

BOMP-CHICKA-BAH-WAH

Chet heard his phone. "Hey, I got a booty text from Lorna the glow stick twirler."

"Is a booty text a bext?"

"It is now."

"Are you going to go hang with her?"

"No, man. She bites too hard, and I wanna hang here and see if our winging gets us both hooked up."

Mark drank. "I promised my neighbors I'd look for a keeper."

"No, dude. Find a one-nighter."

"I don't think so."

"'Cause of your ball bump problem?"

"That. And, well, I've never done a hookup."

Chet's mouth fell open. "You've *never* done a hookup?"

"No."

"You're *twenty-nine*."

"I've always done relationships."

Chet looked like he'd been struck by lightning as his hand clutched the bar. "Red alert! You're suffering from serious serial monogamy. We gotta get you to a one-night-only-craving-hottie stat!

"I couldn't do a hookup anyway. I got an ingrown."

"You've got an ingrown hair in your brain. You're insane. There are so many gorgeous girls around here and you've never played in the hottie-rich fields of the Marina?! That's like going to Vegas and not leaving the hotel room."

"Maybe it's an amazing room."

"You gotta get out of the room. You're living in rectangles, man."

"There's nothing wrong with rectangles. Rectangle walls keep the ceiling solid." Feeling warmer, and looser, Mark realized his head was bob-bob-bobbing like the bar bobble-heads to the beat of the song playing and was talk-talk-talking in time to the rhythm, man. "I like the solidness of a defined relationship like Charles and Vicki got. I like love."

Chet tapped his hand on the bar to the beat. "Dude," Chet said. "Let me spill some T."

"You're always spilling things." *Damn this drink is good.*

"Now I'm spilling truth," Chet said. "Being single is the best. The best. And I gotta stay single 'cause I'm not gonna be a cheater, and I don't wanna be breaking up all the time and go through that terrible mess. So I stay single. Being with a lots of different girls is really the absolute best. We're all still cave-people. Once you accept that you find freedom, and fun."

Mark grinned. "We're more than cave-people. That's the goal, to be more, much more."

"The goal is to have fun," Chet countered.

"So, you've never met a woman where you thought: 'She's the one. I just want her and no one else?'"

"Dude," Chet said. "Honestly. Have *you* actually met 'the one?'"

Mark paused. "I've dated some really great women."

"And being with more than one has made you better, right?"

"It's been a peaks and valleys journey to find 'the one.'"

"And it's the fun of the journey that's awesome," Chet said. "Maybe our universe is just one of many bubbles floating on some high power's frothy beer foam, and the whole point of life is to just have a great time. Every night is a new adventure."

Mark smirked, and drank, and cleared his throat. "There is one thing that's even greater than a plural of women."

Chet leaned against the bar, with raised eyebrows, and a smirk.

Mark smiled. "The *love* I feel with one woman."

Chet stared at Mark.

Mark stared at Chet, hoping he got through.

Chet rolled his eyes.

Maybe not.

Mark pointed up to song playing over the speakers.

"'Loooove Awesome,'" Bonnie sang passing by.

"Thank you," Mark said. "Chet, you should explore what this song is trying to tell us do. It's about love."

"It's about sex," Chet said. "Listen to the bump-bump beat. That's the rhythm of hump-hump-humpin'."

"Monogamous humping. The lyrics are saying monogamy."

"The beat is saying sex."

"Or maybe this song with its bumping beat yet lovelorn lyrics is a deeper message about the conflicting duality between sex and relationship."

Chet stared at Mark.

"Or maybe the booze in these *crazy* drinks is making us way too deep with this song."

"It's making you drunk."

"Maybe it is."

"If you don't hook up then why do you care about your ingrown hair?"

"It's not that I won't hook up, it's just that I never have. I get a woman's phone number, and by the end of our first date she usually wants to be my girlfriend."

"Wow, you move fast."

Mark exhaled out. "I miss dancing," Mark confessed.

"Dancing?"

"I love dancing, like couples dancing. Jill didn't really like dancing, or baseball. But we made it work, for a while."

"You made it *work?* That doesn't sound like love."

Mark took another drink. "Now, I gotta find a new girl-friend to dance with, and *hiccup* ... what was I saying?"

"You're tipsy."

"Hells yeah."

"Did you just say 'hells yeah?'" Chet asked.

"Hells yeah."

"Holy crap, man. I'm taking this drink away from you, before you spill like I spill."

Mark felt his sack glued to his thigh again and wriggled his leg.

"No no, dude. Not now. Look. Bonnie's coming back."

"Oh, she's so nice."

"How's your drinks, boys?" Bonnie asked happy-dappy.

"Spankin' good," Chet tipsily cheered.

"Wonderful," Mark tipsily complimented.

"I'm so happy."

"We're happy you're happy," Chet said.

"And we're all happy that we're all happy," Mark said.

"You guys should be happy that two interested girls are standing right behind you," Bonnie said.

They turned around and saw two very pretty women looking at them. One in a tan dress, one in red, and both with high heels and sparkles in their eyes. *Wow.*

"Have a happy," Bonnie said, and happied away.

The two women smiled.

Chet smiled back.

Mark tensed. One of these women might be his next girlfriend.

"Hi," they said, cheerfully.

Then the tan-dress-woman batted her eyelashes at Mark. "You're so handsome that I bet my friend that you're a movie star."

Chet smiled proudly at his wingman.

"Sorry," Mark said, oddly nervous, and definitely feeling tipsy. "I'm not a movie star."

"You could be."

"Gosh, thank you," Mark said. "I go to movies sometimes. I've been going by myself for lately. It's not as fun. Do you like *Field of Dreams?*"

"Um, I think *you two* look like movie stars," Chet charmed.

They rolled their eyes and laughed.

"Nice both meeting you," Mark said, enjoying the pretty face of the woman talking to him, and her long hair, and sparkly eyes, despite her scary blue eye shadow. He felt his head bobbing to the beat, and palms sweating. He held onto his drink. "I'm happy, I mean, I'm Mark." *That was a strike, dang.*

"Mark's a little shy," Chet cut in.

"I'm Mark."

"You said that."

"And he's tipsy."

"And gorgeoussss."

"I'm Chet."

"I'm Miranda."

"I'm Panda."

"Miranda and Panda?" Chet said. "Outstanda."

Slight smirks.

"What are you ladies drinking?" Chet asked.

"Yukon Dew Me," Miranda answered.

"A Slow Comfortable Screw Against The Wall," Panda purred.

Mark raised eyebrows.

Chet smiled ear to frickin' ear and quickly changed the subject to travel. Probably so he wouldn't have to tell them he was drinking a paddle-me drink.

They learned that Panda was visiting from some European city they'd never heard of and she was a very flexible circus performer.

Chet gave Mark a grin.

Mark smirked. Katy Perry sang "California Gurls" as he found out that Miranda lived way out in the Sunset district, that she didn't like the outdoors, unfortunately, and worked for a company that sold really unhealthy TV dinners, unfortunately, and she burped, un-classily, and garlicly.

Maybe he could still make a relationship with her work.

And even though she didn't like rock climbing, looked like she was getting bored, and stuck her finger down her throat when he said he was a lawyer.

But maybe they could somehow be happy together. Maybe?

Mark saw Chet smirking every time Miranda trashed something Chet knew Mark loved. Alternatively, Chet's conversation with Panda sounded like it was going really well for him. Chet and Panda both liked drinking and dancing, though she'd be leaving back to Europe soon, which Chet probably really liked, no complications.

Chet grinned. "Would you ladies like to take my poll?"

BOMP-CHICKA-BAH-WAH sound.

Chet glanced at his phone, and his eyes flew wide.

The Beatles' "A Hard Day's Night" began blasting and everyone in the bar went "*woooo*," and started dancing! Everyone except Miranda.

Mark tapped his toe to the beat. "You wanna dance?"

Miranda sneered. "I hate dancing."

He could still make this work. "Do you like baseball?"

"I hate baseball."

He could still make this work.

Dancing elbows kept bumping them.

Miranda looked annoyed.

But he could still make this work. Somehow. "So, Miranda," Mark said. "Have you ever thought about living on Chestnut Street, where all the fun is?"

"Dude," Chet said, excited. "We gotta go."

"Go?"

"We gotta go."

"Go where?"

"Outta here."

"I don't wanna go."

"We gotta go."

"But Miranda and Panda."

"This is more importantanda."

"I'm staying," Mark said.

"You wanted to stay home, now you wanna stay here?"

"You wanted me to go here, now you want me to leave?"

Chet leaned close to Mark's ear and whispered. "Dude, you're drunk and saying crazy stuff you shouldn't say."

"I am?"

"Yeah. I've got to get you outta here."

"Really?"

"*Yeah,*" Chet whisper-shouted. "Trust me."

"Oh," Mark exclaimed, worried about what crazy stuff he may have said, and definitely feeling warm and floaty. Maybe Chet was right. What a good friend. *Hiccup.* "Miranda, Panda, I'm so sorry but Chet needs me to go. But can I get your number?" He felt Chet's hand unable to wrap around his bicep and unable to budge him.

Miranda smiled and handed Mark her business card.

Mark smiled at his maybe-future-wife. "Thanks." Then, way behind Chet, he hurriedly bumbled through the dancing crowd toward the front door, but bumped into a wall and fell onto a table, spilling the drinks of a group of bare-shouldered women who all laid hands on his bod and asked if he was all right and asked him to stay, experiencing a variety of different women's hands and voices at once. *Nice. Chet would be proud.* But he politely explained to them that he got Miranda's phone number as he grabbed a handful of his pant leg and wriggled around to unstick his dang balls, and the ladies shrieked!

So much for an easy-going evening.

"Isn't a Galactic Fucker Upper fun?" Bonnie said from the bar.

Too Galactically fun to even find the door.

"Thanks. He needed some fun," Chet said to Bonnie, laughing and racing back and body slamming Mark's body out the door and back into the night.

Chapter 4

HOLY TALLYWACKERS. This night was off the hook.

Cold air and bar neon turned bare legs blue as Kris felt Bren's hands on her arms, hurrying her through dark and colorful Cow Hollow, and onto their next adventure.

"Well," Kris said. "So far we've bumped into our old buffoons, danced with new ones, and been in a bar fight. We're off to a wild start."

"Yes." Bren sighed. "By sunrise we'll be on the FBI's most wanted list. Awesome."

"I wanna go back and kick that girl's ass who said 'fuck you' to me." Kris turned around.

Bren blocked her. "No ass kicking. You need to grow beyond that crap."

"You gotta stand up to people who do you wrong."

"Not with fists," Bren said, steering Kris back around. "It's time to go see Holly."

"You never fight back."

"I solve problems calmly."

"Too calm," Kris said. "That girl needs to be pinned in a leg-lock like when I tackled that shoplifter."

"You were drunk; it was a mannequin."

"Is that why no one thanked me?"

Bren smirked. "It's why I hustled you out of that store. It's why I just hustled you out of Back Scratch. You lose your temper, especially when you drink, and then we can't go back to places. There's five restaurants on this street we can't eat at anymore, and now one bar."

"Hey," Kris said. "If we can never go back to that bar again, then now you can bang Barry. You're welcome."

Bren shook her head as she walked. "Calm down. And you need to chillax before you get arrested again. You don't want *two strikes*. Do you understand the sports lingo?"

Kris exhaled and kept walking toward the faint pretty purple of twilight.

Clack ... clack ... clack ...

"10 ... 9 ... 8 ..." Kris counted.

Delicious neon, and streetlights, and car lights stretched down Union Street, framed by mixed-shaped little buildings lit streetlight-yellow with dark windows because no one was at home.

"7 ... 6 ... 5 ..."

Everyone was out and about, walking in groups, bunching outside bars, gabbing, laughing, and hanging out, holding hands or eyeing for a hookup, all under a big, magical-looking moon above all the sparkly nightlights where anything could happen.

"4 ... 3 ... 2 ..."

Yeah, their paradise was much funner than a jail cell. That would be a bad change.

"... 1."

She felt Bren's hands release off her shoulders. "You gotta stop worrying about me," Kris said.

Then, at the corner of Union and Laguna, in front of them they saw a guy push his friend sitting in an office rolling chair across Union Street as the friend laughed out "Weeeeeeee!"

"Hey," Bren said. "There's your chance to ride a Segway."

Kris smiled. "That looks like an early model."

They watched the Segway guys continue rolling over Union's other sidewalk and down Laguna Street's hill, as Kris's eyes saw a girl sitting on the Laguna's side street, in the dark, in a foofy red skirt and pink t-shirt, sitting on the sidewalk, her back against the hard concrete of the two-story building, with her face buried in her hands, and crying. "What the hell?"

"Oh," Bren said. "We should check on her and ..."

Kris quickly ran across the street, dodging cars, passing the bright jewelry store window and rushed down the hill into the dark.

Clack-clack-clack-clack.

Kris dropped down to the girl.

"Hey there. What's wrong?"

The girl's head popped up. Her young-twenties face was soaked with black mascara tear-streams, her hands gripped her knees, and the despair in the girl's big eyes melted Kris's thumping heart.

"It's all right," Kris told her. "What happened?"

No answer. Just woeful eyes and quivering lips.

Kris quickly looked around for a culprit but didn't see anyone. She latched her fingers on the girl's cold hands. "You can talk to me, sweetie."

No answer.

"Did someone hurt you?" Kris's blood boiled.

The girl's mouth opened. "I'm not a *drama queeeeeeeen!*"

Kris tilted her head. "*What?*"

"He called me a 'drama queen.'" Sobbing. "But I'm not."

"Who?"

"Huck."

"Who's Huck?"

Sobs.

"Is Huck your boyfriend?"

"Not anymorrrre," she super-sobbed.

Kris exhaled. Her right ear heard Bren *clacking* down, and her right hand reached out.

Always-organized-Bren pulled out a pack of Kleenex.

Kris grabbed it, yanked out a wad of tissues, and wildly wiped the girl's mascara-smeared cheeks like a fluttering bird to a tickled face, smudging all the tears off her.

The girl looked *WTF surprised.*

Kris grinned at the girl's Bart Simpson tat on her upper arm as she cleaned and cleaned her face.

"Let her keep her nose," Bren said.

"I'm being thorough."

"I wish you'd clean your room that thorough."

"I wish you'd keep watch."

Bren pulled out pepper spray and looked around the dark side street.

"It's gonna be alright," Kris said as she cleaned. "Heartbreak is only the shattering of your most treasured core, no big deal. Did Huck get engaged to some trollop he just met?"

"Um, no."

"Then you're doing better than me."

"What's a troller?"

"Have you been drinking?" Kris asked her.

"No. I can't afford anything."

Kris got most of the mascara smears off and saw an adorable girl staring back at her with a smile so grateful that it tore Kris's heart apart. "What's your name?"

"Calli."

"Hey, Calli. I'm Krista, Kris for short. She's Brenda, Bren for short."

"I'm Calli, for long."

Kris smiled.

"So, what happened? Did your boyfriend cheat? Dump you? Did you catch him screwing a vacuum cleaner?"

The girl half-smiled, then re-frowned. "I doinked it up."

"Doinked what up?"

"Me and Huck. I doinked us."

Kris wondered what doinking she did. She didn't see any bruises. "Did he hurt you?" Kris pursed her lips.

"No." The girl tussled her long hair away from her face. "I sorta cheated on him. Then he left. And now I'm alone, and homeless, and I only have $9 left, so I'm gonna have to go back to Licking."

"*Licking?*" Kris and Bren both blurted.

"Licking, Missouri."

"Ooooh."

"I'm from Ohio. We're neighbors," Kris said.

"Oh cool."

"Bren's from Boring, Oregon."

Bren gave Kris a look.

"It's boring?"

"The town of Boring."

Calli chuckled through her tears. "Is Boring boring?"

Bren smirked. "So boring that I yearned to escape and come to San Francisco."

"I totally get that," Calli said, her eyes brightening. "I've been dying to escape Licking, but I had to stay and be the noise-maker for my family's haunted apple orchard tour side-hustle and also help with grandpa's hog breeding business. Did you know that pigs can have a half-hour orgasm? I call it an orgas-ham. I usually have a soda while I watch. Anyway, I met Huck a few weeks ago at the Thirsty Badger when he was passing through from some town called Prizzon on his way out here to visit his brother. And I thought this is divine installation – heaven sent me an angel to leave Licking and I gotta go. Grandpa sent all the hogs to live happily in Hawaii to pay his friends at the casino, and the sheriff shut down the orchard tour, so I was free to be free. And I hopped in Huck's truck. The trip was really

fun, seeing all the states. But ever since we started living in his
brother's we've just been arguing."

Kris and Bren looked at each other. *Who was this girl?*

"Huck promised we'd drive out here and have fun. But he's
just been hanging out at his brother's place eating cookies and
laughing. I kept wanting us to go dancing at San Francisco clubs,
but Huck kept ignoring me, so I tried to get his attention by
flirting with other guys, but, instead of appreciating me more,
Huck kicked over the pigeons steaks on the grill and then Huck
called me a 'drama queen' and took off in his car. And his brother was toothless, not my type. So I came here. I love your polka
dot top and green skirt."

Kris smiled and stuck her tongue out at Bren.

Bren rolled her eyes.

"But I'm not a 'drama queen.' I don't wanna cause trouble. I
just wanna have fun and live and love and *feeeeeeel* ... feel everything! I wanna *live. Now. While I'm young.* I'm gonna be *twen-
ty-three,* and then *twenty-four, and twenty-five.* I wanna have a
ton of fun before I have to get old and real and responsible and
stuff. And San Francisco seems like so much fun. I wanted to
come here and see all the fancy dress boutiques, and cupcake
shops, and awesome bars. But Huck just wanted to hang with
his brother. And the makeup store here is huge."

Kris nodded. "Yeah, but it's tough to go in there after you
sleep with the cashier's boyfriend."

The teary girl chuckled.

Bren shook her head.

Kris sighed. "I didn't know he had a girlfriend ... I think."

"You are dressed so beautiful," Calli said. "Is that dress Gucki?"

"Gucki?"

"She means Gucci," Bren said. "No, it's just a sales rack dress."

"You're both so pretty."

Kris grinned at Calli's also non-matching fashion, a pretty red vintage skirt worn ironically with ripped, black fishnet stockings and white tube socks, along with cheap, torn sneakers.

"Do you dress this awesome all the time? I bet you do. I bet your lives are awesome and I bet you go to awesome parties."

Seeing and hearing this excited newbie to SF was wild, like looking back down a road and seeing how just how damn far she'd traveled. Other young twentiers gave perspective, but this little Midwesterner was like a déjà-frickin'-vu.

Calli folded her arms. "I thought California would be hot."

"Not at night," Kris said.

"Aren't you cold?"

"Yes," Bren blurted.

"But we look hella sexy," Kris joked.

"Yes, freezing-chic is very in here," Bren said.

"You should go inside somewhere and get warm," Calli said.

"What are you gonna do?" Kris asked.

"I don't know. I guess I'll go back to Concord."

"*Concord?*" Kris and Bren both blurted.

"You took BART fifty miles to sit here in the dark?"

"Thirty miles," Bren corrected.

"Whatever."

"I wanted to see this fun neighborhood, and *party* like a 'California Gurl,'" Calli said. "But now I feel bad that I did bad to Huck, and my family will be mad that I left and now I'm on the sidewalk, and they'll think I'm even more of a mess, and I'm too embarrassed to call them and ask for money, and now I'm totally *homeless!*" More tears.

Kris's heart pounded her ribs. She exhaled and stood. "Get up, Calli."

Calli stood up.

Kris looked little Calli in the eyes. "Forget dumbhead-Huck, forget feeling bad. Crap happens. You're an awesome girl and you're gonna rock this town. And I'm gonna help you."

"You are?"

Kris cleared her throat.

Bren sighed.

"My parents were super strict," Kris said. "And the day I graduated high school I snuck out a window, pawned their rare spoon collection for cash, and jumped on a train to as far away as I could go, and I ended up in San Francisco. Finally *free*. And broke as fuck. I flirted with dudes so I could stay at their places, but they'd always dump me for a girl who had money for their drug habits, and I ended up crying on a sidewalk in torn sneakers too. But a nice woman, Hazel, saw me and invited me to live in her house, along with a bunch of other girls new to the city. I lived with Hazel and seven misfit roommates in this kinda crappy house in San Francisco where we had to wash dishes in the bathtub. It was like a new family, a sane family, and figured out how to like, you know, live normal. I worked crap jobs, and dated some non-addict guys, then somehow talked my way into a job as a nanny for rich fuckers. I earned enough cash to share an apartment with a nurse on Union Street with Zelda, and she helped me get into nursing school, but I got kicked out. And then my roommate Zelda moved to New York and Bren moved in, and Bren suggested I go to physical trainer school. I did! Now I have awesome friends, a great apartment, a family of patio plants, I do a weekly exercise vlog, and I make bank as a physical trainer for even richer fuckers. I went from nothing to everything, 'cause of a kind stranger and relentlessness!" Kris threw her fist to the sky like a champion!

Calli tilted her head.

Kris stared at Calli. Did she not understand anything she said? Kris put her arm down. "Calli, you're who I was. You gotta do what I did. Stop crying and start working. Start at Hazel's house. You'll be safe there. And work your way up into a great life in San Francisco as a tough cookie no one can F with."

Calli stared unblinking at Kris.

"I know what you're thinking," Bren said to Calli. "It's not a brothel. The place is actually pretty nice, if you like hippie tie-dye decorations and listening to Hazel sing the soundtrack to *The Sound of Music* all the time."

Calli stayed unblinking.

Kris found a mess of cash in her purse and stuffed the warm green into Calli's cold hands.

Calli's eyes popped.

"I'm giving you two hundred bucks."

Calli looked like she'd never seen so many twenties at one time.

"That's enough for food and a little extra to get started building a life in SF."

Calli's mouth fell open. "You want me to wash dishes in a bathtub?"

"Or ..." Bren said. "Calli could come with us."

Kris slowly gave Bren a look. "What?"

"Let her come with us."

"But I just gave my big speech."

"And it was good. Calli, wasn't it good?" Bren said.

"It *was* good." Calli nodded wildly. "But kinda freaky."

"Don't take Calli to Hazel's crappy house. Let Calli come with us."

Kris's mouth dropped. "What the dingle-balls are you doing?"

"I'm being nice."

"*I'm* being nice. I'm giving her a place to stay."

"That house is a crap hole. Hazel let girls live there just because she hates cooking and housework."

"You want me to live in a crap hole?"

"It's paying your dues. Calli needs to go through crap-times and earn her way up to Cow Hollow to truly appreciate how awesome it is."

"I can totally see how awesome it is," Calli blurted.

"Starting low builds character. Toughness. She won't get tough if we let her party in Cow Hollow now."

"I have character," Calli said, jumping around.

Bren chuckled. "See she's already got character. Let her stay with us for a bit."

Kris scoffed. "I can't believe you wanna let a stranger into our super-organized home. What if she doesn't read your reminder notes and forgets to flush?"

"I got a good vibe about Calli," Bren said. "I think she'll flush."

"I'll totally flush," Calli cheered.

"This girl needs to learn to be tough in this world."

"I like *your* world."

"Calli likes our world."

"Who wouldn't?"

"Let's show her our world," Bren said. "If she sees how great Cow Hollow is from the inside then maybe *that* will motivate her to try even harder to 'work her way up through life.'"

"Why are you being a butt about this?" Kris protested.

Bren hugged herself, rubbing her shivering bare arms. "When I graduated college and moved here and was in massive debt you didn't kick me to Hazel's; you kindly let me live with you."

"And after seven years I'm still trying to teach you to stand up for yourself, not cower behind me from your asshole-ex."

"Standing up for oneself doesn't mean yelling and hitting."

"Standing up means not letting anyone make you cry on the sidewalk."

"I'm standing up," Calli said. "See? I'm not crying anymore."

"She's been through some tough stuff already. Let her come have some fun," Bren argued. "Besides, you don't know what she's gonna spend that $200 on. She might blow it all on lottery tickets or drugs."

Kris spun to Calli. "Are you gonna blow it on lottery tickets or drugs?"

"If I say 'yes' can I come with you?"

Kris grimaced.

Bren grinned. "She's not you."

"She's very similar."

"It's cold. It's late. And she's scared. Let her come with us."

Kris pursed her lips.

"*Roommate compromise*," Bren said. "She can crash at our place one night, and then be 'tough' tomorrow."

"Oh *please*," Calli said. "*Please, please, please, please*, Kris. I won't be drama queen, I *swearrrrrrrr*."

Kris looked at Calli's sweet puppy dog face. Then looked at Bren's sympathetic face. Then looked back at Calli's super hopeful eyes gently punching her heart. Cars passed. Distant talk and laughter. A chilly breeze blew Kris's shivering bare skin in the moonlight. "All right," Kris sighed. "You can come with us."

"YEEEEEEEEAH!" Calli hooted.

"Just for tonight," Kris made clear. "One night of fun. Then you live in crap."

"Cool," Calli cheered. "Oh my God! You're so so great!" Calli shrieked and hopped and hopped and hopped and hugged each of them. "Thank you soooo much."

Bren smiled at Kris, as if she was proud of her.

This was such a bad idea.

Now with them taking care of Calli, their night looked like they were leaning less towards passion and more towards pancakes.

"There's so many cute guys around here," Calli said with a huge grin. "Will you help me hookup with one?"

Or leaning more towards passion.

"For now," Kris said to her, "let's focus on you texting your family and telling them you're all right so they don't worry, and then we'll get you into a nice warm bar."

"And show her a great Cow Hollow night," Bren said.

"Oh, thank you!"

Kris hoped this wasn't a huuuuge F-ing mistake. "When's the last time you ate?"

"I don't even know."

"I wish I had that burger from the bar."

Bren reached into her purse and pulled out a thing wrapped in napkins.

"OMG, Bren. You're so on the ball."

"Wow," Calli said. "Your purses are full of magic."

"They might be full of vomit later," Kris said, as she unwrapped her burger. *Oh wow.* It smelled so good and spicy. She could feel Stacy's emptiness *wanting* it. But Kris didn't go with her gut and instead handed it's tempting greasiness to Calli.

The big smile on Calli's face actually warmed Kris way more than booze or horniness.

"You're so nice. Thank you!" She began scarfing down the bunless-burger.

"Damn, you must have been starving," Kris said.

"I bidn't eben rebalize," Calli said with a mouthful of the beautiful burger.

Grrrrrrrrowl.

"Shush, Stacy."

"Who's Stacy?"

Chapter 4

DANG, THAT DRINK was strong.

Mark wobbled through the Marina's carnival of colorful neon lights, smiling, clutching Miranda's business card, hoping the cold night air would sober up his drunktitude so he could make it up his stairs and face-plant into his bed. "Well," Mark said. "We found out Jill's in a new relationship, we did the bar scene, and we met new women." *Hiccup.* "Let's go home."

"No way, dude," Chet said, walking fast and waving him on. "We're not done tonight until we're both bumpin' junk with beautiful babes."

"No junk bumping. I found my next girlfriend, and I'm gonna call her tomorrow."

"No you're not. Miranda's a dead end street. And she's probably meeting some other guy right now anyway."

Mark stopped. "Then I should go back to her." Mark turned around.

Chet raced around and blocked him. "Forget Miranda."

"She's nice. Her shampoo could replace Jill's by tomorrow night."

"No, you knucklehead."

113

Chet tossed his hands in the air. "You shouldn't let a new girl-friend move in. At least not for a year. What is wrong with you?"

What was wrong with Chet? Living with a woman was the best thing ever; why delay?

"Hey," Chet said. "Did Miranda give you her business card?"

"She did." Mark smiled and showed him.

Chet snatched it and ripped it to pieces.

Mark's heart dropped. "What the heck are you doing??"

"She's no good for you," Chet said as he ran up the street and tossed the business card confetti down a drain.

What? "Chet. I can't believe you did that? What is wrong with you?"

"I'm helping you."

"*You're* the knucklehead. That's my next relationship you just threw down the sewer."

"No she isn't."

"I gotta go back and re-get Miranda's number." Mark turned around again.

Chet raced around and blocked his way again "Trust me, man. From now on all your girl choices have to be approved by me."

"Miranda was great."

"She's not great for *you*," Chet insisted. "Miranda hates danc-ing and baseball and you were willing to settle for her? That's ridiculous."

"She's a nice person."

"That's not enough. You want a good fit, right?"

"I just wanna be happy."

"No, you just want to be with someone. *Anyone.* And Miranda's not gonna make you happy. She's wrong for you; so is Panda. They both said they hate lawyers. Deal breaker. Done."

Mark thought about all that. It *would* be nicer to have a girlfriend who liked stuff he liked, but that would be asking for the moon. The only way to maybe find a woman that matchable was to do the online dating thing, and that stuff felt so mechanical and unromantic. No, meeting a woman had to be real-life, authentic.

Chet pushed on Mark's big arm with two hands until he got him turned around and walking east with him again. "I figured out why your relationships don't last," Chet said. "You pick the wrong girls."

"I pick great women."

"You just picked the first girl you met so you don't have to be single. You swing at every pitch, any pitch. I bet that's what you did with all of your ex-girlfriends."

Mark started to argue ... then thought. *Hmmm.*

"I watched you ask for the phone number from a girl who actually hates what you enjoy," Chet said. "You were willing to completely throw your life away for a bit of romance. You move too fast, man, with the first girl you meet, not 'cause you love the girl, it's 'cause you love love, more than the girl."

Mark's drunktitude didn't quite understand.

"You gotta be way more selective," Chet said. "You need deal breakers. Stop negotiating your love life. Don't settle. Don't be afraid to be single, and be picky."

Mark just stood, thinking, re-seeing his entire love life.

"You need to break you love habit and focus on appreciating a girl, as many as possible." Chet raised his phone and showed a pic of three women. "That's Vanessa, Sara, and Jane. And we're gonna go meet up with them. Vanessa bexted me in the bar and invited us."

Mark tilted his head. "That's why we left? So you could have sex? You said we should leave the bar because I was saying drunk, crazy things. I thought you didn't 'false advertise.'"

"I didn't. You *were* saying drunken, crazy crap in there, asking Miranda if she'd was interested in moving to the Marina. I had to get you out of there. *And* we're gonna go see these girls."

"I'm going home."

"No you're not. You owe me. I just saved you from years in the wrong relationship. You owe me more Pap-a-Dap, and wingmanning me to woo Vanessa."

"Who's Vanessa?"

"Vanessa's *the* hottest hottie in the whole Marina. She finally bexted me, with the best bext I've ever been bexted."

"If she bexted *you* then you don't need me."

"I *do* need you," Chet insisted. "You don't understand. Vanessa is my fantasy girl that I finally found in reality."

"Really?"

"Yeah. I get Vanessa and you hookup with her two best hottie friends, Jane and Sara. *Two.*"

Mark rolled his eyes. "You want me to wingman *two* women?"

Chet grinned ear to ear. "You're welcome."

"I'm a winger, not a swinger."

"You are tonight."

"I'm not."

"I got no single friends. I *need* you to swing."

"No way."

"I need you to woo her friends away so I can woo Vanessa."

"Woo?"

"Yeah," Chet explained. "To woo: to flirt, to charm, to romance."

"You romance?"

"Sure. Just not for years, like you do."

"I've never wooed two."

"Tonight you woo two."

"I don't wanna woo two."

"You gotta woo two."

"I can't woo two, I've never hooked up with one."

"Shoot for the moon!"

Chet's word "moon" suddenly gave Mark an idea. He realized exactly who Chet needed. A perfect, fully functional wingman who could woo two while Mark could be by Chet to see if Vanessa and his friend had more-than-a-hookup couple chemistry and, if they did, *encourage* that; this bext could blossom into a beautiful romance, a long-term love, a marriage, and Mark was now eager to help his new friend finally feel the greatest wonderfulness in life, and get Chet to not bug him anymore to go out every frickin' night. At the corner of Chestnut and Pierce again, in the orange neon of the busy gourmet burger place,

Mark typed a text for a wingman, a "wext", then got a wext back, and smiled.

"What'd you just do?" Chet asked.

Keeping his commitment to be a wingman tonight, Mark gave him a grin. "I'm helping you."

"How?"

"He's on his way."

"Who?"

"The right man for the job."

Two minutes later a dude came towards them, strutting like a skinny John Travolta in *Saturday Night Fever*, but skinnier, handsomer, neatly trimmed hair, and seeing the Marina's Gap and Starbucks stores through thick-framed hipster glasses. He was sportin' fashionable slacks and a stylin' shirt, dressed to impress, and his shoes as shiny as the confidence in his eyes. Mark recognized him from the family picture his coworker Rick had in his office, and Mark hoped all the "master of romance" stories Rick had told him about the dude were true. Chet was frowning.

The dude was smiling. "Yo, bro's."

"This *dude*?" Chet exclaimed.

"This dude." Mark shook the dude's hand. "Good to finally meet you, man."

"You too," the dude said.

"Your bother told me that you were in town now."

"I am."

"You got here fast," Mark said.

"I was Tinder-datin' right across the street at the Delarosa, bro," the dude said with a smile.

"Oh yeah?"

"Yeah."

"Thanks for coming," Mark said.

"Thanks for the invite," he said to Mark. "Your text helped me bale out of a downhill date. She was eye-candy, but me and she had no chem. The sex would have been meh. I need more than meh."

"My friend Chet has more-than-meh in mind."

"Oh yeah?"

"He needs a wingman, actually a swingman," Mark said. "And since your brother was telling me about all the dating you did back East, I thought of you."

The guy grinned. "You thought right."

Chet thumb-pointed. "This skinny guy's gonna help me?"

"Be nice," Mark said. "Chet, this is Skip."

"*Skip?*"

"I'm Skip." Skip offered his hand for a shake.

Chet carefully shook Skip's thin hand, as if scared of crushing it. Chet looked skeptical of Skip, eyeing him up and down.

"Skip is my coworker's brother," Mark explained. "Skip just moved here last week and doesn't have many friends yet, so this is a great opportunity for us to help him make friends while he's helping you. And you two can become friends. Everybody wins."

"Thanks, bro," Skip said.

"Skip's brother's always telling me Skip is a Casanova."

"Oh, I'd call myself a Romeo."

"He's also got a great job. He just moved here from Washington."

"State?"

"D.C."

"Born and raised there?" Mark asked.

"No. I was born in Funny Town, Texas."

"What?"

"Where?"

Skip smiled. "I grew up in Austin, but I was born in the car while passing through Funny Town."

Chet tilted his head. "I need to know more about you, Skip. What's your job?"

"I'm a lawyer."

"Like Mark?"

"Different."

"Sports?"

"Space."

"What?"

"Skip's a space lawyer."

"What the hell's a space lawyer?"

"Laws in space," Skip said. "I prosecute little green space aliens."

"What?" Chet panicked. "Mark, did you bring me a crazy guy?"

Skip laughed.

Mark laughed. "Skip's joking."

"You're joking?"

"I'm joking."

Chet breathed.

"Space law's a real thing," Mark assured him.

Skip handed Chet his business card. "I negotiate international agreements and territorial disputes pertaining to non-Earth celestial bodies."

"What?"

"He decides who owns the Moon."

"That's a job?"

"Oh yeah."

"In San Francisco?"

"Oh yeah," Skip said. "I hooked up with a firm out here after I visited my brother and completely fell heels over head for this city. I moved to the Marina a week ago and I love it here. It's –"

"Out of this world?" Chet mocked.

"Exactly."

"Glad to know some people are still moving *to* the Marina," Mark said.

"Dudes."

"Except," Skip continued. "The city's light pollution makes the stars tough to see. We should all take my telescope out of the town sometime to see the stars better."

"Great idea," Mark said. "Any excuse to get out of the city and hike and camp and rock climb and now to stare at the stars. Except Chet doesn't really like to leave the city." Maybe Chet could be his city-friend and Skip could be his out-doors-friend.

"*Dude*," Chet said.

"Yeah?" Mark said.

"Forget the stupid the stars. You're supposed to be helping me."

"I'm helping you."

"Helping? The Pap-a-Dap of Marina girls wants wooing and you send me the space lawyer from Funny Town?"

Mark laughed. "Calm down. Skip's got a rep for wooing."

"*I'm* not wooed by him yet."

Skip looked confused. "I'm supposed to woo *you?*"

"Not me. Woo a girl," Chet said.

"What girl?"

"The most amazing girl ever."

"I'm wooing the most amazing girl ever?"

"No. *I'm* wooing the most amazing girl ever," Chet stressed. "You're wooing her friends."

"More than one? Sweetness."

"Except, I'm not sure you're the right guy for the job."

"Why not?"

"Well. You're not really ... buff."

"Chet, be nice," Mark said.

"I'm being real," Chet said. "He's got no muscles."

"So?"

Chet proudly displayed the pics of Vanessa and her friends to Skip.

"Wow, those girls are as hot as the sun."

"That's how A-level this gig is. And the sexy one in the middle wants *me*, finally," Chet explained.

Mark smirked, and thought that negotiating between Chet and Skip would be much easier without the Galactic F-er Upper in his system. "Chet, I'm sure Skip can talk to Vanessa's friends if that's what you need him to do."

"I need him to be big and desirable so the girls will keep talking to him."

"You don't think I can woo?" Skip said with a grin.

"Skip, I don't mean to offend," Chet said. "You seem nice and you're probably really smart since you work with the Moon. But this opportunity with Vanessa is *the* most monumental moment of my life. I've been hot for Vanessa and trying to hookup with her for almost a year. She's flighty and this is my big one-and-only chance to impress her. So I need quality wingmen to charm her two friends. And when Vanessa sees her friends are in good hands for the night then she'll feel free to be with me."

Skip laughed. "Is he kidding me?"

"Chet, you're being ridiculous, and kind of not nice," Mark said.

"It's okay." Skip shrugged at Mark and smirked, as if enjoying Chet's doubt, as he stepped up with all the wingman-ish swagger that Chet probably wished Mark had, and opened his arms toward Chet as if grandly presenting himself. "Dude, I'm your *dude*."

Chet shook his head. "You're not buff."

"Give me a minute, I'll do some push-ups."

Chet chuckled. "He *is* funny."

"He's a nice guy," Mark said.

"But dude."

"*Dude*," Skip assured him. "Don't judge a book by its cover. Remember when Luke looked at the Falcon and said it was junk and it turned out to be the coolest thing ever? I'm the Falcon. I'm the best wingman ever." Skip pulled aside the collar of his dress shirt and revealed an eye-catching maroon hickey on his neck. "That's a fresh one from a girl I met at lunch and invited me back to her place for an afternoon delight."

Chet's eyes got wide, and his mouth grew a grin.

Skip pushed up his glasses with a finger. "I ain't jacked like Mark, but I don't need to be," Skip said with swagger in his voice. "I got charisma. I got game. And, dude, I got your back."

Nice. "Sounds like a good deal," Mark negotiated. "What'dya say?"

Chet stared at Skip, then at the time on his phone.

Night sounds. Cars motoring. People talking. Moon moving.

"Fine ... okay."

Skip smiled big. "Cool."

"Good," Mark said.

Chet looked down at his bulge in his pants. "Heads up, buddy, we might get let into Vanessa-land tonight."

Mark rolled his eyes. But it felt good to bring Skip and Chet together. Maybe they could even be friends. He grinned at this interesting team.

Chet looked *really* hopeful at his team.

Mark paused, now realizing he had to go with them to make sure Chet wasn't going to be not-nice to Skip, and going back to his empty apartment and being alone would be awful. It'd be better to go to more bars than being home alone. So much for bed.

"Let's get walking," Chet said.

"Yeah," Skip agreed. "It's so cold my balls are freezing."

"I bet Mark's balls are *really* freezing," Chet joked.

Mark smirked.

Skip looked confused. "Why are your balls *really* freezing?"

Chapter 5

KRIS GUIDED Calli's little shoulders west down Union Street's neon kaleidoscope of cool bars with lines-out-the-door and music blasting. Like hanging onto a wild, zigzagging rocket, Calli whooshed her body left and right gawking at all the crowded venues on both sides of the glittery street, the bars, the restaurants, while this wide-eyed girl in her hands asked a million questions about every fun place they passed and how she'd just read about all these cool bars on this thing she'd tried for the first time recently called "the internet."

Wooooooooow, Kris thought. *Calli was a hoot, but really naïve.* Kris didn't remember being as clueless about things when she also left a small Midwestern town. It was as if Calli's family had reeeeeeeally sheltered her from the world, waaaaaaaaay too much. It was like watching a released house cat experience grass and trees and internet for the first time. Kris suddenly felt a strange caring need to chaperon clueless-Calli through all this big city newness. The too-trusting little zig-zagger might get mixed up with not-nice people or date a douchebag who dumps her for a Leeeesa. Kris held onto Calli even tighter as they walked through Cow Hollow's pretty nightlife, past bars and cafés, and the –

"Oh no," Kris blurted, as she stopped. "Tula's Trinket Shop is closing."

"It is?" Bren said.

"Look at the sign: 'going out of business sale.'"

"No more chicken snow globes for us."

"Damn. Everything's changing," Kris said. "We gotta buy a bunch of their stuff, to keep them in business."

Bren shook her head. "We'll buy none of their stuff, because you can't even walk through your junk-filled bedroom as it is." Bren guided Kris's shoulders forward, while Kris guided Calli's.

"*Roommate compromise*," Kris said as they walked. "We'll buy one last thing there as a souvenir."

Bren sighed. "One small thing."

"We'll go halfsies on a gumball lamp."

"Nope."

"A unicorn coatrack."

"Nope."

"A Hello Kitty pool table."

"A *small* thing."

Kris gasped. "*A disco ball.*"

"A disco ball?"

"Oh yeah, that's totally what we need."

"For all the disco-ing we do?"

"For our bathroom."

"Our bathroom?"

"Instead of my plants," Kris said. "We'll hang it up high from the ceiling so my dancing can't knock it over."

"A disco ball?"

"Bathroom time with Debbie the Disco Ball would make you less stressed while you wait for me and make things so fun. Showers would be magical. Brushing hair would be a party. Oh, Bren, imagine peeing among spinning stars!"

"I'd get dizzy and fall off the toilet."

"We'd put a seatbelt on it for you."

Bren grinned.

Kris laughed.

Calli smiled. "You guys bicker."

"I think we banter," Bren said.

"I think we'll be bathroom disco dancing," Kris said.

Calli did her own kind of dancing outside every lit up place they passed. She two-hand waved "hello" to grinning eaters at tables outside upscale Perry's, pointed at the glamazons packed outside Blue Light bar, applauded the sporty hunks outside rollicking Bar None, and bounced by all the lipstick-marked Appletini glasses at Betel Nut's open-doored, festive-red-tabled foodie and drink extravaganza!

Jeez, it was like literally hanging onto the mid-west-meets-big-city-girl she once was when she first jumped off the train and ogled at all these glitzy party palaces, reliving that *zing* of excitement, and suddenly catching a holy-shit-clue that that was ten years and a hundred shoes ago. She watched her Gucci ankle boots striding steady beside Calli's dirty, racing-all-around sneakers ... *and saw how much had changed.*

Wow.

"I'm so happy!" Calli shouted. "My tiny town has nothing like these lights and laughs and long lines and pretty peeps dressed chic and gorgeous buildings and cool bars and so much WOW I wanna dance! Can we dance? Which bar is best for dancing? I wanna dance with hot sweaty guys all night and and and and I'm so happy!"

Bren and Kris shared a look: *Wow, this girl sure perked up.*

And people say *I* have energy, Kris thought as she kept her hands locked on Calli and facing her forward.

Bren turned into a tour guide. "Calli, this eatery is where a guy choked on chicken and Kris saved his life."

"He choked his chicken?"

"He choked *on* chicken."

"And this place has great crab," Bren shared with her. "This is where we once met some guys and we pretended to be from Australia."

"You speak Australian?"

"Um, yeah. But our Aussie-faking all went to heck when *they* turned out to be from Australia. But then we found out they were faking Australian too."

"Did you hook up with them?"

Kris smiled. "I went down under."

"Under where?"

"You said underwear."

"Yeah." Calli stared blankly.

"Never mind

"Calli," Bren said. "You're should come to brunch tomorrow."

"Yay!"

Kris frowned.

BLEE-DEE

Bren looked at her phone. "Another text from Holly."

"Hey everyone, another text from Holly!" Kris hollered to the neon neighborhood. Drunk partiers outside of the bars "whoooooooo"ed back wildly for no reason.

Bren rolled her eyes.

Kris grinned.

Bren read Holly's text aloud as they walked: "Sittin g by the front winndow. Wow, four grammatical errors and *ten* emojis. Holly's tipsy."

"For serious? Holly let herself get tipsy?"

"We should meet up with her before she runs out of emojis." Bren texted Holly back that they were on their way to see her.

"Who's Holly?"

"She's a friend. We're on our way to meet up with her at a really fun club," Kris said.

"Yay!" Calli clapped. "Will there be hot guys?"

Kris raised her eyebrows.

Bren chuckled. "Imagine a male-model runway after-party, and none of them have read Dickenson."

"*Wow*," Calli whooped. "What's Dick in Sand?"

Bren's eyes went wide. "Tomorrow I'm giving a box of books."

Calli smiled. "Cool."

Kris pushed both dawdlers onward past all the stylish places packed with pretty people that Calli said she had only seen in magazine pics of Hollywood award parties, the "cool-crowd" she'd always dreamed of partying with. Kris kept her walking.

Bren kept them stopping to say "hi" to friends waiting in lines outside the hoppin' bars and restaurants along the way. Hugged, gabbed, gossiped, and Bren kept introducing everyone to their "new friend Calli."

Calli's face lit up like the sun every time Bren called her "friend."

Kris pulled Calli along, oddly finding herself now the one to keep them on schedule, as she kept their party moving, walking west, across Fillmore Street, turning right down the hill, and popping in and out of the Mauna Loa Club, and Comet Club, and Cellar Door, and Pizza Orgasmica, and Balboa Lounge, quick-hello-ing with friends, like usual, Calli probably getting the Cali experience she had traveled all the way here to have. Then they crossed back across Fillmore again, hello-ed at Eastside West tavern, and Matrix, then walked back up the hill a bit, and full-stopped at the big two-story building, lit up like a colorful, crowded carnival, with letters above the front glass door shining the infamous bar's name: Big Hoopla Bar.

Techno bass beats boomed out of the open door, and the club looked spectacular as usual. Calli ogled all the pretty lights and pretty people and the bright classy nightclub, clearly seeing that this was *the* hot spot in town.

They got into the long line out front beside the front window and Kris spotted Holly sitting on a sofa inside. Kris tapped on the glass and Holly's silky, blue shoulder-showing dress gracefully turned around toward Kris, and she waved with an open-mouthed smile and pointed toward the front door.

Not about to wait a half-hour in line, Kris guided Calli past dress-shirt-jeans-and-dress-shoes guys and mini-dress-skin-showing girls up to the front of the line. She heard Bren's footsteps reluctantly following, knowing that Bren hated cutting, but Kris knew that Bren was aware that her bestie would make a BIG LOUD scene if Bren stayed in line and refused this special treatment.

Calli looked worried. "Can I get in? I'm not dressed as cool as all these girls."

Kris gave Calli a wink, and gave the tight-shirted doorman a BIG hug! "Dylan," Kris cheered, then gripped his grapefruit-size biceps. "Holy crotch-candy, I can feel how mega-muscled my workouts are getting you."

His smile stretched up to his sideburns. "Yeah, baby doll. You're gonna get me benching SUVs."

"Hell yeah. You're looking beef cakey."

"And you're looking fine as divine in your skimpy skirt."

"Thanks, sugar." Kris pulled Calli close.

Then Dylan's smile fell sideways seeing Calli's under-dressed-for-the-club thrift store clothes.

Kris leaned her elbow on Dylan's boulder shoulder. "It's okay, handsome, she's with us," she blew gentle into his ear.

Calli smiled big at "she's with us" and shakily handed over her driver's license.

Kris finger-combed Calli's tangled, jungle.

His fingers held Calli's I.D., as music thumped and sidewalk people passed.

Kris could feel Calli's shoulders trembling with worry that she wouldn't get in, her whole future in the hands of this nice, but frowning door guy.

Kris tensed, *ready to cause a scene.*

Dylan grinned. "*Licking?*" He laughed, then winked at Calli as he handed back her card. "You just made my night, girl. Have fun."

Kris smiled and gave his grapefruits a "thank you" squeeze.

He kept laughing.

"Thank you, thank you, thank you!" Calli jumped up and down.

Kris's hands quickly steered her bouncer away from the bouncer and got her through the open door, out of the chilly night, and into the warm wonderland of wow!

Kris watched Calli actually slow to a *halt* now in full view of the glitzy epicenter of San Francisco's in-crowd, still unsure about letting a newbie who hadn't earned it see just how damn glorious life can be from the inside. But it was pretty heart swelling seeing this torn-sneaker girl's eyes pop as wide as her open mouth taking in heaven on Earth: the beautiful colors, beautiful clothes, beautiful bar, to the beautiful DJ's pulsing thump-thump-thumps pumping hard and inspiring dress shoes and high heels to dance. But there was no room to flail about in this big but crowded-cozy place packed with pretty people, plush couches, and cocktail tables with pink and purple drinks picked up and sipped by super sexy partiers showing-off bare shoulders, flicking hair, and flirting with muscled dress-shirt hunks. So many hot hunks. All over this warm-sherbet-orange-lamped lodge from the large maroon-ish velvet-padded walls to the kickass classy, shiny bar where supermodel heart-throbs and hotties shook, poured and served mingling singles and laughing lovers in this glorious paradise!

Seeing Calli's huge smile re-pumped Kris's love this magical place too. It really was great. So many laughs and lays from here. Back Scratch was a nice start of their night, but this place was the peak of the nightlife mountain, with a view so spectacular she never wanted to climb down. But they couldn't linger on Everest too long tonight or Calli might get attached. She steered Calli through the tight, talky crowd, sliding passed fabrics of Chanel, Dior, and through plumes of perfume and cologne and armpit, and through an orgy of voices, a vorgy:

"what's her deal?" "his parents are in oil"
"your extensions are boss" "private equity"
"I was like 'no way'" "turning thirty"
"he took me sailing" "OMG you're so savage"
"Balmain" "bandwidth" "Botox"
"now it's an eyebrow salon"
"love"
"Pilates" "text 'em and have 'em join us"
"World Series" "$5,000 rent" "wedding" "swag"
"hashtag" "so fetch" "vjazzle" "dick pic"
Such Marina girl things to say.

They squeezed their way around, and then back up toward the front windows.

Kris saw Holly still guarding several reserved seats by the front window.

Dazzling Holly sat elegantly upright in her sexy/sophisticated royal blue dress, like a perfect window display for the club, with a sparkling blue cocktail in her long thin fingers as she confabulated with a glamorous-looking couple, while Holly's boyfriend sat staring at his phone and not his girlfriend.

Kris, Calli, and Bren approached and overheard Holly's royal conversation with the gorgeous couple.

"It's a come-hither motion," Holly was saying to them.

"Heeeey!" Kris cheered, feeling soberer than a half-hour ago.

Holly smiled, excused herself, and floated up from her comfy couch, pitter-pattering her pumps over to give warm greetings gracefully without spilling a drop of her blue Bombay Sapphire.

The couple moved on.

Hug! "Heeeeeeeeeey, Krista!"

Hug! "Heeeeeeeeeey, Brenda!"

Kris leaned out of the plume of Holly's sweet perfume.

Holly looked at them, smiling. "I'm so happy you're finally here. How are you two?"

"Not nearly drunk enough," Kris said.

"How's your night so far?"

Kris smirked. "Exes, buffoons, and bar fights."

"A typical Saturday night," Bren said.

"You have to tell me *everything*," Holly's said. "I love hearing your adventures."

"We'll start with our latest adventure." Kris looked around and found Calli wandering off open-mouthed towards the Ralph Lauren-shirted, tall hunks. Kris hooked her arm around her every-moving mini-me and scooted her away from their wolfy-grins.

"Hol, this is Calli," Kris announced over the loud burnin' beats.

Calli's eyes lit up like seeing a movie star.

Holly's eyebrows raised seeing Calli's tattered clothes, and a Cheeto in her hair.

Kris picked it out and tossed it.

"*Hey, my drink,*" someone said.

"Calli," Kris said. "This is our friend Holly."

"Hiiii," Calli greeted her loud and smiley.

"My goodness. You're a ... surprise," Holly said, her gorgeous lips pronouncing each syllable with exquisite diction. Holly smiled and gave her thin hand to Calli who shook it so happily that Holly's drink in her other hand sloshed around. Holly held her drink from her dress and smiled big at this little firecracker. "It's very nice to meet you, Calli."

"Nice to meet yoooooooou," Calli cheered as she looked Holly up and down and looked all around at all the everything going on, then clapped her hands to her cheeks in awe like the *Home Alone* movie kid.

Holly's smile turned toward Kris and Bren. "Soooo. What is happening right now?"

Bren grinned. "We found Calli on the street."

"I found her."

"She's visiting."

"We invited her along."

"Bren invited her."

"She's staying with us."

"One night."

"So we're showing her how fun the Marina is."

"For one hour," Kris said. "Then Bren's taking her back to the apartment until morning while I go find some passion. After I eat a hundred mini crab cakes here."

"One hour?" Bren protested. "But it's our anniversary."

"I know, but *you* invited her, so you're taking her home. And one hour is plenty of time to get a taste of this awesomeness before it's too heartbreaking to leave it."

"You sound like a parent. How did that happen?"

"I don't wanna be a parent, but you made me into a parent."

"She doesn't need a parent," Bren argued. "She's twenty-two."

"She's new. From nothing. Suddenly in everything. I remember wanting all this. She needs a parent. And you're too passive to be a parent, so now I'm the responsible one, and I say you'll take her home in an hour so mama can get some dick."

Holly slid in. "It's not polite to talk about Calli in front of Calli."

They looked at Calli who was looking around.

"Calli," Holly cooed.

Calli kept looking.

137

"Calli."

Calli kept looking.

"Calli!" Kris hollered.

Bren shook her head.

Calli spun around. "Yeah?"

Holly grandly gestured to the cushy seats. "Please come sit with us."

Calli smiled huge. "Cool."

"Welcome, welcome, welcome," Holly said with stretched open arms, like a refined circus ringmaster. "I reserved this whole section. Everyone please ..."

Calli plopped down next to Holly.

"... sit."

Bren and Kris sat down on plush cubes facing Calli and Holly and Holly's boyfriend, who was still staring at his phone.

Holly smiled, sat up straight, and looked like a pretty picture in the big window's frame, the club's light positions striking her silky dress and hair just right to both shimmer splendorously, turning her into a shining star, soooo intentionally, even her lipstick color coordinating with the club's burgundy walls.

"This cushy seat is like a big purple cloud of awesome," Calli said, wiggling her butt on it. "Much more comfy than the concrete sidewalk."

"Sidewalk?" Holly said looking at Kris and Bren with raised eyebrows.

Kris and Bren nodded.

Holly turned back to Calli. "They're magic seats," Holly joked. "They recharge your whole spirit with positive energy the longer you sit your tooshie on them."

"They do?"

"No," Holly said and laughed. "But wouldn't that be great?"

Calli grinned. "You're funny, and so glamorous, but nice and stuff. You're *all* so nice. Maybe California girls aren't all hellcats like the beauty parlor ladies say."

They all grinned.

Kris also grinned at Holly's raised eyebrows-stare studying Calli like seeing a space alien beside her. Instead of keeping one eye on the social scene around them (glancing for celebs, exes, friends, and frenemies, constantly aware of who was there, who they were with, what they were doing, what they were wearing, who might be talking about her and why), both of Holly's spinning eyes kept scanning Calli's unusual attire, but the queen of the Marina remained polite as ever. "Calli," Holly said. "This is my boyfriend, Collin."

Collin looked up, nodded to them, sipped his champagne, then re-stared at his phone.

Kris scowled.

"How are you, Holly?" Bren said.

"I'm doing great. Even greater now that you two are here."

"How many places have you been to tonight, Holly?"

"Oh my gosh. So many. Collin and I have had such a fun evening so far."

Collin yawned.

"Yeah, we got your silly texts," Kris said.

"Silly? Oh no. Did I text something embarrassing?"

"No," Bren said.

"Twenty emojis," Kris said.

"Twelve," Bren corrected.

"Oh no. Did I over-emoji?"

"Of course not," Bren assured her.

"It's good to see you tipsy?" Kris said.

"Oh no. Am I tipsy?"

"You're fine."

"You're texts were kinda tipsy."

Holly put down her drink.

"We had a cow named Tipsy," Calli said.

They looked at Calli.

Kris grinned. Now the window display looked enjoyably more diverse. What a wild sight seeing Holly's classiness beside Calli's whateverness, and, *ugh,* them beside Collin's solitudeness. "Hey, Collin," Kris hollered. "Doesn't your girlfriend look hot as hell tonight?"

Collin looked up, looked at Holly, looked at Kris, nodded, then looked back at this phone.

Jackass.

Holly kept smiling.

"You do look amazing," Calli said. "Are you a supermodel?"

Holly grinned. "No, but thank you."

"Holly works in marketing," Bren explained.

"For my family's company," Holly said.

"She's being modest," Kris blurted. "She's a grocery store baroness."

"Wow."

"I'm not a baroness."

"Is Collin a baron-er?" Calli asked.

Holly grinned again.

Collin stared at his phone.

"Collin is a Hendeross," Holly said. "His family is in footwear, the finest in the world."

Collin lifted up his shoe.

"Wow," Calli said.

Collin lowered his shoe back down.

It was the most energized Kris had ever seen him.

"My family's in ice cream," Calli said. "Goat ice cream."

"Ooooh," Holly said with her head tilted.

"What's your family in Bren?"

"My dad's in a double-trailer truck somewhere, and my mom's in and out of marriages."

"What's your family in Kris?"

Kris smirked. "Insane."

Bren and Holly nodded.

"But your grandparents are adorable," Holly said. "I loved meeting them."

"They're a different crazy," Kris said. "When they came back from borrowing your car to Napa they said they weren't used to a car with talking navigation, that it was their 'first time with a British lady,' and she kept 'taking them down strange roads,' and they were 'playing with her buttons' but 'she kept making noise,' and they 'couldn't get her off' so they finally pulled over and 'double-teamed her.' Then they asked me why I was choking on my coffee."

"That's adorable," Holly swooned.

"And they love you, Holly," Kris said.

"I was worried they thought I was a hoity toity snob or something."

"Stop being so insecure."

"It's my default position."

Grrrrrrrrowl.

"Shush, Stacy. Hey, let's get some food."

"Calli," Bren said. "Holly grew up in San Francisco. And she has a fun apartment on Chestnut Street. It's the main street of the Marina with all the bars, boutiques and cupcake shops."

"Awesome."

"Holly is the hub of this whole Marina wheel," Bren continued. "She knows everything about everybody."

"She does? You do?"

"Bren is hyperbolizing."

"Hyper what?"

"You do know everybody."

"Do you know a lot of the people in here?" Calli asked.

Holly nodded.

Calli smiled. "Ooo. What do you know about them? Who secretly has the hots for who? Who's doing who?"

Holly gave a tight grin. "I can't say."

"What can't you say?"

"Anything." Holly's fingers elegantly zipped her lips. "I never gossip."

"But I love this place," Calli said. "I wanna know everything."

"You won't hear secrets from me."

"Holly is a *Non-Gossip Girl*. She knows everyone's dirt yet says nothing," Bren said.

"That's why people can tell me things, because they know I won't tell those things."

"Ever?"

"Ever," Holly said. "I'll tell my friends if I know a guy is all right to date or not; I just won't say why."

"*Non-Gossip Girl* wouldn't be an exciting TV show," Kris said.

"Not as exciting," Bren concurred. "Things would happen, but they wouldn't be gossiped about."

"Right."

"Holly puts on fun rooftop parties," Bren continued.

"Parties on rooftops? Wouldn't people slide off?"

Bren smirked. "No. Parties on the flat roof of a three-story building."

"Ooooh," Calli said, with a worried look on her face. "I couldn't go to high up roof parties. I'm afraid of heights."

"Oh," Bren said. "Well, you could stay safely in the center of the roof. You'd wanna go to Holly's big parties. They're lit up so beautiful, with a DJ, and lots of fancy people to secretly poke fun at. Holly's an amazing party hostess. She's like a female Gatsby."

143

"What's a Gatsby?"

Bren gasped. "The character. The book. The movie. Oh jeez, I'll loan you my Gatsby."

"Does it vibrate?"

Holly leaned over to Kris. "Why is Calli wearing tube socks with fishnets?"

"For fun?"

"And a ballerina skirt with a t-shirt?"

"It's all part of her style."

"*Style?*"

"There are different kinds. Let's get some food," Kris said, really feeling hungry.

But Holly had already turned back to her non-mini-me. "So, Calli," Holly said, smiley. "Tell me all about you. What brought you to San Francisco?"

"Huck and his truck."

"No, I meant why did you come to SF?"

"For *fun*," Calli said, sitting up and smiling. "California looked so fun on the TV. So dazzley. And, ding dang, it sure is. Look at all this pretty. But now that I'm in it with these shoes I feel like poo on a pie."

"Like what?"

"I've always wanted to be dazzley. I wore glitter at the bar, but it'd fall in my beer. The toilet looked like a sunny day with stars."

"What?"

Kris grinned.

Stacy grumbled again. Kris saw a cocktail on a table no one was drinking and snatched it and fed Stacy, as the ice cubes fell on her face.

Bren shook her head.

"You have so much verve, Holly said to Calli. "Are you an Aries?"

"I'm a Licker."

"A *what?*"

Bren laughed. "She's from Licking, Missouri."

"Oooh. I got different pictures in my head. I'm onboard now."

Stacy gurgled the vodka-something.

"I meant what's your star sign?"

"I'm a Gryffindor."

Holly grinned. "No, I mean, when's your birthday?"

"Oh, August 18."

"Oooh, you're a Leo." Holly said.

Kris saw lipstick on the rim of the glass that wasn't hers and decided not to give a damn.

"I just knew you were a fire sign. Because you've got chutzpah."

Calli touched her face. "Where?"

"Where's my drink?" someone said.

Kris burped.

"I'm so sorry, my friend's kinda tipsy," Bren said to some girl.

"I'm so happy you brought me here. You're the awesomest. Twenty minutes ago I was sitting in the dark and now I'm sitting in the coolest club in the coolest city with the coolest peeps and feeling cool, actually *cool.*"

"We think you're cool," Bren said. "Don't we Holly?"

"You're certainly growing on me," Holly said.

"You are so sweet," Calli said. "I've always felt like this kinda outsider, I've got six older sisters and I kinda get lost in the mix. So I learned to do some stuff to make me stand out a bit. I can wiggle my boobs, ears and nostrils while I move only one eye, do the wave with my arms and say the alphabet backwards as President Kennedy. Wanna see?"

Calli did it.

Mouths dropped.

"I can do other tricks too, but not in public. I also learned how to DJ but the tractor sat down on my daddy's leg, so while it got better I helped run our family's Licking Ice Cream Parlor and Horse Tackle, while my mama worked as a stuff-below-the-belt doctor, and the orchard work with my sisters, while me and my ex-beau Billy got cured from the mystery pants rash he developed, and I was gonna study to be a tattoo artist 'til I realized they don't rub those pictures on."

Holly listened with raised eyebrows.

"And the sheriff shut down the orchard, and Daddy's leg got better, and he went back to the ice cream scooping, and I was helping with Grandpa's hogs, and I also applied for a job as a head assistant but when I got to the man's house the job wasn't what I thought it was gonna be. And then I met Huck and he said he needed a hand on his drive out here so I came with him, but then the hullabaloo with his brother and Huck kicking out the grilled pigeons, but I just wanted his attention, and his brother's thingy wasn't nothing to write home about, not that I'd write home about it, Ma and Daddy would frown at that postcard. This is such a crazy town, walking from the train tonight I saw a lady with a pink dog, I didn't know they came in pink, it was by that big bar called Parking Garage. We had a dog, named Bubbles. She liked to bite bubbles. One time she tried to bite a bubble and bit the mayor in the danglers. Well, I never did see Bubbles after that. They sent her to Hawaii ..."

Holly sat silent, then leaned over to Kris again. "She's a *delight*. And she's homeless?"

"Not anymore."

"Where's all her things?"

"In her bag."

"What's in her bag?"

"Tampons, a flip phone."

"A *flip phone*. Oh the poor girl. What's going to happen to her?"

"She's staying with us tonight, and then –"

"Oh," Holly exclaimed. "If she's going to stay we should help her, spruce her up, burn those clothes, take her shopping, and get her a smart phone."

Kris shuddered. "That's the last thing we should do."

"I'll take her to Jazmin and get her hair beautified. She would look so cute with peek-a-boo bangs. We'll have Nikki do her nails, Jared do her makeup, Sofia whiten her teeth, and ... my gosh, is her bag *denim?*"

"Yeah."

Holly *gasped*. "Ooooh, Kris, we have to help her."

"She's not a project," Kris said.

But Holly had leaned back to Calli.

"... so the doctor pulled the flashlight out of him."

"Calli," Holly said.

"Yeah."

"Let's get you some of that *fun* you came here for." Holly did a come hither motion.

A server rushed over.

"We would like the crab cakes, short ribs, shrimp ceviche, olive-watermelon-feta skewers, charcuterie & cheese board, three chocolate mousses, a Lemondrop with four tiny umbrellas, bourbon and Coke in a martini glass, a Paradise for Calli, a glass of Dom Pérignon '95 Rosé for Collin, and ... oh what the heck, one more Bombay Sapphire. On my tab."

Server girl smiled and rushed off.

"Jeez, why didn't you just say 'we want everything on the menu?'" Kris said.

"We didn't get the almonds."

"You're gonna spoil her."

"Good," Holly said. "Then maybe she'll stay with us."

Kris frowned.

Calli smiled.

"Now Calli," Holly said. "My friend Rolanda is looking for a roommate. Maybe you could move in with her."

What? Kris's ears perked up.

"Really?" Calli cheered. "Does Rolanda like to stay up late and sexy dance?"

"Well, I can't say," Holly said.

"Oh right."

"And I could talk to friends and help you get a job. Perhaps a dress boutique."

"Oh wow." Calli said to Holly.

What was happening?

Bren smiled. "Holly could totally help you get a job. Holly knows *everybody*."

"*No*," Kris exclaimed. "I'm sending Calli to Hazel."

"What?" Holly said. "Out of the question."

"It'll be good for her."

"That run-down place? Oh, no no no no no," Holly said. "Calli, we'll find you a cute Marina apartment, a roommate, and a fun job. You'll love it here."

"Yaaaay!"

Noooo.

Holly nodded.

Calli smiled.

Bren smiled.

Kris put her hands to her head.

Things were changing.

Holly's eyes were sparkling. "My horoscope said I would meet a fascinating new stranger today and here you are."

"Here I am."

"Here you are," Holly said. "This has to be fate."

"There's no such thing as fate," Kris said, waving her arms and smacking some guy in the dick. "You guys are out of control."

"Are you okay?" Bren asked hit-in-the-dick guy.

"Calli needs to stay in that run-down place," Kris continued.

"I'm so sorry. My friend's kinda tipsy."

"Calli would have much more fun with us," Holly said.

"You just had a vasectomy?"

"I don't wanna wash dishes in a bathtub," Calli said.

"Oh, I'm glad you're just joking about the vasectomy."

"Calli is still too sweet for the big city," Kris argued. "She needs to toughen up in scarcity not Burberry, under steady supervision, and –"

Food arrived. Trays and trays of colorful appetizers and cocktails got splayed all over their low, candlelit table like a little gourmet carnival.

Calli's eyes popped wide! "What is all this?"

"Food," Bren said.

"It's too pretty to be food."

"Enjoy the pretty," Holly said with a royal hand wave.

Calli dug in!

Holly smiled.

"This food is so good!" Calli said.

"I'm so glad you like it," Holly said.

"I don't even know what it is but I never wanna live without it!"

Oh dear.

"It's magic food," Holly joked. "It makes you so enlightened that you never wanna go back to cheap burgers."

"Totally true," Calli said.

Totally trouble. Kris grabbed her bourbon.

"It also helps you be psychic and lose cellulite."

"Really?"

"No, but wouldn't that be great?"

Calli laughed and chewed and swallowed and drank and looked like she might *cry* with happiness.

Watching Calli cramming down lots of pretty, Kris drank her bourbon and crammed crab cakes. Stacy sure appreciated *finally* getting fed something solid, appreciated it more because she was made to wait. "I'm just saying," Kris said. "Hazel is a no-bullshit, protective, keep-you-on-the-right-path chaperone. I'd be a mess if Hazel hadn't helped me."

"We're on-the-right-path people too," Bren said.

Kris swallowed her third drink, looked at Bren's four umbrellas, and Holly's unspeaking boyfriend, and sighed.

"We don't have to settle this now," Bren said. "Let's just relax and have a nice night, okay Kris?"

Kris exhaaaaled, and tried to relax, and counted down from ten, then dipped her crab cake in her bourbon.

"I know what we'll do," Bren said, cheery. "Tomorrow we'll take Calli on a road trip,"

"Leave the city?" Holly said.

"We'll drive up through Sonoma and drive down Napa, without teaming Holly's British navigator, show Calli the wine country. And we'll see how things go."

"Road trip?" Kris laughed, a relieving laugh. "You are hilaaaar-ious."

"Why?"

"Do you remember me and you *trying* to do a road trip?" Bren smirked.

"Do you not remember this?"

Holly grinned.

"Where'd you go?" Calli asked.

Kris downed the rest of her drink and sat up. "In 2010."

"2009."

"Whatever. I wanted to be on *The Amazing Race* TV show. Holly wouldn't do it. Bren considered it, but under the condition that we do a trial run. So we decided we'd drive to my hometown in Ohio and back, my first time home since I left at eighteen, very monumental. Bren went into over-planning mode and color-coded a map she made, I'll say that again, *a map that she made*, detailed down to the exact rest stops we'd stop at, and I tolerated it, 'cause I wanted to do the race. I wanted to see if me and Bren could not kill each other while traveling, if her anally-organized craziness and my non-analness could work together."

"You did what?" Calli asked.

"To see if we could work together enough that we could travel around the world for free and win."

"So how'd you guys do?" Calli asked.

Holly laughed into her drink.

"We spent an hour –"

"Ten minutes."

"Arguing what song to play as we started our trip."

"It was important," Bren said. "It was historical."

"And you were hysterical, and not the good kind."

"I was completely calm. *You* were hysterical."

"I was fun," Kris said. "I wanted to start our trip blasting Third-Eye Blind's 'Semi-Charmed Life.'"

"Which has nothing to do with the theme of a road trip."

"It's the funnest song ever. Fun was the theme. And Bren wanted to start with the boring 'Take Me Home Country Road,' when we were *leaving* home."

"No, you nut," Bren corrected. "I wanted Carrie Underwood's 'Let's Get Out Of This Town,' because we were getting out of this town."

"Oh. My song was still better, upbeater."

"More upbeat, but not as apropos for the moment."

"Fun moment, fun song. It was apropos-able."

Calli's sparkling eyes watched them and listened.

"So," Bren said. "Our spirited song-debate went on for a while. Then finally we did what we do, we compromised. Neither of our songs would be played, and we would just choose a song at random."

"And we ended up with Renaissance fair music."

"It wasn't Renaissance," Bren corrected. "It was a ballroom dance piece from my "Pride and Prejudice" soundtrack."

"Oh God help me. It was minstrels tooting flutes as we finally fucking pulled out of the parking spot at 7AM, 'cause someone woke me at 4AM."

"Because someone," Bren said. "wouldn't pack her crap until the morning, and I knew it'd take you two hours. And it took you *three*."

Holly dabbed a napkin to her laugh-tear.

"So," Bren said. "The ballroom music."

"Minstrel music."

"Wasn't the perfect tone to start our trip."

"It *was* the perfect tone: crazy," Kris said. "Our whole trip was crazy. You constantly bugging me to not speed yet to get to a specific town by a specific time so we stay on schedule, not knowing how to change a tire, not letting me flash my boobs at truckers, not letting me jump off the motel roof into the pool, not to mention arguing over where to drive, where to eat, and where to hide the pot when I got pulled over for speeding. And all that arguing causing so much chaos between us that we only made it to Reno before we turned the stupid car around and came back."

Bren rolled her eyes. "But if you would have just followed my rules, instead of fighting them, then we would have been an efficient team that could have gotten to Ohio, gotten on the Amazing Race, and won."

"But having no fun along the way."

"Efficiency is fun."

"Not without boob flashing or Third-Eye Blind."

"*I'm changing the subject!*" Bren hollered.

People looked.

Bren laughed.

Kris laughed, and tossed the bourbon sprinkles from her empty glass at Bren.

Bren ducked, dipped her fingers in her Lemondrop, and flicked wet sprinkles at Kris.

"All right you two," Holly said, arms outstretched. "Peace."

"I'll do a road trip with you, Kris," Calli cheered. "I'll flash boobs at truckers with you."

Kris smiled and high-fived Calli.

"Oh dear," Bren said. "Two Krises in one car? I do need to rethink my road trip idea."

Holly's smile sipped another gulp. "Calli," she said. "Was your road trip as wild as theirs?"

"I don't think so," Calli said.

"Is Huck coming back?" Holly asked.

"No. Before he drove off in a huff, he said he was gonna make a run for the border, but first stop in LA to see this big hotel where they filmed his favorite movie *Pretty Woman*."

Holly nodded as she drank. "I know where that is," she said. "That's by the apartments I recommended to Bren if she moves to LA, and –" Holly stopped talking, and clapped her hand over her mouth! Then looked at Bren. Then Kris. Then back at Bren.

What?

Bren's face fell.

Life shifted.

"If Bren moves to LA?" Kris asked.

Holly quickly put down her cocktail.

Bren chugged hers.

Kris stared at Bren who wasn't meeting her eyes. *Holy dick snap.* "Wait. Bren. Are you moving to LA? Are you moving out??"

Bren just ... stared at Kris like a deer in headlights then put her empty glass down, and flew her hand to Kris's arm. "Yesterday I received a job offer ... a promotion. To the LA office."

Kris's heart *dropped*. "LA?"

Bren hesitated. "Yes."

"You were offered a job in LA and you didn't tell me?"

Holly touched Kris's other arm. "I'm so sorry I told you. I drank too much. I can't believe I *gossiped*."

Collin rolled his eyes.

Kris wanted to shake his head off his shoulders. Back to Bren. "Did you not tell me because you're *taking* the job?"

"I haven't decided."

"You're moving away?"

"I haven't committed to moving. That's why I didn't tell you. I'm still deciding."

"You're leaving me?!"

"I haven't decided."

Kris sat super still, wondering, woozy, cheeks burning, volcano rising, seeing Calli's face looking as confused as Kris felt.

Calli touched Holly's arm. "Can the magic food fix this?"

Holly patted her shoulder. "No ... but wouldn't that be great?"

"*Roommate compromise*," Kris said. "... you don't move."

Bren looked at the floor. "There's no compromise this time."

This was way too much change. What to do? Count to ten? Count to a *thousand*. Make Bren stay. Make her know how much it would suck to be without each other, by bailing on Bren. Kris tried to stand, but her legs were wobbly noodles.

She grabbed the arms of two muscly dudes standing beside her and yanked herself up, regained her legs, pushed away the grinning dudes, and stormed off toward the restroom!

David's engagement? Calli chaos? Bren leaving?

This was the craziest Saturday night!

Chapter 5

MARK'S HICCUPS tasted like strawberries as he followed Chet and Skip past crowded bars and bright restaurants with chairs up on tables, feeling a little less F'd up and a lot less lonely with another new friend with them. This was cool, being part of a team. Yeah, that's something his video game couldn't give him: camaraderie, the great feeling of belonging, even if the game they were now playing was Let's Get Chet Laid, and – "Oh no," Mark said. "The rubber chicken is closing."

"What?" Skip said.

Mark stopped. "The rubber chicken store. That's what I call it." Mark stared at the "Closing Soon" sign. "It's a magic shop that sells magic stuff, Halloween costumes, and rubber chickens."

Chet ran back to them. "What the hell are you guys doing?"

Mark pointed. "The rubber chicken store is closing. It's a magic shop that –"

"Oh, I don't care," Chet said. "We gotta go."

"But don't you see what this means," Mark said. "All the stores on this street are normal restaurants, bars, and banks. This is the one rubber chicken store. It's good to have variety."

Skip guffawed. "Like a skinny guy among muscled dudes?"

158

"Yeah," Mark said. Mark and Skip bumped fists.

Chet rolled his eyes.

"And now it's closing. This is so sad."

Chet held up his phone, showing the selfie of Vanessa and her friends.

"All right. We're coming," Mark said and started rewalking his big shoes east through the glitter of Chestnut Street, slowly sobering.

"I wouldn't worry," Skip said as they walked past happening hot spots. "I'm sure another kitschy store will come along. Neighborhoods are always changing. Where Delarosa is now used to be a restaurant called Fuzio pasta, this movie theatre opened in 1928, then it became Cinema 21 and was remodeled in 2006."

"You just moved here, how do you know all this?" Mark asked.

"I love the Marina," Skip answered. "I read all about it online. I love knowing its history."

Chet rolled his eyes.

Skip continued tour guiding. "This cupcake store space used to be a cookie shop, and the Piper Bar can be seen in two popular movies."

"And how many blowjobs have I gotten in Piper Bar's bathroom?" Chet asked.

"Um ... that info wasn't online."

Mark laughed.

"Seven," Chet informed them proudly. "Hey, history *is* fun."

Skip frowned.

"*I'm* a part of the Marina's history too," Chet said. "I'll give you the *real* tour. In that bar I met a French tourist who took me back to her hotel and let me help with foreign relations. In this bar I made-out with Mimi who took me home and let me prove I could make my finger disappear. And in that bar across the street I happied Hanna under a table while she talked on her phone with her mom about their home-hamster-cremation gone wrong."

"That bar's been there for forty-two years."

"And I've had sex in its bathroom four awesome times!"

Mark shook his head laughing as they gave him the G *and* X-rated history of Chestnut Street. Wikipedia pages certainly didn't have all the special memories so many people had in these special places. Though that might be a good thing.

BOMP-CHICKA-BAH-WAH sound.

Chet looked at his phone.

"I got another text from Vanessa: 'Coming?' she says." Chet smiled and typed: In there soon. Then he walked even faster as they turned the corner by a crowded bar/restaurant that Skip informed them was once Faultline Brewery, then Cozmo's Corner Grill, and was now Circa. Chet's fast feet seemed to give no Fs about Skip's history lesson as they headed up Fillmore where they crossed the wide six traffic lanes of Lombard Street into sparkly Cow Hollow, as Skip continued tour guiding how this neighborhood got its name because there were cows here in the 1800s.

Chet stared straight ahead as they passed a long line of pretty partiers outside Kelly's Tavern on their right, packed and playing loud country music. Chet gave his rated-X tour as he bragged about how he met Ally here who took him out to the alley and showed him her trick of leaning against a wall without touching the ground as he kept his posse walking south past busy Balboa Café, and past packed Eastside West Tavern, past Matrix, to finally arrive at Big Hoopla.

If they could get in.

The line was long and Chet's patience short.

They walked to the back of the twenty-person line.

"Wow," Skip said as he looked at the inside of the bar through the big glass windows.

Mark looked too, at all the stylishly dressed twenty-somethings inside holding cocktails, and noticed the smiling, stylishly dressed women sitting and drinking on the other side of the glass.

"This is my kind of place," Skip said smoothly.

"Damn," Chet said. "It's gonna take a half-hour to get in."

"The line usually moves along," Mark assured him.

"We gotta get in *now*. Every minute Vanessa's without me is an opportunity for some other dude to woo her."

"Don't worry; she texted *you* specifically. She'll wait."

"She could change her mind."

"Why don't you just text her?" Skip suggested. "And tell her you're out here."

"I'll look weak if I can't get in," Chet said. "I gotta seem impressive."

"You need to calm down," Mark said, calmly.

161

"I need a miracle," Chet said, looking around frantically, and then up at the Moon. "Oh awesome Moon so bright, I wish I may and might, get in so I can bang with Vanessa tonight."

"You're supposed to wish on stars," Skip said.

"Are you Chet?" a voice said.

Chet looked around and then saw the doorman staring at him. "Yeah, I'm Chet."

"Vanessa's expecting you." The doorman waved him up.

Chet's face lit up like Christmas, and gave a big thumbs up to the Moon, then sneered at Skip. "Moon wishes work too, space-boy." Chet grabbed Skip's arm and rocketed past all the frowns of all the waiting nightlifers to the front of the line and whipped out their I.D.s for the doorman.

Mark stayed at the back of the line, not comfortable about cutting in front of everyone.

Chet waved Mark up.

Mark shook his head.

Chet waved!

Mark shook.

Chet marched back to Mark. "What the hell?"

"I don't feel right about cutting in line."

"We're VIP."

"It's unfair."

"Get up here, goody two-shoes."

"I'll get in here fairly and meet you inside."

Chet scrunched his face. Then unscrunched into a smile. "I have an announcement," Chet said to all the people in line.

"My friend here has an issue with his ball. I'd like to tell you aaaall about it."

"Dang you," Mark said, laughing.

Chet grinned.

Mark reluctantly walked to the front of the line, and handed his ID to the doorman.

The doorman put up his palm. "That's okay. I don't need to see it."

Dang. Mark felt as old as the hills, and felt like a jerk for cutting in line, and still slightly tipsy from his F-er Upper as he put his wallet back in his pants and walked through the open door and stepped inside the heart of the Marina's nightlife.

"Have fun," the doorman said.

Mark hoped they would as he and his friends entered the very crowded club. A group of laughing people squeezed toward the door and Mark moved aside for them, then, "Ooof," felt a hand *hit* his dick.

"Are you okay?" a sitting woman said to him.

Mark laughed.

"I'm so sorry. My friend's kinda tipsy," she said.

"Good thing I didn't just have a vasectomy," he joked.

"You just had a vasectomy?"

"No, I'm joking," he assured her. Then he saw the talkative, dick-hitting woman ... she seemed really intriguing ... just something about her.

Chet pushed Mark forward, urging him farther into the club and away from the intriguing woman and into the mess of high-end fabric-covered bodies. Mark remembered all the times Jill and he had come to this popular club and it felt odd to be here without her, and then how claustrophobic packed clubs made him feel and why he rarely went to them and missed the great outdoors as he hesitantly followed Chet through the tight, trendy crowd fizzing with trendy chatter, tratter:

"what's her deal?" "angel investor" "doggie playdate"
"engaged" "homerun" "nosejob"
"merch" "pole class" "he's heaven on toast"
"that's so *Bling Ring*" "now it's a shoe store"
"happiness"
"super pricey" "clients" "why are you sober?"
"went to Spain" "ghosted me"
"house party" "VIP" "upload"
"D-listed" "mansplainer" "*another* dick pic??"

Same old Marina-talk.

Skip eyed the ladies.

Chet eyed everywhere, frantically looking for vivacious Vanessa. Looking and looking and looking and –

FLASH!

Mark turned toward the camera phone flash and saw a woman in a tight orange dress and long hair laughing with two other women in skirts doing selfie-posing. They looked like the women in the picture Chet has shown them. Vanessa must be the woman in orange, Mark thought. Vanessa swayed playfully wild in her sexy, sexy skin-showing mini mini-dress deep in the back of the club among the hubbub, like a secret treasure, a this-is-

THE-hot-girl-every-guy-yearns-to-find-and-grind-when-he-parties-in-Cow-Hollow siren made even more tantalizing with the club's flashy orange cocktail in her orange-nailed fingers as she laughed loud with her girl squad.

And her squad was surrounded by a dozen grinning guys.

But Chet had something these other guys didn't: *an invite.* Mark watched his roommate smile huge and wave his wingmen to follow as he fixed his invisible tie for confidence, and strut his brown shoes to the sexy techno beat, and smilingly approach Vanessa by squeeeezing between all those drooling dudes.

"Vines are *tooootally* the future," Vanessa said.

Then Chet and Vanessa's eyes met.

Chet's sparking eyes clearly hoping she was *his* future.

"You're finally here!" Vanessa cheered. "Thanks for coming!"

Chet winked at her. "How are you, *beautiful?* You look *amazing* tonight." He walked straight to her.

She zoomed to him, stilettos tapping, drink and phone and arms wrapping around him, pressing against Chet, popping a huge, giddy smile on his face in an awesome, welcoming hug that none of these other frowning dudes were getting.

Mark smiled at Chet happily getting hugged by the drink sloshing happy hugger. Then Vanessa's eyes zipped to him over Chet's shoulder, her eyes flew wide, and she flew out of her hug with Chet and flew right for *him!*

Mark felt her press her pilate-toned body tight to him, her hair/perfume mix smelling like a coconut Christmas, and saw Chet's flabbergasted face as she kept hugging him, and hugging

165

him, and hugging him, and he knew they had a problem. *This was not good.* Vanessa made a nest against his chest and he looked at Chet's face growing wilder with worry. Mark stepped back and gently peeled her off him like Velcro.

"I'm soooo glad you came, Mark!" Vanessa gushed to his bewildered face.

"Do you know me?"

She laughed loud. "Oh my God, *yeeeah* I know you. You're Bigfoot."

Mark and Chet glanced at each other, then back at Vanessa.

"I'm Bigfoot?"

"Yeah. The elusive hunk no girl can catch 'cause you're always in a relationship."

"Do people really call me that?"

"Yeah. You've never heard that?"

"Nope."

"Well, you're Bigfoot." She looked down at his big dress shoes and smiled "Oh yeah, definitely."

Oh, Mark thought, was that why Awna commented about his shoe size?

Chet cleared his throat. "And this is Skip. He's in charge of the Moon."

"Hi," she tossed to Skip then turned back to Mark and gushed some more.

Skip smiled.

"Uh ... uh ..." Chet stammered. "How did you know Mark was coming here with me?"

"My friend Awna talked to you guys earlier and texted me."

Uh oh, Mark thought, Vanessa had summoned Chet only to meet him, not Chet? Chet was gonna hate him. Would Chet move out, leaving Mark living alone again, just when they had become good friends? No, he thought, he couldn't hurt his new friend. He –

Vanessa kept on talking as her hands patted Mark's wide chest. "I have been dying for this day since Cora told Katy who told Misha who told Gina who told me that you broke up with Jill," Vanessa gossiped. "But I was in New York for three months and I came back to SF just for *you*, and I heard that Jill was going on dates with Gary and then Malcom and then Paul, and I soooo worried that she would backslide to you, but then Mora texted me that Jill's now locked with Jack and I was like 'whoo hoo!' And I hope it lasts 'cause Jack has been such a flight risk. He bailed on Hannah after two weeks, and Jenny after one, and rumor-has-it clandestine kissed Mona, and if it doesn't last then I worried you would backslide, so I thought I *gotta* claim you before you could backslide and ... you don't remember me, do you?"

Mark's head was spinning. Jill dated who? And who? "I'm sorry, Vanessa, have we met?"

"Hella yeah. At parties. And we've taken group pics before."

"We have?"

"Yeah, but you were always with a girlfriend, you butt." She swatted his shoulder. "But now you're *single*! And I'm *single*! And this is soooo boss!"

Mark raised an eyebrow.

167

Chet dropped his jaw.

The rejected dudes frowned even frownier and Chet was now one of the rejected frowners.

Vanessa waved her drink around as she talked and texted and snuggled against Mark and - *FLASH!* - clicked a selfie of them together. Then clicked four more until she got the perfect shot for posting.

FLASH! FLASH! FLASH! FLASH!

Mark blinked, blinded.

"Yes!" she said. "This is awesome-sauce! I'm totally gonna In-sta-Snap-Face-Tweet this." She did, fast as lightning.

"I thought yesterday was national selfie day," Mark said.

"Everyday is selfie day for me," Vanessa said, as she hit record on her camera and videoed her and a still-blinking Mark. "Heeeeeeeeey everybody, I have tracked down and captured the infamous Bigfoot! Whoooooo! Mark! *The* Mark! Yes, And now he's mine. You're my BF, my BigFoot!"

What the heck was going on, Mark thought?

Chet's face wondered what hell was going on.

"Say 'hi,' Mark."

"Hi, Mark."

Vanessa over-laughed. "He's soooo funny. And gorgeous! Marky, you soooooooo gotta come to my party this week. I'm gonna live stream it. It's gonna be savage!"

"Savage is good?"

"Savage is lush!"

"Lush is good?"

"Lush is raise-the-roof amaze-balls!"

"Ah."

"What would be amaze-balls is if she did something *without* filming herself," the young woman in a beige mini-dress beside Vanessa said.

The other young woman beside her in a pretty blue top and skirt tapped her on the shoulder. "Jane, today I saw Van take out the trash *without* filming it."

"That's shocking! You should have filmed her not filming to prove that her non-filming happened."

"But she'd probably want to post that film of her not filming, which would make the moment moot if it did get filmed. So it's better that I didn't film it."

"But now she's filming our talking about her not filming and when she posts this film everyone will know she didn't film so her not filming will not be a pure un-filmed moment."

"I'm lost."

"And I'm too bright for your shade," Vanessa said, sneering at her posse. "Mark, these two hecklers are my backup dancers." Vanessa laughed and laughed. "I jest, these are my new roomies Jane and Sara."

"Hi," Jane said.

"Hi," Sara said.

"Nice meeting you," Mark said.

Chet still looked bewildered.

Jane just moved up here from LA, and then Sara's gig just ended and she came up here too," Vanessa told him. "Jane's my sister."

"What?" Chet said. "I didn't know you had a sister. I didn't know you lusted for *Mark*." Chet's whole world looked sideways.

Vanessa didn't seem to notice as she over-laughed and over-awed over Mark. "Is it true you jumped in front of a bear to save your girlfriend?" Vanessa said.

Mark shook his head. "That's hyperbole."

"That's *hot!*"

Chet waved at Mark wildly as if signaling that he needed an emergency meeting with his supposed-to-be-helping-him wingman, to figure out a new plan while Chet pushed Skip forward, maybe to talk up all three women to keep all the other jackals away. "Ladies, this is my awesome friend, Skip. Skip, this is Sara and Jane."

"Hi," Sara said.

"Hi," Jane said.

"   ," Skip said, just staring at them like a deer in the head-lights, staring and staring until finally Skip squeaked out "hi."

WTF?

Now Chet *really* looked worried. He smiled big to the girls like everything was still just totally, totally awesome! And then he yanked Skip aside.

Vanessa talk-talk-talked in front of Mark. Her fast-moving mouth was oddly interesting to watch, but Chet and Skip's chatter beside him was far more entertaining.

"Skip," Chet whisper yelled. "What's going on, man?"

"I lied."

"What?"

"I *lied*," Skip confessed. "I'm no good with girls. I'm terrified of them."

"What?" Chet panicked. "You told us you dated all the time."

"I *lied*."

"You *lied?*"

"The hickey I showed you, I made that with a vacuum cleaner hose."

"*What?*"

"I'm sorry I lied."

Dang, Mark thought, Skip said he was a "Falcon" but instead he was liar. Mark's heart sank, feeling bad that he'd set Chet up with the wrong guy for the job, and yearning to fix this. He held up a finger to Vanessa. "I'm sorry, Vanessa. Bigfoot needs a minute." Mark turned around to Chet and Skip. "Okay, gents, what's going on?"

"I *knew* 'space lawyer' sounded ridiculous," Chet said.

"I *am* a space lawyer; that part's true," Skip said. "I only lied about being confident with girls; I'm not. And I lied about having a date tonight; I didn't. I never have dates. I'm too intimidated by girls to date. I have panic attacks. But I'm trying to get better. I memorize stuff about the Marina for conversation, but I never hookup 'cause I'm too scared to talk to girls. I hang around outside of the cool bars but I'm too afraid to go in. But tonight I'm *in*. This is a huge step for me. My therapist says I need to put myself in social situations to slowly get over my gynophobia."

"You have a gyno?" Chet asked.

"I have a fear of women."

"I have a pain in my chest," Chet said.

Dang. Mark had accidentally stolen the woman Chet wanted and gotten him a faulty wingman.

"I was so excited that you guys chose me to come along with you. I didn't wanna let you down. I wanna get over my fear, so I lied to you. I thought I could do this. But these girls, oh my gosh, these girls are so *beautiful.* I can't woo for you. My head is ... spinning."

"*Are you .... fricking .... kidding me?*" Chet whisper-shrieked over the shocking situation he was in now: Vanessa had tricked him, Skip had tricked him, and in two minutes his whole perfect plan had IMPLODED! Vanessa lured him here for Bigfoot and the Falcon might faint!

Skip tipped over.

Mark grabbed onto his arms and propped him up. "Chet," Mark said, leaning close and letting the loud music cover their conversation. "I want you to know I'm not trying to take Vanessa from you."

Chet rolled his eyes. "You're gonna try. No one rejects Vanessa."

Mark opened his mouth to say more, but Chet leaned close to Skip's ear. "Now you listen to me, you skinny goofball," Chet said to Skip. "The happiness of my penis is riding on tonight working out with Vanessa and I need you to not be a fearful fainter but be the over-confident pretender that foolishly fooled me into to bringing you here. Got it?"

"I can't pretend with these girls," Skip said. "They're so beautiful."

"Don't focus on a woman's beauty," Mark suggested. "Look at her eyes. See the human in her. One human to another."

"They're more than human; they're *angels*."

"Angels who fart just like us," Chet said.

"They don't fart."

"They fart."

"No way they fart."

"They fart and sneeze and blow their beautiful noses. Just keep that in mind when you talk to them."

"Talk about *what?*"

"All your Marina history crap."

"My mind is blank, I can't remember anything."

"Just ask them questions."

"About what?" Skip asked.

"Travel."

"Travel?"

"It's exotic and will make them feel exotic and associate you with exoticism."

"I'm not exotic."

"Be confident."

"I'm not confident."

"Be cool."

"I'm not cool."

"Pretend you're cool."

"How?"

"Do what I do, pretend you've got a 12" banana."

Mark smirked. *This is was Chet's winning strategy?*

Skip paused. "Is twelve inches even possible?"

"Pretend it's possible. Pretend you got a footer. Feel the length lounging down your leg."

"Which leg?"

"It doesn't matter. Feel the weight. Feel the *confidence.*"

Skip leaned to one side, and scrunched his face.

He looked like a moron, but at least he was standing. "Or," Mark said to Skip. "You could talk to them without all the shenanigans and just be yourself."

Chet's eyes flew wide. "Noooo," Chet countered, grabbing Skip's shoulders. "Be better than yourself. Be like me."

Mark just shook his head.

"Now," Chet said to Skip. "I'm gonna talk to Mark while you talk to Vanessa and her friends about travel and you focus on your footer and if you feel faint remember they fart."

"Oh God."

Chet turned Skip around and nudged him forward. "Game on."

Skip breathed a big breath and stayed scrunching and leaning towards his pretend twelve-inch as he zombie-walked back to the group of overwhelming angels and almost fell over *again* seeing Vanessa hoist up her shirt and expose so much exhilarating skin to show Mark her latest cute tattoo.

Chet gaped and held up Skip.

Mark hesitantly took a look.

Vanessa smiled at Mark's eyes seeing her naked flesh. Then she playfully dropped her shirt and continued to flirt. "I would show you the tiny tattoo of a butterfly on my inner thigh, but tonight is 'No Panty Day.'

Chet's tongue almost unraveled to the floor, then his eyes flew wide watching Vanessa pull Mark closer then turned her only-skirt-covered bottom toward Mark and index fingered over herself. "And I was thinking of tatting a sprinkle of little stars across my glutes," she said.

"Seriously?" Jane cynically sighed.

"Yes, seriously. And they'll be astronomically accurate."

"Your glutes?"

"The stars."

"So your ass will be a planetarium?"

"Not planets. Stars."

"You know," Jane said. "If your ass gets bigger the stars will stretch farther apart like the expanding universe."

"The universe is expanding?" Sara asked.

"My ass is not expanding."

"I said 'if.'"

"I do Pilates."

"I don't care."

"You should do Pilates."

"You should stop filming everything."

"I hate when you bicker," Sara said.

"I'm keeping her real," Jane said.

"My sister loves to hassle me," Vanessa said.

"I'm trying to help you."

"Let's change the subject."

"I LIKE TRAVEL."

All eyes zipped to Skip!

Pause.

Skip froze.

Chet cringed.

Skip looked woozy ... and *faint* ... and Mark's hand held him up.

"Do you travel?" Sara asked Skip, with a smile.

Skip's eyes were wide at the girl that was actually talking to him, directly to him, with a smile. He smiled. *Chet's 'travel' advice was working!* Skip leaned towards his imaginary 12". "Um ... I like ... travel," he said.

"That's cool," Sara said with a smile.

Vanessa turned back to Mark.

Chet tried to pull Mark away for a private talk.

Vanessa pulled Mark back.

Chet exhaled.

Skip looked at Sara's smiling face and bright eyes. "H-H-H-Have *you* traveled lately?" Skip asked.

"I flew home for my grandma's funeral."

"Oh that's exciting."

"Exciting?"

"I mean. Um. No. That's not, exciting. Um. So ... she's dead?"

"Oh lordy jeez."

Mouths dropped.

Chet cringed.

Skip was failing.

Chet chuckled. "Skip's a hoot."

"Um," Mark said polite, pulling attention from Skip's verbal flailing. "Vanessa, you're a really cool and accomplished and beautiful woman and I'm very impressed with you. And I am very flattered that you have been wanting to meet me. But I gotta tell you the truth that my friend Chet here has been infatuated with you for quite a while."

Vanessa's and Chet's eyes both popped.

"And Chet was so happy that you bexted him, I mean texted him, and invited him to come see you," Mark continued. "And I'm sorry, but I simply can't involve myself with a woman my friend is gaga over."

There was no negotiating this. Moving in on another guy's woman was a deal breaker, Mark thought. Then continued. "And under Chet's unique humor he's got a good heart and is a really great guy who I'm sure would absolutely appreciate your fun spirit and your lovely tattoos, and definitely your no panties. And I think that you and Chet would really hit it off. And I hope you'll give Chet a chance for exploring a deeper relationship with you. So, respectfully, I'm gonna step aside and let you and Chet talk."

Everyone stood with their jaws on the floor, as if he was the first guy to reject Vanessa!

Mark smiled politely at everyone.

They stared.

Mark smiled "got your back" to his friend.

Chet smiled back at his friend, as if Mark was the greatest wingman ever.

Vanessa looked at Chet.

Chet looked at Vanessa.

Vanessa videoed this crazy twist, as she took a step closer to Chet.

Mark breathed easier, backing away, seeing Chet with Vanessa, and Skip with two angels, and feeling like the greatest wingman ever, as that intriguing woman in the polka dot top who hit is junk earlier bumped past him on her way to the restroom.

Chapter 6

KRIS PLUNGED through all the people, crashing past Cosmos and bare shoulders, and some hot girl filming her and her friends, with techno beats blaring and her heart breaking as she busted into the too-small, two-stalled restroom.

"Ooof," some girl said.

Crammed in with four glittery girls waiting for the two occupied stalls and six more preening girls at the two sinks and big mirror that showed Kris's frowning face as she stood shaking in the middle of this crowded ladies room, where the horrible truth fully sunk in, that her bestie-roomy-rock-of-her-life was about to leave her, forever.

No.

She couldn't handle this loss and hurt.

How could this be happening on a Saturday night, on their roommate anniversary?

Bren rushed in.

Kris stared at her. "What the fuck?" Kris cried out.

The room froze quiet.

"Please don't freak out," Bren's said.

"I'm freaking out!"

Bren looked at the freaked out girls.

"You're moving to LA? For a job? You're ditching me??"

"I'm not ditching."

"You're ditching."

"I haven't decided."

"You're breaking our friendship."

"I'm considering the job offer."

"That you kept secret."

"Because I knew you'd freak out."

"Of course I'm freaking out."

"Which is why I didn't tell you while I'm deciding."

"When would you move?"

Bren took a deep breath. "Right away."

Kris stood, breathing hard, not knowing what to say, wanting to say anything that would make Bren stay. "I can't match my clothes without you!" Kris's shouting shook the bathroom stalls.

"You never take my fashion advice anyway."

"But I like hearing your logic."

"So you can rebel against it."

"See," Kris argued. "You know me so well. I'll never find a friend as in tune with me as you, or one who will tolerate all my being-late. I need you every day."

"We could video chat."

"Everyday? From LA?"

"Sure."

"It won't be the same."

"I know it won't. It's a compromise."

"It's a sucky compromise, as sucky as minstrel music."

"I ... I hate this too," Bren said. "I'm sorry. I ..." Bren pulled out her inhaler.

Ah, damn.

Bren sucked a hit. And breathed.

Kris reached to rub Bren's arm, but than yanked back her hand. "Wait. Is that why you needed your inhaler tonight? You were super stressed about this secret?"

Bren breathed deeply, and nodded. "... Yes."

Kris breathed a big breath.

"I'll visit you all the time," Bren bargained. "And Holly can help you."

"I need *you*, *here*. I need my daily Bren-banter."

"We can banter by phone."

Kris wanted Bren to stand up for herself, but not to *her*. "After Zelda moved out on me for New York we never talked anymore."

"I've roomed with you longer than Zelda. You and I are closer."

"You'll be gone."

Bren sniffled.

"Are you moving 'cause I'm messy? Just get your own apartment in SF."

"The job offer is in LA; I have to move."

"There's still awesome guys here in SF. You'll find one, I swear. You don't need to move to LA to get Ryan Gosler to build you a house."

"I'm not leaving for love, though LA does have a bigger dating pool," Bren said. "It's a huge career jump. It's regional manager."

Kris gaped. "You're choosing the perfect job and potential for love over *ME?*"

The girls in the stalls stayed hiding, probably too scared to come out. A glitter of needing-to-pee girls had built up by the sinks, listening, watching, and wiggling legs.

"I would take the job," a girl said.

Kris backed that bitch up against a wall!

No other opinions were offered.

"Calm down," Bren pleaded. "You're gonna literally scare the piss out of them." Bren turned to the girls. "I'm really sorry, my friend is tipsy."

"I'm not tipsy," Kris shouted. "I'm drunk. And I'm pissed off. And shocked. And ... fucking sad."

Bren started to reach toward her, but then folded her arms.

Instead of kicking a stall door, Kris exhaled. "Is this why you kept trying to hurry me out of our apartment tonight?"

Bren nodded.

"You knew this would be our last night of fun without me knowing you're leaving. You're not really horny."

"I am horny!" Bren shouted.

All the girls looked at her.

"But I'm even more wanting to share this last night out with you if I leave."

"Wow," Kris exclaimed, suddenly realizing. "Is this why you wanted Calli to come along with us tonight?"

Bren froze and stared back at Kris.

"It is." Kris felt duped. "You thought Calli could be my new roommate."

Bren nodded.

"Oh my God."

"You're both from the Midwest, you both like to party. She's the perfect roommate for you."

"*You're* the perfect for me," Kris argued. "Our differences are what makes us work."

"I think we actually have more stuff in common," Bren said.

"Then don't leave."

"I don't know."

"Who's gonna scare your bad boyfriends?" Kris argued.

"I can take care of myself."

"No you don't."

"I handle things calmly."

"Too calm."

"I don't wanna fight."

"Learn to fight. I'm fighting for *you*. What about Clark the Clock? And Tammy? And Fern? You're going to break up our whole family."

"You're the one who names them. I give you custody."

"What about *me?* I'm the funnest BFF ever."

"I know. It's not you, it's me."

"How can you leave me?"

"I wish you could move with me," Bren said. "But I would never ask you to leave San Francisco."

"I love SF. I'm never leaving. You know that," Kris said. "It took me years to build up all my moneybag clients. I'm not moving and starting over from scratch."

"I know," Bren said. "That's why I'm not asking you to move with me. But I would want to you come with me, so you can't be as mad."

"I'm still mad!"

Bren's shoulders deflated.

Kris stopped talking, realizing her anger might chase her friend away. She breeeeathed and refocused. "10 ... 9 ... 8 ..."

Bren staring at her.

"7 ... 6 ... 4 ..."

"5," Bren said.

"5 ... 4 ... 3 ... 2 ... . 1." Kris staring at Bren. "Please don't move away. Don't break us up."

Bren wiped away a tear and looked away.

Kris saw hope. She stepped closer to Bren. "We need each other. I keep you fun and you keep me organized. Apart, I'll be bedlam and you'll be boring. We know each other."

Bren looked back at Kris with wet eyes.

"You know I can't handle change."

Bren looked like her heart got punched. "I do know. And this is the hardest decision I've ever had to make knowing that my plan would break your heart. And this is breaking my heart too. But ... I just don't know."

Uh oh. Bren had the same look on her face as she had when she'd considered letting Kris bring a real life fir tree into their apartment for Christmas, but later admitted that she'd already made up her mind. Had Bren already decided to go LA? Bren *was* gonna leave her. This sadness ... *sucked*. Kris huffed a big exhale. She would *not* be abandoned by a best friend again. She would leave Bren before Bren could leave her. She flung open the bathroom door. Then stopped, and stared at Bren. "Now we can't have our disco ball. And that would have been awesome."

Bren just stared at her.

Kris stormed out.

Happy music and smiling people all around her. She pushed past the hot filming-girl again and marched through the damn crowd and plopped down beside Calli.

Holly went on and on about being sorry she'd babbled about Bren considering moving, and to please not be mad ... *this was surreal*.

Kris sat silent, arms folded, staring at the wood floor, thinking about everything Bren had said and everything she had shouted back at Bren, and feeling betrayed and abandoned. Her swirling thoughts stirred up their neighbor, Madeline's, motto: "Live it up while you can." But how could she live it up without Bren. She felt so lost, maybe as lost as Calli had felt earlier tonight. She was back to being alone, as empty as her one and a half empty cocktail glasses, and this crappy feeling reminding her how harsh life can be. And ... maybe she didn't want sweet Calli to feel such horrible harshness.

"You okay, Kris?" Calli asked.

Kris looked up and saw Calli's concern wilting that usually happy face, and not liking it having to wilt. "I'm great, sweetie." Kris snatched her bourbon off the table, pouring help into herself until ice fell on her face again.

Calli laughed.

Kris looked at her laughing and grinned, happy to see her happy again, and yet also aching, realizing Calli couldn't be her new roommate. She wasn't Bren.

Chapter 6

MARK STOOD beside Chet, no longer between his friend and Vanessa, hoping he worked things out so Mark could go back home. For now, he stood ready to help Chet if needed.

"Soooo ... ," Chet said, coolly. "... how was New York?"

Vanessa waved her cocktail. "What the hell did you tell Mark?"

"I-I-I told him ... just ... stuff."

"Did you tell him to stay away from me?"

Mark shook his head.

"Not at all," Chet said. "I didn't even know you liked him. He told you I liked you and declined you all on his own."

Vanessa scowled at Mark, then sighed huge at her shoes.

"Besides," Chet said. "You and Mark aren't a good match. He's still got a big shampoo and he doesn't like being filmed. Whereas I don't mind being filmed at all, in fact I have ideas."

Vanessa smirked at Chet, and flipped her hair. "So," she said. "*You* like me?"

Chet looked like a deer in the headlights. Then he shifted his weight to his side. "Well, babe, I ..." He paused, looking at Vanessa's hard stare, then looked Mark.

Mark bumped his elbow to Chet for encouragement.

Chet rolled his eyes to the ceiling, but then signed and turned back to Vanessa's unflinching stare. "Yeeeeah," Chet exhaled to her, like a layer of ice had melted off his heart. "Of course I like you. Who wouldn't want you? You're the tops, the best, the babe men crash their cars staring at. You're *Vanessa!* You're *MY* Bigfoot."

Wild pause.

Vanessa's red, glossy lips grew into a big smile.

Mark grinned. Chet was doing fine. But Mark heard Skip wildly rambling and saw him sweating like a rainstorm.

"... and did you know the bendy straw was invented in San Francisco? And it was patented in 1937, the same year the Golden Gate Bridge was finished, and –"

"Skip!" Jane interrupted him.

Skip froze.

"Breathe, man."

Skip inhaled ... and ... exhaled ...

"You look like you're gonna pass out," Jane said.

"You okay?" Sara asked him sweetly.

Skip looked panicked that she was touching his arm, and also loving it.

"Are you gonna faint?" Jane said to him.

Mark prepped his hand to hold Skip up, but Jane's hand grabbed Skip's arm.

A woman was touching Skip's arm! He looked both elated and dizzy.

"What's wrong? Do you need to sit?" Sara asked.

"... I ... I ... I ..." Skip stammered, then looked over at Mark.

Mark looked at Skip and just nodded.

Skip's eyes flew wide, and he looked like he might melt into a puddle of goo ... but instead he nodded back, straightened tall, took a deep breath, and turned back to the worried-looking angels. "I–I–I'm trying to impress you ladies," Skip confessed. "With my knowledge of the Marina and travel talk. Because I think you're both awesome. I'm sorry if I seemed like an idiot."

"Oh, you're adorable," Sara cooed to him.

"I thought I'd have to give you CPR," Jane said. "Sara would probably give you mouth-to-mouth."

Skip chuckled. "Oh, then I would totally pass out. You see, I ... I have a fear of talking to women. It's ... it's really bad."

"Ooooh, you poor thing," Sara cooed again, as she stretched her arms out and cradled Skip into a big hug.

Skip's eyes flew wider!

"Don't hug him too much, he might really pass out," Jane joked then rubbed his arm.

Skip smiled HUGE at Mark as *two* women were touching him!

Mark quietly laughed. Okay, both his friends were doing fine, without shenanigans. Mark breathed a proud exhale, and quietly wished he had a woman to hug too. Water. With his friends now fine, he could go get water.

Mark squeezed his way barward through the singles crowd, feeling very single, not his favorite feeling, not entirely thrilled to be in this solo scene again, but trying to stay positive, though it was getting harder to stay hopeful. Sliding past flirting couples, smirking at the awkward connections, envying the happily flowing ones, wondering if he would ever really find a happy flow with a girlfriend that wouldn't end, that just kept on flowing happily for years and years and years. Maybe he just wouldn't make a connection like that, he thought, but he did make it to the big, beautiful, but crowded bar, confused about love, life, and the future.

Under the warm-orange glow of the hanging stylish cylinder bar lamps, Mark's eyes beheld the two endless dark wood shelves lit up and packed with booze bottles behind the dark wood bar, multiplied by a mirrored wall and made enticing by supermodel-looking bartenders grabbing, flipping, and pouring them like skilled circus performers. The fun sight and the tantalizing smell of beer and gin reminded him of all the fun nights with all his ex-Marina girlfriends. And yet, here he was again, alone and looking for the next woman to share more fun nights with, hopefully the last woman he will share all those fun nights with. He wondered who she would be.

Wait. What about that intriguing woman he saw when he walked in.

Mark paused, and wished he was completely sober again. Or maybe he should just go home?

"You're the guy my friend hit in the crotch," a voice said.

Surprised, Mark looked to his right and saw a young woman in a black mini-dress looking up at him. Caught off guard, but he recovered with a smile. And then he recognized her from when he entered the bar. "Oh, right."

"Sorry my friend smacked your package," she said.

He grinned. "Your friend's got a good punch."

"She does self-defense."

"She does it well."

"And you did not get a vasectomy, right?"

"I didn't. I was joking. That's how I work through pain, especially impacts to Elvis and the Band."

"Who? Oh, you name your stuff too?"

"Too?"

They stood in silence.

The silence grew awkward.

He saw her lean into the orange glow from above. She had a mascara streak down her face like the trail of a tear. "Are you okay," he asked?

Her hand quickly wiped her face and she took a breath. "Yeah. I'm – I'm great."

He gave a grin. "Are you really?"

She looked up at him and exhaled a long exhale, then smirked. "No. I'm not," she admitted. "This night kinda sucks."

He nodded.

She grabbed a napkin off the bar and wiped her face more. "How's your night?" she asked.

He chuckled. "Well, I'm not a fan of the singles scene. But I'm single, so I'm back in the scene, hoping to not be single for long, but my roommate tells me to take my time, but that just means more time being confused about who to date and who not to date, and I'm just too tired to be confused anymore tonight. So I'm just gonna drink some water, and then go home."

She stared wide-eyed at him. "Wow. Honesty. In a bar."

He grinned. "What better place?"

She half-smiled.

He took a conscious breath. Remembering Chet's advice, he restrained himself from wanting this new woman to be his girlfriend to save himself from loneliness, and first find out if they were compatible. "I'm Mark."

"I'm Jen Itaylia."

Mark stifled laughter. He paused, unsure, not wanting to offend. But ... no way. "Is that your Bond girl name?"

She laughed. "It's my *bar* girl name."

He laughed. "Well, Jen –"

"It's Bren."

"Bren?"

"Bren."

"Bren, do like the outdoors?" Mark ventured.

She rolled her eyes. "When necessary."

Uh oh. That was not an encouraging answer, he thought. He really tried to not think he could still make things work between her and him.

"Mark, do you like books?"

He cringed. "Not for fun."

"Crud," she said, then sighed.

He sensed that was *her* deal breaker. He hung onto the bar, resisting the urge to make a connection between them work anyway, but maybe there was still a slight chance. "I read law books."

"Ew," she said, then covered her mouth. "I'm sorry. That was rude."

He grinned. "That's okay. It was honest."

She put her hand on the bar. "That just sounds so dry. I don't understand why anyone doesn't like reading for fun. Romances, mysteries, thrillers. Why is it so hard to find a guy around here that's on the same page as me ... pun intended." Her eyes wandered his face. "What do you like for fun, besides the outdoors?"

He smirked, then felt his cheeks blush warm. "Reality shows."

Her ears perked up. "Reality shows."

"Yeah."

"Really?"

"Yeah."

"And baseball," Mark said.

"Baseball?"

"Yeah."

"And you're a lawyer?"

"Yeah."

Her head tilted. "What kind of law do you practice?"

"Sports."

She ... paused. "Sports?"

"Yeah."

"You're a sports lawyer?"

"I am."

"Really?"

"Yeah."

"For baseball?"

"Mostly. I negotiate contracts for baseball players."

"Gosh." she stared hard at him. "So you go to Giants games a lot?"

"All the time."

Her face brightened up, and her whole head looked him up and down, staring at his shoes, then back up to his eyes with such intensity now. "What else are you into?"

"I like sports video games, hiking, camping, rock climbing."

She literally spun around in a circle then grabbed his arms tight. "Jackpot!" she exclaimed. "You are *NOT* going home."

Confused, he watched her wave-wave-wave the bartender over.

"A water for him," she ordered, "a Matchmaker for me, and a Coke in a martini glass."

Mark tilted his head. "Who's the third drink for?"

Her no-longer sad face spread a big smile. "Your soulmate," she said.

He ... he ... he drank his water.

Chapter 7

THIS NIGHT was crazy-balls, Kris thought. David engaged, bar jackasses, Calli joining, Bren leaving, and now feeling really alone. Her heart felt pummeled. Now this Saturday night sucked. But no more, she decided. Everything needed to go back to normal. *Right now.* She hopped up and grabbed her phone to text Hazel.

Bren jumped in front of her.

What the hell?

Bren smiled.

How dare she smile.

"I'm gonna make you happy again," Bren said with a clap of her hands. "I brought you someone." Her hands pulled a wide-chested, green-shirted, movie star-handsome guy in front of her.

A guy? "You picked up a guy?" Kris hollered.

Bren poked her head out from around Mr. Tall Dark And Fuck-Me-Now.

Kris put her hands on her hips. "After you break my heart you go pick up a guy?"

"He's not for me," Bren said. "He's for *you.*"

"*What?*"

Bren kept smiling. "Instead of bringing you a Coke and Maker's Mark, I brought you a Coke and a *real* Mark."

Kris looked at this eye-candy man-gift and ... and kinda liked what she saw.

"Hi," she said.

"Hi," he said.

Real-Mark smiled a gorgeous smile and his arm, as thick as her thigh, extended a martini glass of cola toward her, beautifully, but in a bonkers situation.

"Bren, you think you can mend my heart by bringing me the hottest guy in the world?"

Mark smiled. "I can't possibly be the hottest."

Kris paused and looked over his poundable chest, up to his thick, grippable hair, kissable chiseled chin, and his starry eyes looking at her so nicely that she felt the warmest whoosh tingle up thoughts of exactly how she'd climb him. "I'd bang you," she said.

"Really?"

"Really."

"We should probably get to know each other first," he said.

"You think so, huh?"

"I'd love to get to know you," he said, smiling, his voice deep as a valley. "Because, if you don't mind me saying, I think you're really intriguing."

Holy fuckadoodles. Was life trying to overload her with everything tonight? "Mitch," she said.

"Mark," he said.

"Mark, I am soooo not in the mood for a smooth talker."

He chuckled. "I'm not a smooth talker at all. I'm just saying that when I walked in the club you caught my attention, and it'd be great to talk with you."

"Talk about what?"

"Well," he said. "Bren says that, like me, you're into rock climbing and reality shows."

"And cricket powder," Bren said.

"And cricket powder," he said.

Suddenly everything was waaaay too surreal. And Bren was way too smiley for a heartbreaker. Kris tossed up her hands. "Bren, I'm supposed to be happy again 'cause you brought a hot dude who likes climbing and cricket powder for me to bang?"

Bren rolled her eyes. "He's not a bang. He's a good one. You know, a '*good one*.'"

A '*good one*,' Kris thought, doing a double-take.

She saw Bren give her the secret thumbs up sign that she had Googled Mark and he hadn't killed anybody. Holly stuck her head around his hip and nodded her approval of Mark, as the knower of everybody. And Calli just ogled at Mark's butt.

Then Kris took another look at this mountain of man-candy, and ... and Calli might get to hang out in Heaven just a little longer while Kris's curiosity explored just how 'good' this one was.

"Well done, Bren," Holly said, smiling once again. "He sounds like a perfect boyfriend for Kris."

Boyfriend?

What was happening?

Kris stared at smiling-Mark.

This night was getting even more crazy-balls.

MARK'S POINT OF VIEW

What a wild night, Mark thought. Jill with Jack, the Miranda fail, Skip afraid to flirt, Chet afraid to love, and now feeling his pulse pick up talking with this fascinating new woman. His heart felt dizzy. Hoping everything turned out happy for everybody. Maybe it could. And for him if he didn't ask this new woman to move in with him right away, and instead he smiled at Kris and simply offered her the glass of cola.

Chet zipped in front of him.

What the heck?

Chet smiled.

Why wasn't he with Vanessa?

Chet gawked at all the ladies. "Dude, the S.S. Vanessa sank, but you got us a lifeboat full of hotties," Chet said as he fist-bumped Mark's shoulder.

What the heck? "What happened with Vanessa?"

"She only wants a boyfriend," Chet said. "But I'm not getting tied down."

Mark shook his head. "But you wanted Vanessa so badly."

"As a hookup," Chet said. "Besides, she still likes *you*."

Uh oh.

Chet kept gawking at Bren and Kris. "And it looks like you found yourself a new two to woo."

Kris and Bren both rolled their eyes.

Dang. Chet was making another mess. "It's not like that," Mark said to Chet. "Bren apologized to me at the bar because Kris accidently hit my junk, and then Bren thought I should meet Kris."

Kris raised her eyebrows. "I hit your junk?"

"As I walked in the door."

"Oh," Kris said. "Is that why I'm intriguing?"

"No, no. It's not like that," he explained. "I was intrigued by your exuberance and beauty, and then Bren said you like the outdoors, and the Giants. And Coka Cola," Mark said as he extended the martini glass of Coke to her again.

Her vibrant eyes looked at the drink, then up at him, with a smirk. "Nice segue," she said.

He grinned. "Thanks."

Her hand with the green fingernails lifted the drink from him and slurped a gulp while eyeing his eyes, and then him all over. "I like your hair."

"Thanks."

"I like your shoes."

"Thanks."

"I like your shirt."

"Thanks."

"What's a cock ring?"

"What?" he said.

Bren laughed.

Kris grinned. "I told Bren I'd ask a guy that tonight."

"She did say that," Bren said.

"Now I'm even more intrigued," he said.

"I bet you are," she said, smiling at him, as if he'd passed some sort of test.

He smiled back at her.

"*Do* you know what a cock ring is?" she asked.

"I don't," he said.

Chet smiled. "This girl is *wild*."

Mark cleared his throat to signal Chet to be more respect-ful. "Kris likes the Giants and the outdoors," Mark said

"I do," Kris said.

Chet nodded and fist bumped Mark's shoulder. "You have my approval to talk to *this* girl."

Mark smirked. "Gee, thanks." Then he turned back to Kris as his mouth slowly curled ear-to-ear as he stared at this fasci-nating woman in an unusual combo of polka dots and leather, who liked stuff he liked, and spoke with a fearless spirit he envied and couldn't get enough of. He stared at her piercing eyes that couldn't hide a world of kindness behind them. He stared at maybe his next girlfriend, and tried so hard to *not* get her phone number too fast, or lift his leg.

He turned to talk more. This night was getting so much better.

"There you are," Vanessa said, as she danced over and start-ed filming Mark again.

Uh oh.

"Skipster's in the hoooouse?" Skip sang, with his arms around Jane and Sara.

What in the heck?

Mark looked at Kris.

This night was getting wilder.

Kris's point of view

Kris saw these people who seemed to know Mark standing around her sitting friends, as tonight's wackiness suddenly doubled in size. How did Mark know the camera-girl, Holly's fremeny? That wasn't good.

"Hello everyone," Holly said, once again in hostess-mode, as she stood up and opened her arms, handling camera-girl being there so politely. "I'm Holly. Are you friends of Mark's? Wonderful. This is Kris and Bren and Collin and our new friend Calli. Please join us," Kris overheard.

Everyone sat.

Kris re-sat on her cube, thrown by all this new stuff happening, and totally wishing there was bourbon in her cola, as Mark sat his beautiful bod on the cube beside her, and set his water glass near the center of the group's table beside them.

Holly come hither-fingered and ordered more food and drinks for their new guests.

"I'm Skip," a guy said to Holly. "This is Jane and Sara."

"I'm Jane. She's Sara."

"Oh right."

"Great to meet you," Holly greeted. .

"That's Collin," Calli said. "He's a shoemaker."

Collin winced and raised his shoe.

"I'm Chet."

"I'm Jen Italia."

Chet's jaw dropped!

Camera-girl sat in an orange dress, filming them all.

Jane pointed at her. "You probably know Vanessa," she said.

"I do," Holly said, sweet as a Cosmo. "Are you Vanessa's sister?"

"Yeah," Jane said.

"I love your fish tattoo," Calli said.

"Thanks," Jane said.

"My uncle's also got a tattoo on his arm that he calls his 'trouser trout,' but it doesn't look like a fish."

"Uuuum," Jane said.

"*That's* what sculpture I could make, a beautiful fish," Sara said. "I'm thinking of making art out of lint?"

"I've got some in my belly button if you wanna start there," Skip said.

Sara laughed.

"Soooo, Jen Italia," Chet said. "You look amazing tonight. What'da you do for ... *fun?*"

"I read about three new books a week, Bren said.

"We have so much in common," Chet said. "I read too."

"Really?"

"Yeah, I got a whole library in the bathroom."

Kris had to understand who's side Mark was on. "What's your deal with Vienna?"

"Vanessa?"

"Yeah, her."

"Oh, you know her?" he said.

"I know *of* her. Are you friends with her?"

"I just met her tonight," he said.

"Oh." *Good.* "Then why is she filming you?"

Mark sighed and smirked. "I'm Bigfoot."

"What?"

He grinned. "I'm told that's my nickname. I guess I'm always in a relationship, and it's rare to see me single, like it's rare to see Bigfoot."

"Really?"

"Yep."

"So you're single?"

"I'm single. And, unhairy."

"How long have you been single?" Kris asked.

"Four months."

"Four? That's a while for a Bigfoot who's supposed to be rarely single."

He nodded. "It's been mentioned to me by a few people that I tend to jump into new relationships too fast. And ask new girlfriends to move in with me too soon. I like living with a girlfriend. And I don't like being alone. So this time I tried to not rush things, hoping that my next relationship would be better for it, and, you know, last."

Wow, she thought. He was being honest and forthcoming with info. Shocking info. Kris tilted her head at him. "You only do relationships?"

He nodded. "This is true."

"Seriously? You don't do a casual fling?"

He felt like misfit again. "Nope."

"No hit and quit."

"Nope."

"No wham and bam?"

"Nope."

"No dick and duck?"

"I've never heard of that one, but nope."

"That's crazy."

"It's simple."

"So, I'd have to have a relationship with you to climb your mountain and sit on your peak?"

Mark chuckled. "That's quite a visual. I'm afraid so."

"Why don't you fling?"

"A fling's not my thing."

"Have you had a fling?"

"No."

"Then how do you know a fling's not your thing unless you have a fling?"

"Because I need more zing than a fling. I need ... you know ... love."

Kris recoiled. He said *love*, in a bar, on a Saturday night? "*Love?*"

He nodded. "Love."

Kris winced. "Yikes."

Food and drinks arrived.

"Please," Holly said. "Help yourselves."

"Thanks," Skip said.

Their guests dove in.

Vanessa filmed the food, then panned her camera to Mark.

"Um, hello, Vanessa," Holly said. "I see you're back from New York."

Vanessa lowered her camera. "Hi," she said.

Holly handed Collin a bruschetta.

He nodded, then munched it while looking at his phone.

Kris scowled at him again.

"Maybe," Sara said. "I could make a lint portrait of Van, to thank her for letting us stay with her."

"Sara, please make some cheesy lint art," Jane said.

"So you read men's magazines on the toilet?" Bren asked.

"And *travel* magazines," Chet said.

Bren swung her eyes away. "Hi, I'm Bren."

"I'm Jane. This is Sara and Skip."

"I'm Sara. He's Skip."

"Oh right."

"Very funny," Skip said.

"Is that an orange camera?" Calli said to Vanessa. "I've never seen an orange camera before, and you've got an orange dress, orange shoes, and orange fingernails. You must like the color orange. Before I got my boobs I put oranges in my bra and went to the county square dance, but I danced so hard my oranges fell out and rolled across the dance floor, and one got kicked, bounced off the banjo player, and knocked the Pabst can off the Christmas tree. The other orange got picked up by Billy Bart Button who brought it back to me, and we ate my orange-boob together in the moonlight."

Vanessa looked at Calli like ... *What?*

"Hey," Kris hollered. "Is it Vanessa?"

"It's Vanessa," Mark said.

"Vanessa," Kris hollered. "Stop filming Calli."

"I'm not," Vanessa said.

Mark smiled at Kris.

Holy damn doodles. Why did he have to be a relationship guy? She couldn't go down that road right now, or maybe ever again, it hurt too much, even though Mark was a hot, polite reality-show-watching, climber, cricketer, hunky-hunk, and who ... who just felt so nice to sit by, for some reason. *Hmmm.* Kris noticed Holly watching her like a fairy godmother, smiling at her talking with Mark. Kris watched him tap his big shoe to the beat the DJ played. *Hmmm, did he like to dance?* Kris smirked at Mark's eyes are her. "Are you looking at my drink or my clothes?"

"Oh," he said. "I was just looking at you."

She grinned. "I drink bourbon and Coke from a cocktail glass to feel rebellious. And my clothes mismatch 'cause I don't care if they match. I just wear what I feel like wearing."

He tilted his head. "Oh," he said.

"What?" she asked.

He nodded. "We went to Mingles Bar earlier. Maybe that's why all their decorations are so random, not to please everyone with everything, but they just decorate with all the random stuff that they like."

"What?" she said.

He smiled. "You're helping me see things differently."

She grinned and slurped her Coke in a cocktail glass, seeing that he was a classier guy than the bar bozos who usually hit on her. She wondered if he did details like Barry. "I haven't seen you in here before," she said. "Are you new?"

He chuckled. "I haven't been new to anything in a while. But I'm glad you think so." He picked up his water glass and drank. "Meeting you is new," he said. "It's a very nice new."

"I'm a nice new?"

"Yes."

"You're a nice new too."

"I'm glad to hear it. Do you hang out here much?" he asked.

She laughed. "I pretty much live here. Here and all the other bars around. I'm very much a Marina girl: I Pilates, I brunch, I dance. Do you dance, Mark?"

"I dance."

"That's great."

"Swing."

"You're a *swinger?*"

"Swing dancing. And ballroom."

"Oh. That's not so great. I mean do you like rave and house dancing?"

"I like couple's dancing."

Of course he did. "So," she said. "You don't like to go to dance clubs?"

"Not really."

She winced. "Yikes."

"Helloooo, I'm Chet. Who are you?"

"I'm Calli."

"You look amazing tonight."

"I look like my mama. And she looks like her mama. My family were Europeans. But now we're Lickers."

Chet jaw dropped again.

"So, you two were coworkers in LA?" Bren said.

"Yeah," Jane said.

"We worked at a movie studio," Sara said.

"What's LA like?"

"It's a beautiful hell," Jane said.

"But it's pretty amazing," Sara added. "If you need a hippopotamus at 2AM for a movie set, you can get one."

"Well, I might be moving there for work," Bren said. "But I won't be needed any hippopotami."

"Oh, we can totally help you find an apartment in LA," Sara said.

"Really?" Bren said.

"You could live with Candy," Jane said. "But she's kinda messy."

"I've grown to not mind that," Bren said.

Kris's heart hurt.

Chet sat with his mouth open while listening to Calli.

"My sisters and I used to play 'Hide the Salami.' They'd hide a salami in the barn and I had to go find it, and if I found it they'd let me wear one of their pretty dresses that could be worn to both church and Beer Day square dances."

Chet's jaw dropped *again*. "*We* should travel together," Chet said.

"But I don't need to travel anymore," Calli said. "I love it here in San Francisco."

"Hey, Chuck," Kris hollered.

"Chet," Mark said.

"Chet," Kris hollered. "Don't flirt with Calli. She's off limits."

Chet's face wilted.

"And Scott."

"Skip."

"Skip, you stay away from her too."

Mark smiled at Kris.

"And Vanessa. Stop filming us."

"I'm filming Mark."

Kris almost said don't, but she didn't want to fight about a guy she couldn't be with ... but maybe she could have as a client.

Kris looked at Mark's beautiful bod up and down. "Do you have a trainer?"

"I don't."

"You built your body all by yourself?"

"My dad played baseball. He taught me how to work out."

"Really?"

"Yeah."

"Is your dad in the majors?"

"He was. Kansas. Then we moved when he got traded to Wisconcin, then Florida, then Oakland. Now my parents live up in Santa Rosa. Mom teaches dance. Dad watches a lot of TV, but he still works out."

"I think you should let me be your trainer. I could get you looking even better." Though he looked super, super tip-top already, she thought.

"You're a trainer?"

"I'm a physical trainer," she said. "And damn good. Got my own business. And I've got Pacific Heights clients."

He smiled.

She liked that he smiled."

"That's awesome," he said, as he set his glass down on the small table, then looked back to her.

She winced and shivered, then quickly grabbed his glass and moved it further to the center of the table, and looked at him. "I hate it when glasses are near the edge. It freaks me out. I don't know why."

"Oh," he said. "I apologize."

Wow, an apology. That was new. She set her glass down too, next to his in the center, and sat glassless with him, now nothing between them but space. Mark did *not* look around at other girls while he talked to her. He didn't lose his temper when a guy bumped into him and spilled his water. He was polite, and calm as cool could be. And, Mark didn't wince at the stuff she said. He tossed his stuff right back at her, like playing catch, super fast, so fun. This was a nice change. "What do you do?" she asked him.

"I'm a sports attorney."

Holy butts. "Really?"

"Yeah."

"What sports?"

"Mostly baseball players."

Her heart did a somersault. "Do you love baseball?"

He chuckled. "I eat, sleep, and dream it," he said.

Holy bongo booties. "You're built like you could play it."

He winced. "I played in college. I tried to go pro, but ... I didn't make it."

She sensed an embarrassment behind his eyes when he said he didn't make it. "You tried to be a pro ball player like your dad? Make him happy?"

Mark sat up. "*Wow,*" he said, with a grin, then chuckled. "You don't hold back."

Uh oh, she thought, did she overdo it? "Um," she said. "How often do you go to Giants games?"

211

"All the time."

Kris smiled. "That's great."

"I'm glad you think so."

"Did you go to the game today?"

"I did."

"Me and Bren went today too."

"Cool. It was a good game to go to."

"I know. We finally beat the Marlins. And I finally tried the fried chicken sandwich," Kris said.

"Was it good?"

"It was a home run."

"Nice."

"Thanks."

"What's your go-to food at the stadium?"

"Usually a vegetable sandwich," Mark said.

"Vegetables? Are you a vegetarian?"

"No," he said. "Sometimes I'll get the ahi tuna or salmon."

"What about cheesesteak?"

"No."

"A meatball sub?"

"No."

"A bacon-wrapped, beer-battered, cheese-dripping bratwurst?"

"Nope," he said. "I only eat healthy at the ballpark."

"What? That's crazy."

"It's my style. I wanna feel sharp and good at a game, and that's how I do it."

"Don't you ever indulge?"

"Oh yeah," he said. "At home I'll scarf down burgers, bar-beque, and chili quesadillas. But, being at the game, it's like I'm at work, and I gotta be my best at work."

"So," she said. "If we went to a game together I'd be noshing a pizza piled with pulled pork and nachos, with ranch dressing falling on my knees while you're eating an eggplant?"

He grinned and nodded. "Probably."

She winced. "Yikes."

MARK'S POINT OF VIEW

Mark was nervous that Kris kept saying "yikes." Not a good sign. But his friends looked like they were all smiles.

"You look amazing tonight," Chet said, grinning.

"You look nice too," Holly said. "This is my boyfriend, Collin."

Chet sighed.

"Holly," Skip said, handing both Jane and Sara bruschetta, and giving them each a wink. "Vanessa said you hang out here a lot."

Holly smiled politely. "This has been one of my favorite places for a while."

"Oh," Skip said, playfully wiping Sara's lips with a napkin. "You've been in the Marina for a while?"

"I've been in San Francisco all my life."

"Really," he said. "So you must know SF history. Were there really cows in Cow Hollow?"

Collin looked at his phone.

"LA sounds both fun and frustrating," Bren said.

"As much as we're glad to leave LA, it'll always been special to us," Jane said. "'Cause that's where me and Sara met."

"And where we fell in love," Sara said, as she leaned across Skip and kissed Jane on the lips.

Chet's jaw *really* dropped.

So did Skip's.

Mark grinned at their bewilderment.

"It's Jane and mine's two-year anniversary next month," Sara said, very smiley.

Bren smiled. "Congratulations."

Kris smiled. "That's awesome."

Holly smiled. "Wonderful."

Calli smiled. "Wow, they kissed, like the Katy Perry song."

Kris grinned.

Chet and Skip looked at each other like: "Now what'da we do, with no ladies here left to woo?"

Kris looked back at Mark, just staring at him, sipping her soda cocktail, her eyes flicking all over him. "Rocking climbing," she quizzed him. "Group or solo?"

"Pairs," he answered.

"*Amazing Race* or *The Bachelor*?"

"*The Bachelor.*"

"Cricket cakes or cricket shakes?"

"Shakes."

"A night in the bars or a night at home?"

He liked the intensity of her stare. "A *romantic* night at home," he answered.

Kris leaned back, sighed, and turned to Bren. "Is this a joke?"

"No."

"You got my hopes up."

"What'da you mean?"

"He's a really nice guy, but the opposite of me on everything. You brought me an un-flingable dude, who doesn't do dance clubs and only eats brussell sprouts at ball games?" Kris shook her head. "He's a pretty horse I can't ride."

"You could if you put a saddle on him."

"Kinky."

"That's not what I meant. You two have so much in common."

Kris rolled her eyes. "Just because people have stuff in common doesn't mean they'll *click*."

"It's a great start."

Mark saw Chet sitting over there watching things fail for Mark too. At least they had video games waiting for them at home.

"But we have too much stuff *not* in common," Kris said to Bren. "I can't get with this guy."

"Because you're looking for a reason to not get with him, because you know he'd be great for you, and that freaks you out, because it might mean a relationship longer than four months, maybe even marriage."

Kris opened her mouth, but nothing came out.

Bren nodded. "Sorry about mentioning 'marriage,' Mark. I don't mean to freak you out too."

He grinned. "I'm not easily freaked out. I am looking for marriage."

Kris whipped her eyes back to him, her wide-open eyes, definitely looking freaked out.

Dang. He didn't want her to wince and say "Yikes" again. He got the message that this was not his soulmate, even though there was some really great vibe going on. *Oh well.* "Sorry to put my marriage-seeking out there on a Saturday night," he said to Kris. "But I like being up front. No misunderstandings. And I really like your up frontness too, Kris. That's something we've got in common. But if we're too different on everything else then you're probably right, we're not a good match."

Kris stared, then exhaled. Relieved?

Mark felt a deep ache in his chest, but muscled up a smile. "Well," he said sticking out his hand toward her. "It was very nice meeting you."

Kris took a breath, then nodded, and shook his hand.

Her hand was really lovely, with a really impressive grip.

"Nice meet you too," she said to him.

They let go.

They sat in silence, not looking at each other anymore.

Bren folded her arms and shook her head at them.

Chet shrugged his shoulders at him.

Mark sat, disappointed. *Huh, this was new, heartache without a relationship.*

"You're not having much luck with girls tonight?" Vanessa said.

Chet gave her a grin. "Well, the night's not over yet."

"Why don't you want a relationship?" she asked him. "Is it because you're still in love with Lana?"

Chet shot straight up.

"Who's Lana?" Calli asked.

"The girl who dumped Chet right after she won that popular TV talent show and went on to win all those big music awards."

Chet's eyes and mouth went wide, and he shrunk on the couch.

Holly slightly scowled at Vanessa.

Mark felt his mouth fall open. "You had a girlfriend?"

"Yeah," Chet slowly exhaled.

"You were in love?"

"Yeah," Chet exhaled again.

"That's amazing."

"That's brutal," Kris said. "She dumped him when her career took off. I know how that feels." Kris stared at Bren.

Bren shrunk in her seat.

Holly clapped her hands, unsubtly pulling attention from the heavy vibe. "Skip," she said. "To answer your question from earlier, yes there were once cows in Cow Hollow in the 1800s."

"She's changing the subject!" Kris hollered.

Mark grinned at Kris pointing out what is usually not said.

Skip leaned towards Holly. "So there were really cows?"

"Yes there were."

Skip smiled. "And I read that this bar has a lot of history too."

"It does," Holly said.

Calli sat up straight and smiled at everyone. "The barber in town got the Rolling Stone music magazines and he let me have his whole collection, and I read aaaall the Rolling Stones, and I remember reading that all kinds of famous bands played here, like Cute Condom."

Everyone stopped and stared at her.

Calli smiled big at all the eyes on her. "I don't know worldly stuff," Calli said. "But I know music stuff."

"You *do?*" Kris said.

"Sure," Calli said. "Pop music's what I read about when I'm in bed, or on the can."

Holly smiled.

"Is anyone gonna eat that last broosketta?" Calli grabbed it and munched.

Everyone stared silent.

Kris and Bren looked at each other with mouths open.

"That's interesting," Mark said. "Earlier tonight, Chet and I heard one of their songs: 'Love Awesome.'"

"Huh," Kris said. "Me and Bren heard that song earlier too."

"Weally?" Calli said with a mouthful of bruschetta, then swallowed. "That's a cool coincidence. And Kris and Mark met in the place where they used to play concerts." She crunched another bite. "It's like destiny."

Kris and Mark looked at each other.

Kris watched Mark smile at her.

"That is a cool coincidence."

Kris rolled her eyes. "You believe in destiny?"

He chuckled. "Not really," he said, as Skip put his drink down by the edge of the table.

Kris *cringed*.

"I'm a pretty pragmatic person," Mark said, as his hand casually moved Skip's glass away from the edge and to the center of the table, and kept talking, as if what he'd just done wasn't a big deal. "I do make a wish when I blow out birthday candles though, but I never do grow wings."

Kris paused, staring at the glass that Mark just casually moved away from the edge for her ... *amazingly*. Then her eyes slowly lifted up to his, and he just looked at her, clearly oblivious of the *amazingness*. Did he really have no idea how much what he just did meant to her? Moving her glass. It was incredibly kind. He remembered, and was aware. And he *cared*.

Her heart suddenly ached. But in a new way. A *good* way. A really good way at this really '*good one.*'

Uh oh.

Why did he have to be a relationship guy?

219

Mark's point of view

Mark noticed Kris suddenly look blank-faced with her mouth open. Did he say something wrong? Did he offend her by saying that he didn't believe in destiny?

But then her lips curled up.

Oh good.

Then she leaned toward him, her beautiful face eclipsing everything.

Oh my.

Her hands softly landed on his thighs.

Oh wow.

He inhaled her glorious, green apple shampoo-scented hair.

Oh yes.

And her perfect mouth opened by his ear. "I'm glad you didn't become a major league player," her sweet voice said. "'Cause then you might not have been here tonight for me to meet you."

Ooooh wow.

His whole being *buzzed*.

She became an angel.

His heart restarted, like a whole new life, and pounded so hard.

Her words were like salvation from years of regret. Did she know the bold gift she just gave him? Did she know how much more he now had to restrain his yearning?

Don't ask her to move in yet.

Don't ask her to move in yet.

KRIS'S POINT OF VIEW

"I don't think Kris wants you to film them," Calli said.

Kris looked across the table.

Vanessa's camera pointed at them.

"Hey. This is a private moment," Kris scolded. "I told you to stop filming us."

"I'm not," Vanessa said. "I'm filming Mark."

Kris jumped up. "You're gonna film the inside of your ass."

Kris stepped toward Vanessa.

Holly leapt up and put herself between them. "Whooooa, you two."

Mark smiled.

"It's orange dress vs. polka dots," Jane said.

"My bet's on polka dots," Sara said.

"I don't know," Jane said. "Van's nails get scratchy."

"Kris," Bren said as she flashed her fingers.

Kris ... exhaled, while she glared at Vanessa. *10, 9, 8 ...* Then she saw Mark staring at her. *Damn.* He just saw her lose her shit. Did she just scare Mr. Amazing away? *7, 6, 5 ...* And the hottest thing about him was that he was caring. She wanted more of his caring. Suddenly she didn't care if they had stuff in common or not. She slowly sat back down on the cube beside him. *4 ... 3 ... 2 ...* Maybe she could change him, maybe open up his world to dance clubs, barbeque at ballgames, and maybe she could be his first fling! If she hadn't scared him off ... *1.*

Mark's point of view

"Why don't we all explore another bar?" Holly said, smiley with her arms wide, as she gave Kris a look. "We can all get some air."

Everyone agreed and got up.

Mark tossed cash on the table.

And some others did too.

Calli rummaged around in her bag, then held out her $9 to Holly.

"No, no, Calli," Holly said. "That's very sweet, but I've got this."

"How can I repay you?"

"Just have the night of your life."

Calli smiled. "I am."

Mark was too. Looking at Kris, feeling more sure about her than anything ever, and couldn't stop smiling, because now he finally knew how you know when someone is the one: *you just know.*

Kris looked at him. "Me yelling at Valerie."

"Vanessa."

"Vanessa," she said, then sighed. "People say I have too much 'energy.' I'm working on it."

He raised his eyebrows. "What'da you mean?" he said. "Don't change. I like your energy."

She did a double-take. "You do?"

He smiled at her, this unexpected woman. "People say I rush things. I'm working on it," he said.

Don't ask her to move in yet.
Don't ask her to move in yet.
She stared at him, intensely.
He waited for Kris to wince again and say "yikes."
But instead, she downed her drink, stared at him again, and said with a big exhale: *"Ho ... ly ... fuck."*

Chapter 8

KRIS SAT staring at remarkable Mark. Staring *stunned*. Feelings tingling down into deepness in her she didn't even know was down there, and setting up camp, while thinking that he was the most amazing guy she'd ever met. What the H-E-double-dicks was happening? Did she just find Mr. Right? While bantering about bratwurst and *The Bachelor*? She was gonna have to scold the horoscope people 'cause they didn't mention anything like *this* going down tonight. This feeling was unlike any other she'd felt before with any dude, a fuzzy, fun feeling of ease and awesomeness vibing all through her, urging her to do more than just mount him, but to melt with him, as everything else in the world whooshed away except his nice eyes, in a silent hum of wonderful, as she watched him stand up tall beside her, tower over her like a mighty gorgeous mountain, then with a kiss-a-licious smile, offer her his big hand.

She ... she ... she did *NOT* take it.

Instead she jumped up on her own, as tall as her 5'7-ness could, her eyes at his chin, buzzing with shock, flashed a polite smile, and bolted the hell away from him, through the crowd, out the open door, and back into the safety of the night!

224

The freezing night.

The chilly air iced her bare arms and legs, telling her how hot and sweaty her bod had been with this new guy. Enough steam probably rose off her skin to fog up San Francisco as she cooled in the quiet, refocused, and breathed in freshness, loving the feeling of her ankle boots flat on solid rock sidewalk, back in reality, looking around at streetlights and shiny parked cars, passing drunk strangers, and her pretty-dressed friends walking out to join her. Like waking from a wild dream.

But, holy fuzzy butts, then Mr. Dreamboat walked out and onto the concrete sidewalk to her, very real, and still looking very reMarkable, and looking right at her with his *relationship-eyes*. More wonderful feelings. And freaked out ones. "Are you all right?" he asked.

She had no F-ing idea how to answer that question, as she turned and followed behind her, no, not her, now *their* now-larger group of tipsy friends, strolling north through the sparkly night down Fillmore's wide sidewalk peopled with lots of other fashionable, tipsy nightlifers, and Mark strolling soberingly beside her, her heart thumping faster than her footsteps, and her mind fling-flanging all over the place as they past more loud, crowded bars and two drunk jocks arguing whose biceps were bigger. Why couldn't she have met some bonehead to bang? Why'd she have to meet a really *good* guy? Mark's goodness and this crazy connection between her and him was way too wild to be real. She gripped her leather skirt, like hanging on to a mile-high cliff, and poked a little more at this

225

too-good-to-be-true dude, hoping to find *something* rejectable about him. "Mark, do you like Christmas or Halloween?"

"Christmas."

"Car or truck?"

"Truck."

"Dog or cat?"

"Dog."

"Paris or Vegas?"

"Skiing in Tahoe."

"*Casablanca* or *Weekend at Bernie's*."

"*Field of Dreams*."

Damn. He was killing it.

"Wigs or handcuffs?"

He smirked. "Who wears the wig?"

"I haven't decided."

He smiled. "I like my own hair, and I've never done handcuffs, so I'll wear those."

Super-tingles.

"The Beatles or The Beach Boys?"

He grinned. "The sultry twang of Sheryl Crow's electric guitar and spicy barbeque on a foggy San Francisco night."

Holy tickle tackle. This was getting real. "What'd you give your mom for Mother's Day?" Please say something stupid and end this insanity, she thought.

"I drove up to Santa Rosa and brought my mom some flowers," he said.

Oh damn.

"And I cooked her a seafood stew dinner."

Oh damn.

"And I got her a framed vintage movie poster of *Singing in the Rain* that I had signed by some of the crew members."

Mother fucker. He was even great to his mom. Tingles. And trouble. Time to turn over the BIG frickin' stone.

"How long did you date your ex," Kris blurted out.

Mark looked over at her with a raised eyebrow and a grin, as if liking her going for the jugular. "Eight months," he answered. "About four months longer than it probably should have, because I try to make things work."

Hmmm. "And why did it end?" Her heart beat harder, fearing both another perfect answer or a total deal breaker. *Was there cheating? Arguments? Did his girlfriend catch him humping the vacuum cleaner?*

"Asteroids," he said.

"What?"

He grinned. "The day after Valentine's Day an asteroid entered Earth's atmosphere and exploded over Russia. Then, just sixteen hours later, *another* big asteroid narrowly missed Earth by 17,000 miles, closer than any rock its size. Jill and I talked about the coincidence of *two* big space rocks happening on almost the same day, and somehow we got into whether she wanted to be with me, and if I wanted to be with her, during an end-of-Earth asteroid, and we both respectfully decided no. I guess we didn't have as much in common as we needed to, and I guess I should have noticed that before I asked her to move in with me."

"You broke up over asteroids?"

"We did."

"17,000 miles is a long ways away."

"Surprisingly it's not," he said. "The moon is 240,000 miles away. If my foot is the moon and my head is the Earth the asteroid passed us at my neck."

"Where's yer-anus?"

Mark broke into laugher.

What a goofy reason for breaking up, she thought, but, dammit, not a deal breaker, both thrilling her and freaking her even more. Luckily Calli was there with comic relief. She grinned at Calli's cartoonish reactions to everything new: jam-packed bars everywhere, pretty neon, hundreds of twenty-somethings walking and talking and texting in stylin' clothes, sidewalk cooks grilling sizzling meats outside the bars, the line out the door for a late night pizza slice, a passing SUV limo with bachelorette partiers "*woooo*"ing out the sunroof. Calli "*woooo*"ed and waved back as their group all crossed the headlight-filled six-lanes of Lombard Street and turned right. Kris remembered seeing all this fun for the first time ten years ago, and seeing Calli see this old-hat stuff made it feel like ten years ago. *Yikes.*

Then Calli danced among bubbles that a purple-haired girl was blowing, and Calli playfully bit at the bubbles. "That's what my doggie used to do," Calli said.

Kris grinned.

Then Calli started flirting with a drunk douchebag guy looking at Calli like she was prey.

Kris un-grinned.

No fucking way.

Kris barged between them, hooked Calli's arm with hers, and kept Calli with her. But walking with Calli, and possibly Mr. Right beside her, felt bizarrely like a family, and oddly kind of enjoyable, and Bren looked back and smiled at them all, and, *whooooa*, this was way too weird. Kris hooked Calli's arm with Bren's. "Calli, walk with Bren while me and Mark talk and keeping riding this vibe to find out if we're a good match."

MARK'S POINT OF VIEW

Mark tried to calm his big smile so Kris wouldn't think we was a loony weirdo as they walked through the golden bar window lights together. He just felt so much awesomeness to meet her and hang out with her. It was awesome that she was still hanging out with him. It was awesome that her brisk non-high heeled walking speed able to keep up with his strides as they began outpacing their group together. It was awesome that her pretty voice and refreshing bluntness actually said out loud that her goal was to keep seeing if she and he were a good match, *wow*. And it was really awesome to be with a Marina-loving woman who fearlessly said exactly what was on her mind with no subtle hinting or games, and who was also feeling their vibe. *Jeez Louise,* he almost stayed home and missed out on meeting her; *that* would have been loony. What a rush of *whaw yoo* to

229

find her, and, *oh man,* what a feeling of responsibility to not screw up this great but delicate moment, like not stepping on feet when dancing. Though Kris might step on his feet right back, which was so flippin' exciting about her, she dished it right back at him. Life with her would be a hoot. He'd start that life right now if he could, start by holding her hand.

But he didn't offer his hand again.

Instead he just kept his hand-fantasy to himself, so she wouldn't skedaddle away from him again, and really hoped that she also thought they were a good match. "What'd you give *your* mom for Mother's Day?"

Kris winced. "A Prada purse."

"Wow. You're a nice daughter."

"I wish she thought so."

"How could she not think so?"

"My family thought I was a looooser for so long while I was just getting by. Now I save up and send them spendy bling to prove that I'm a success, worthy of their love and all that stupid stuff."

"They shouldn't need bling to love you."

"Well, when your family is nuttier than a vasectomy doctor's office 'cause they all saw a UFO and started a wacky cult for the planet Zoondangles, you're not dealing with people who do normal."

Mark looked at her.

She bit her lip. "And I've totally scared you off, huh?"

He grinned. "Heck no, you just keep getting more intriguing."

"Really?"

"Did *you* see the UFO?"

"No, I was in the house with my *boyfriend's* cigar-shaped object."

He chuckled.

She chuckled at his chuckle. "Why do people who see a UFO say it looked cigar-shaped? Why don't they just say 'it looked like a dick?'"

"Well, that might start a very different cult."

"That's true."

"But my family being part of a dick-cult would be even harder to swallow."

He laughed.

"Oh my god," she said. "I didn't even mean to say that. Oh shit, my therapist's gonna love that one." She laughed, then winced. "So, UFOs and swallow-Freudian slips. Are you freaked out yet?"

"No way," he said. "I'm fascinated. And I'm curious how much more your therapist can take after you say that you've now met Bigfoot."

Kris laughed

Mark smiled. "And I'm glad you didn't see the UFO. If you had we may never have met."

She grinned. "You're taking my wild stuff really well. Better than most. Better than my ex."

"Is your 'wild stuff' why you broke up?" Uh oh, he thought, was asking that too personal? *But why was this amazing woman single? Was her and her ex not a good match? Did he screw around on her? Did he not like cricket powder?*

"*The Star Wars,*" she said.

"What?"

"I like *The Star Wars,*" Kris said.

"*The Star Wars?*"

"Yeah. On April Fool's Day, David thought it'd be funny to play some prank on me by poking fun at my family's eccentric-ness. So he dressed up as one of those alien dudes and jumped out at me, hoping for a laugh. But he got a scream and a chest kick."

"Oh no," Mark said.

"Oh yeah," Kris said. "I was freaked out. It was instinct. I slammed a kick into his chest, and he went flying, landed on my skateboard, whooshed across my apartment, and whooshed out the door, onto my patio, into my plants, causing Cathy the Cactus to fall on his alien junk."

"Oh no."

"Oh yeah. My 'too much energy' was pretty much the last straw for him and he dumped me. A real dick punch to the heart."

Mark nodded. "I'm sorry." Note to self, he thought, don't surprise her dressed as an alien.

Self to Mark, her ferocity was *awesome.* She was a *warrior.*

Mark grinned. "Did your boyfriend bruise his coccyx?"

"He did."

Mark rolled his eyes. "I was trying to be as funny as your 'Uranus' joke."

"Oh wow," Kris said, grinning. "Well, your joke fizzled."

"It did. I can't top Uranus."

"You could if you go home with me," she said.

"Ooooh." Mark laughed.

Kris laughed.

"Now you've got two funny jokes," Mark said. "I'm so far behind."

"You could be behind if you go home with me."

"Ooooh. That's three."

"No. It'd just be us two."

"Oh jeez. You're on a roll."

"I could be on something else if you go home with me."

Mark smiled, as she laughed, and he stopped talking, so far behind her funnies. Then realized that she just invited him home with her, *three times. Jeez Louise.* She liked him. *Oh yeah.* This was great. Or was she just being funny? He tried to stay cool, while confused, while they walked up the busy street, in wild silence. "*Star Wars,* huh?"

"Yeah."

"You know," Mark said. "I heard George Lucas got married today."

"Really?"

"Yeah," Mark said. "And the food at the reception was chewy."

"Ooooh." Kris laughed and jumped up and down. "You did it. *You* did a funny."

Mark laughed at her laughing, and took a bow.

They walked.

She smiled. "You still didn't top my anus."

Mark grinned. "I could if I go home with you."

"Ooooh," she cheered and bumped his hip with hers.

Wow, it was *on*, he thought, it was *on*. Whatever was going on between them, it was definitely *on*, definitely a good match. His heart did cartwheels. His hands sweated. And, *wow*, if he was ever gonna go home with a woman the same night he met her it would definitely be Kris. And then the next night, and the next, and living together, and marriage, a chewy reception, and rock climbing together, and happiness forever. As long as nothing went wrong tonight.

He watched Skip count the headlights zipping by on Lombard as they neared the sounds of karaoke-ers singing Elton John's "Tiny Dancer" coming from inside the big, block-long bar they walked towards.

Skip tour-guided. "This whole area of town used to be marshland," he said.

"And I've kissed a guy on that corner, and that corner, and that corner, and this corner" Kris said. "Does *that* bug you?"

Mark shrugged. "No. I've probably kissed a girlfriend on all those corners too. It just means we've both around the block."

She laughed again. "Now you're being funnier than me and that's gonna bug *me*," she joked.

"I'll dial down my funny for you."

"Thank you," she said with a grin, as they crossed Webster Street and arrived at the best karaoke bar in San Francisco: Silver Cloud.

They all showed I.D. to the door guy, who didn't ask to see Mark's. *Dang.* Mark let Kris enter the bar's open door before him. Her playful wink flashed a "thanks" as she passed him.

His heart felt another flip, and he enjoyed seeing her polka dots and long hair, and then a circus of people, lights, and who knew what wild stuff would happen next.

KRIS'S POINT OF VIEW

Inside the bar, people were having a ball. Once again, one of the Marina's most popular bars did not disappoint. Big venue, crowded but roomy, relaxing brown-wood interior, classy hanging Tiffany-style lamps, neon colors, sports on TVs, massive menu, endless alcohol, pinball, Skee ball, hoops, and most of all the place was in full swing with a standing crowd singing their inebriated hearts out along with the girl and guy on the colorfully lit karaoke stage.

Before the new arrivals even went for beverages Kris and the group couldn't help but instantly join *their* tipsy voices with the infectious flair of the happy herd to the enthralling chorus! Hands swaying, abs clenching, lungs launching, the wood floors, beams, tables, chairs, and bar shook from the thunder of a hundred-plus voices!

Except Holly. Kris saw her just shyly mouth the words. Song over. Bows. APPLAUSE!

MARK'S POINT OF VIEW

Their singing together felt like a big bonding experience before their group instantly forgot the moment and scattered to the bar to get drinks as Jane and Skip squeezed through to get their names on the list to sing soon. The rest of their group worked their way toward the bar. Mark waved his hand for Kris to go first through the loud, perfumey crowd, while the next karaokers sang to the sultry twang of Sheryl Crow's "Strong Enough." *Hmm.*

Mark looked at Kris.

Kris looked at Mark.

They grinned at each other in some surreal moment of connection, until thirsty peeps barged between them, separating her from him.

KRIS'S POINT OF VIEW

Surrounded by the swarm, Kris ended up waiting by the bar, Markless, but with her friends and with her hands playfully and protectively on Calli's shoulders in front of her with Calli's head looking-looking-looking all around, clearly loving this party place, and clearly tipsy the way she swaaaayed around and asking-asking-asking even more questions that usual. Calli's tipsy-talking about how she'd like to go to Europe to see skywriting in another language made Holly smile again.

236

She felt Bren's hip accidently bump hers as they both bellied up to the bar. They looked at each other, but said nothing, their achy nothing interrupted by a hot beefcake bartender whose wide Nirvana t-shirt suggested they'd get no '80s pop song titles from him. Kris ordered Calli only a water to much bouncy protest. Kris already sorta had a Mark so she just ordered a Coke in a martini glass, unusually wanting to keep sobering up with all this crazy going on tonight that might get crazier she both hoped and feared. She heard Bren order another Lemon Drop with lots of umbrellas. The last time she ordered one they were friendly and talking, now they stood by this bar just looking at each other, awkwardly, not talking. Bren looked as lost for what to say as Kris felt. Such weirdness between them now.

"I don't have to do my yoga breathing while in L.A. traffic anymore," Sara said, light and laughing. "Now I can get anywhere in SF by bus in only twenty minutes, such less stress. My soul thanks me every lovely day." Sara put her mood ring ornamented fingers to her heart. "Though now I stress about insane rent, and I think Jane might actually miss LA. But isn't that how life is? You can't have everything perfect."

Kris thought the same thing.

Somebody sang Britney Spears, toxically.

Kris saw half a glass of beer on the bar no one was drinking and saw Calli reach for it. Kris pulled her back. "You can't just take stuff."

"No one's drinking it."

"It's just not cool," Kris said, super surprised that she actually said that. That beer did look good, Kris thought, but didn't grab it, and sipped her soda.

Sara started jabbering about LA to Bren again.

Bren glanced at Kris and tried to change the subject.

Kris thought about hollering her change-the-subject joke again but her heart hurt too much, and turned toward Holly and Calli and listened to their happier conversation.

"This is so much *fun*," Calli cheered to Holly. "I love this place. I can't wait to sing. I sing all the time. But I like to change the lyrics. You should hear me sing 'Bootie In The Sky With Diamonds.' Holly, do you like to sing?"

Holly cracked up, laughing more than Kris had seen Holly laugh in a long time. "Um, I don't like to sing in public," Holly surprisingly admitted to Calli.

"Why not?"

"I, um, I don't like the attention on me."

"But you throw parties."

"The attention is on the party, not me."

"I *love* people looking at me. It's fun," Calli said. "Holly, you should let loose and have fun. When you LET LOOSE life feels so much more funner."

Holly paused, glanced at Collin engrossed in his stupid phone, then leaned toward Calli and whispered: "How *fun?*"

Calli smiled.

Whoa, Kris wondered, did Calli like Holly more than her? If Bren left for LA would Calli leave her all alone and hang out with Holly instead? Would Mark grow tired of her energy like most guys do? *Damn.* They all kinda felt like they might leave her, all these great old and new friends in her life. That would super-duper suck. That is not how this should go down. There had to be a way, a way to keep Bren and Calli, and maybe Mark ALL in her life. There had to be a way.

Kris looked over at gorgeous Mark, across the crowd, and wondered what it would be like to "let loose" with him.

"I saw Natalie Portman sing 'I Think We're Alone Now' here in 2007," Vanessa bragged.

"Cool," only Sara said, casually.

Vanessa frowned as if no one was impressed with her, and Kris watched her do a hair flip and dance away from their half of the group and started filming Mark's half.

MARK'S POINT OF VIEW

After the canoodling couple in front of him got their drinks, Mark ordered his water, hoping to soon be canoodling too, with Kris, feeling as over the moon as his moon-lawyering friend's smile looked.

Skip talked on and on about how fantastic it was to talk to Sara and Jane and have them talk back to him nicely, even if they were a couple and he couldn't pursue either of them, it was still such a stellar experience for him, and that with his new burst of confidence he was eager to talk to more women, as Vanessa danced over with her signature orange cocktail prop, and her camera, and she filmed Skip's elation, and Mark's crotch and polite smile.

Vanessa's constant camera on him made him feel like he was on a reality show, of his real-life. This was weird and cool, and annoying. Now he knew he didn't want to be on a reality show, and he could forget the application to be on *The Bachelor* now that he'd met Kris, he sure hoped. "I'm happy for you, Skip," Mark said, getting his water and tipping two bucks, as Chet returned from the restroom, looking not nearly as chipper as Skip.

"You were supposed to help me get *more* girls," Chet griped to Mark. "But tonight I haven't gotten *any* of the girls I wanted."

"Sorry," Mark said. "But there's plenty of women in this bar."

"Are you gonna help me finally woo one?"

Mark hesitated. "I don't want Kris seeing me talk to other women. She might think I'm not interested in her. Skip should be your new wingman."

Two girls sang Smash Mouth, like all stars.

"I got our names on the karaoke list," Jane said, joining them, and putting her hand over Vanessa's camera for a second and grinning.

"Don't, silly," Vanessa said, refocusing.

Chet looked at Jane, and looked at Jane again, and smiled. "Soooo," Chet said to Jane. "You and Sara look amazing tonight. Do you and Sara like to, um, travel?"

Jane rolled her eyes. "We're not interested in traveling to threesome-ville if that's what you're asking."

Chet raised his eyebrows. "Oh, um, what makes you think I was asking that?"

Jane just smirked and went silent.

"Because," Vanessa piped up, "we know that when you talk travel you're trying to make a girl feel exotic and tingly, but Jane's only travel partner is Sara."

Chet's eyes flew wide and looked over at Mark.

Mark did the "I don't know how she knows that" shoulder shrug.

"I heard Skip tell Jane and Sara," Vanessa said.

Chet's eyes zipped to Skip.

Skip bit is lip.

"You told them?" Chet exclaimed.

"I'm sorry," Skip said. "But the more honest I was with them the more they listened and smiled at me, so I told them, you know, everything."

"You broke the rules, you space moron. You lied about being a ladies man, and then you spilled to girls my moves. You're the worst wingman ever."

"I'm sorry," Skip said again.

Jane patted him on the shoulder. "I'm really sorry," Jane said.

"Lighten up, Chet," Vanessa said.

Mark looked over at amazing Kris, across the crowd, and shared a look with her hot stare again, and wondered what it would be like to go home with her, as people applauded, and the DJ announced: "Up next, The Marina Girls."

KRIS'S POINT OF VIEW

Kris saw Jane jump up.

"Here!" Jane shouted, waving her hand.

"Alright, come on up," the DJ said into the mic."

Jane waved at Sara, Vanessa, Calli, Holly, Bren, and Kris to join her up on the stage, just big enough to sport all seven of them.

Kris sprung up, so ready for some normal Saturday night fun, as she hauled Holly up with her.

Holly was in no hurry.

Calli was, as she bounced up on stage with a big, big smile. "I'm a Marina girl now!" she cheered, waving to all the people in the bar looking at her.

Holly looked like she might faint.

"It's all right," Kris said. "Your hair and makeup look awesome, and these lights make your dress shimmer beautifully. Just have fun. No one's gonna think you're a diva."

Holly polite-smiled at the crowd while *death gripping* Kris's right arm.

Kris saw Bren standing to her left. They shared a look. Kris suddenly realized this might be the last time her and Bren ever sing karaoke together. *Oh crap.* They were about to make their last fun memory, under a disco ball that would look great in their bathroom. Lots of feelings. Mad *and* sad.

The DJ handed a microphone to Calli.

Calli literally jumped with joy!

DJ offered Vanessa the other mic, but Kris snatched it! This mic was hers and Bren's.

Vanessa gave her a *gaaaawd* sneer.

Kris gave no fucks.

Hot lights! Huge crowd! Tons of eyes on them. Phones filming them.

Holly started to leave the stage.

But Kris pulled her back, hoping facing her fear would be good for Holly. "Let's do this!" Kris hollered, before Holly could flee, faint or vomit.

DJ pressed play.

Strum strum. Taylor Swift's "22" began.

The crowd wooooed!

Calli wooooed back!

Holly gripped tighter.

Kris was glad she had another arm in case Holly pinched off this one.

Vanessa held out her camera and filmed this moment.

Sara clapped.

Jane smiled.

Bren looked at the lyrics on the screen.

Kris stomped the stage to the beat, beat, beat, beat.

And all seven of them started singing. Holly shyly. Bren medium. Kris loud and fearless! And Calli's voice was right behind Kris's volume as they both let loose for fun and –

BAM!

The chorus kicked in.

And they sang it.

And rocked it.

And they were in it.

Doing this.

Together.

Singing together. Feeling together. Having fun together.

Badass bonding.

This felt like a perfect night!

All rockin' to the rhythm, in their own rhythms: Vanessa S H O W Y ! Holly shyly. Kris BOLDLY! Bren precisely. Calli BoUnCy. Jane calmly. Sara fist-pumpingly!

Kris sang (so off-key) to Mark's smiling eyes. Kris saw Holly trying to hang back, but Kris kept giving Holly as much mic time as Bren and Calli.

Vanessa seemed to really want to have a mic. Jane kept trying to share their mic with Vanessa, but also kept trying to gently pull down Vanessa's camera. But Vanessa looked annoyed at that and danced her way near Holly, squishing Holly to get near the mic that Kris power-held. Vanessa was now the outcast.

Kris kept moving the mic away from Vanessa, on purpose.

Vanessa kept moving closer to the mic.

Holly kept getting squished.

Kris tried to savor this fun moment with her friends that Vanessa was filming. But more distracting than Vanessa's filming was Mark out there in the crowd, staring up at her, and smiling, and looking like a whole new life, a love life, a wonderful, outdoorsy love life together that could end up with her married with sex on a regular basis and a baby bump, but also that love life ripping her away from all this fun, single, party life, forever, ever, and ever. *Holy dick dangles.* Lose her friend and lose her fun all in one last wild night? Too much. Just too, too much. She sweated. Feelings of everything falling, falling, falling, and the mic falling out of her hand as Vanessa tried to steal it away from her sweaty palm. Kris gripped it tighter and tighter as Vanessa squished Holly to get at the mic and Kris kept yanking it away.

Squishing.

Yanking.

Squishing.

Yanking.

Suddenly, Kris witnessed a miracle as peacekeeper-Holly *thrust* herself forward, grabbed the mic out of Kris's hands, breaking up the fight and taking over the song! As if she was showing them how they should properly act in front of crowd and how to put on a good show! Smiling big! Singing loud! Stomping feet! Swinging hair! Hand in the air! Belting to the back wall! And looked like she was finally having *fun* as she let *LOOSE!*

AND HOLLY *SANG!*

AND HOLLY *SANG!*

AND HOLLY *SANG!*

And the song ended.

And Holly kept *SINGING!*

And *SINGING!*

And *SIIIIIIIINGINGGGGGGGG!!!!*

And Holly seemed to realize she was the *only* one singing.

And stopped!

And silence.

And a *HUGE ROAR* came back to her!!!!

And ... *oh God* ... Holly stood stunned, front and center, with all eyes on her!

APPLAUSE! WHISTLES! WOOOOS!

THE CROWD WENT WILD FOR HER!!!!

Holly looked like she had no idea what the heck just happened.

Calli ran over and hugged her so hard!

Kris hugged her!

Bren hugged her!

Holly had actually let herself un-shyly stand out in a crowd!

Actually having the courage to stand up and let her voice be heard!

Holly had actually *let loose!*

And what came back at her this time was *positive* energy!

A flood of love and approval more fun than any cocktail or new dress could give!

And Holly smiled HUGE!

Then looked scared as F! Holly quickly fled off the stage, out of the spotlight before anyone could label her a diva and hid herself among the crowd.

But she couldn't hide from Kris knowing how *WOW* this moment was for her.

Collin didn't seem to know as Holly hid in his arms, her cheek to his chest. He held her nicely, but said nothing, not even 'good job,' just patted her on the back.

Kris couldn't believe his silence. But she wouldn't stay silent and cheered for Holly, joined by Bren, and by Jane and Sara as they all complimented over and over how they didn't know what a fantastic singing voice she had and they all bonded over this amazing moment, all of them except Calli. Where was Calli? Kris panicked. *Where was Calli?* She'd lost Calli!! *Oh God no!!*

"Hi," Calli's voice giggled over the speakers.

Kris spun around! So did everyone in the bar. And saw Calli on stage, solo, with the microphone, and smiling at everyone's eyes hot on her. *Oh thank God she hadn't lost Calli.* Kris panted with relief, then disbelief at what she was seeing and hearing.

"I'm Calli," she said into the mic with a big smile, in front of every staring person in the bar. "I'm new in town and single. I like music and playing *Hide the Salami.* I'm looking to meet a new, fun, cute guy who doesn't have hairy butt checks, and likes music, dancing, and a girl who lets loose, and if you wanna meet me I'm gonna be right over here. *Woooo!*"

Kris, Bren and Holly stood with their jaws on the floor!

"Now *that's* how you make an announcement," Kris exclaimed.

"That's how you attract psychos," Bren warned.

"That's how you be fearless," Holly envied.

A herd of random guys eagerly followed their junk towards Calli!

"Oh my God," Kris worried. "We gotta go stand with her and filter out the jerks."

Calli got surrounded and flirted and smiled like she was in Heaven!

Kris kept Calli close as she and Bren and Holly filtered the twenty flirting guys, as she saw Mark walking towards her, closer and closer, and the DJ announced: "Up next, The Marina Boys."

MARK'S POINT OF VIEW

Mark felt Skip grab his arm and point to the stage. But Mark didn't wanna go sing; he wanted to go talk with Kris again.

"Come on," Skip insisted. "This is gonna be sweetness cool."

Mark saw Kris busy talking with her friends, and Skip was adamant about singing. "All right," Mark said, following his friend up to the stage. Maybe Kris's attention would be with her friends and she wouldn't hear his terrible, terrible singing voice.

Chet was already up on the stage waving at the crowd and advertising himself.

Ladies "*woooed*" at him.

He smiled. Then he rolled his eyes as Mark stepped up on the stage and the "*woooos*" wooed louder.

Mark just smirked at Chet, and looked out to see if Kris was seeing him, but she was still busy talking with Calli. He took the microphone the DJ handed him. Lots of people looking at his friends and him were more like silhouettes in the shine of the yellow and blue spotlights.

Chet grabbed the other mic.

Mark moved to share the mic with Skip, who looked a little nervous again in front of so many ladies. Mark patted his shoul-

der, and some old timey Frank Sinatra song began playing. *Nice.*
Rat-a-tat drums, mellow horns and piano started swingin', and
this might actually be fun, he thought. Then he saw Kris, amaz-
ing-Kris, out there, looking at him, looking at him about to
make an ass of himself. *Greeeeat.*

But this would at least be a good bonding moment for
Chet, Skip, and him.

The lyrics scrolled on the screen.

Chet and Skip sang, not too terribly. Chet loudly. Skip mellowly.

And Mark whole heartedly gave it a go, hoping Kris didn't
go, singing from his gut, swinging for the fences as usual, feeling like a fool, feeling hot and stupid, but not self-conscious
about the two hundred eyes on him, just the two most important eyes he didn't want to see him strike out. Hopefully
she'd see the humor in his trying to be cool for her. *Dang.* His
tongue stumbled over the lyrics and quickly looked back at the
screen, and as he sang the words deep and sonorous, and maybe
in key. *Wow.* These words he was singing were about someone
thinking someone was marvelous. Spot on lyrics to describe
how he felt about Kris. He got into them. He felt them. He
looked up and sang them to Miss Marvelous out there, sang
them from his feelings, into the mic, out the speakers, and
right to her. *Yeah.* Right to her, as if it was just her and him
in this beer-scented wonderland, singing right to her cute ears,
to her beautiful stare, and felt her hearing him, hearing his
feelings. *Oh yeah.* Kris's mouth hung open. She looked moved.

Entranced. Maybe liking him even more than before. *Wow.* This moment was *marvelous.*

Until Chet began stretching his arm in front Skip's face as he belted the tune, blocking him like a diva, bumping Skip backwards, clearly on purpose, clearly still miffed at Skip.

And Skip, sounding more and more confident as he sang, and nudging Chet's arm away.

Again.

And again.

And again.

And this was getting ridiculous.

And then it got stupid as Skip started arm-blocking Chet, and they both got unhinged and started shoving each other.

And finally Mark had to step between these two stooges, push them apart, and negotiate a peace that never got reached as they kept reaching for each other on each side of Mark.

And the crowd seemed to think it was a comedy act and cheered on their buffoonery.

And the song ended with the three of them bumbling off the stage.

Roaring applause.

Mark's arms kept them apart until the two fops settled down. He shook his head, then turned toward Kris, but back on the floor he couldn't see her. Miss Marvelous was out there somewhere. Did she like what she saw and heard? He couldn't wait to talk instead of sing, as he excused himself from Skip and Chet and walked through the crowd to find her.

KRIS'S POINT OF VIEW

Kris saw Mark step off the stage and come towards her. *Emotions, emotions, emotions.* Kris told Holly to guard Calli with Calli's new guy-friend as Kris grabbed Bren's arm and hauled her away, past a glitter of new Marina girls singing Cyndi Lauper, 'cause they just wanted to have fun, and over to the back of the bar by the pinball machines, away from Mark's ears, for a BFF PM ASAP! "I changed my mind," Kris said to Bren. "You can't move to L.A."

"Kris, I'm sorry I upset you."

"Bren, I'm sorry, but you can't go to LA."

"I might go."

"You can't. You gotta stay here in SF."

"Why?"

"Mark is such good news that he's bad news!"

"What?"

"I felt it in the bar. I felt it walking with him. I felt it big time when he just stared at me and sang. Me and he got *maaaagic.*"

"Fantastic."

"Too fantastic. Too much change too fast. I told you, there's still so much I haven't done in life, alone. I gotta *party* now before the whole neighborhood changes. I'm still having fun dating and being single and being free and being me and I'm not ready for the dude of my dreams and get married and preggers like Kate Middleton."

"She's not Middleton anymore; she's the Duchess of Cambridge."

"I can't be the Duchess of Cow Hollow."

"You can't be a duchess 'cause you're being a drama queen."

"I'm not. I'm legit serious. I wanna stay being like Calli and keep partying."

"But you've done an 'ass-ton' of partying for years."

"I'm still not ready to lock down in a relationship, maybe forever," Kris explained. "Mark is *fucking awesome*. And I like that he likes me. I like feeling wanted, wanted by him."

"That's great."

"It's too great. Too soon. Too much."

"It's fine."

"Bren, *you* have to date Mark."

"What?"

"*You* have to date Mark for me."

"Why?"

"I'm not ready for Mark, but I *will* be, so I'm gonna park Mark with you until I'm ready for him."

"*Park Mark?*"

"Park Mark."

"With *me?*"

"With you."

"While you party?"

"Until I'm ready."

"You want Mark to park in my *garage?*"

"No one else is using it."

"So just stuff him in?"

"And when I'm ready I'll yank him out."

"I'm not Pubic Storage."

"It's a favor."

"It's F'd up."

"It's perfect, it keeps you here too."

"It's nuts."

"It's not. He's rarely single so we'll lock him down. You keep Mark off the market 'til I'm ready to take him."

"Criminy jeez. You're out of her mind."

"You always want me to plan. This is a perfect plan."

"A ridiculous plan."

"Relationships are complex these days. Get with the twenty-first century."

"Get with reality."

"Get with Mark!"

"Excuse me," some hot guy said to Bren. "I just wanted to say I really liked your singing up there."

Uh oh, Kris thought.

MARK'S POINT OF VIEW

Mark saw Kris still talking to Bren, talking about him? Maybe talking about the same thing he wanted to talk to Chet about. He tapped Chet's shoulder, and asked him away from some laughing ladies. They smiled at Mark and looked him up and down.

Chet excused himself, and pushed Mark away from them.

Then Mark motioned for his friend to follow him over to the big front windows for a timeout chat with Chet. "I need your help, man."

"Help with what?"

"I think I might do my first one night stand."

"Really?"

"Yeah. But it wouldn't be a one night stand."

"Then it's not a one night stand."

"But it's meeting a woman and going home with her on the same night. Whatever that is."

"That's a hookup."

"Then I might do my first hookup."

"With Kris?"

"Yeah. She was joking about it with me."

"That's *great.*" Chet whapped Mark's shoulder.

"It's very great. But I want her to want to keep seeing me the next night, and next, and the next."

"That's more than a hook up. That's dating."

"Then I want to do dating with Kris. Starting tonight, and if it goes well, every night, for the rest of our lives."

"Of course you do."

"Got any advice for how to do a hookup, one that I want to continue going down the road towards living together, marriage, family, and forever?"

"Yeah." Chet said. "*Don't* tell her what you just told me."

"But Kris likes honesty and upfrontness."

"But, in the throngs of passion, she doesn't want to hear you holler '*will you move in with me?*' That might freak her out."

"Good point."

"And what are you going to tell her about your ingrown hair?"

"Oh no." Mark remembered and worried. "My ingrown hair's down there."

"That'll be a fun thing to share."

Skip tapped Mark's shoulder. "Hey, dude, Bren met some book-reader guy named Roger and we're all going to a party at Roger's friend's apartment."

Cool. A chance to have another fun walk and talk with Kris again, Mark thought, and then a hookup-but-not-a-hookup-hopefully-dating-forever-awesomeness.

Chapter 9

"WHERE THE HELL are we going now?" Kris said, leaving her third bar of the night.

Bren hugged herself in the now colder night air. "We're going to the apartment party at Roger's friends."

"Why?"

"It'll be less crowded and less loud.

"I like crowded and loud."

"You should open a bar called Crowded and Loud."

"What if it's a slow night and it's not crowded and loud."

"Then it'll be ironic."

"I don't want an ironic bar. I want a crowded, loud bar."

"I wanna go to the apartment party."

"Why?"

"It'll be less crowded and less loud."

"I like crowded and loud."

"Somebody else talk now," Bren said.

"Where are we going?" Mark said, joining them outside on the sidewalk.

"We're going to an apartment party at Roger's friend's," Calli said.

256

"Why?" Mark asked.

Bren rolled her eyes.

Kris put her hands on Calli's shoulders and kept her out of reach from this Dan dude Calli picked up.

"Who's Roger?" Chet asked, joining them outside.

"I'm Roger."

"And you're with Bren?"

"I invited Bren. And Bren invited all of you."

"Where?"

"An apartment party," Calli said.

"Whose apartment?" Chet said.

"A friend of Roger's," Calli said.

"A friend of mine," Roger said.

Holly joined them. "Sorry," she said. "Someone was taking their time in the restroom." She hugged herself in the cold air. "So where are we going?"

"An apartment party," Calli said.

"All right," Holly said. "It was getting kind of crowded and loud."

"Is this everyone," Roger asked?

"No, there are still more friends coming," Bren said.

Roger grimaced.

Vanessa joined them. "That bathroom line was long."

"That's what Holly said," Calli said.

"Holly was the one taking her time in the restroom."

Holly polite-smiled.

"*Don't pick on Holly*," Kris hollered.

Roger startled.

Mark grinned.

Vanessa backed away. "So where are we going?"

"An apartment party," Dan said.

"An apartment party," Calli said.

"Who's apartment," Vanessa said.

"A friend of Roger's," Calli said.

Jane and Sara joined them.

"Hey," Sara said hugging herself in the cold air. "Someone was taking their time in the restroom."

"That's what Holly and Vanessa said," Calli said.

"Vanessa was the reason it was long," Jane said.

"I was not," Vanessa said. "It was Holly."

"*Don't pick on Holly.*"

Roger startled again.

Mark grinned again.

Vanessa backed away again.

Jane hugged herself in the cold air.

"So where are we going," Sara asked.

"Who's on first?" Mark said.

Kris grinned.

"An apartment party," Calli said.

"All right," Sara said. "That'd be less crowded and loud."

"All right," Kris said. "None of you are invited to my Crowded and Loud Bar if I ever open it."

"Can I come?" Calli asked.

"Yes, *you* can come."

"Yaaaay," Calli cheered.

"Is this everyone," Roger asked again?

"No, there's still more friends coming," Bren said again.

Roger grimaced again.

Skip joined them, with a girl on his arm. "Hey, everyone. This is Lola."

Everyone stared surprised at her. "Hi, Lola," everyone said.

"Hi," Lola said.

Skip pointed to everyone. "This is Kris, and Bren, and Calli, and some guy I don't know."

"Dan," Dan said.

"Dan," Calli said.

"Dan," Skip said. "And, Holly, and Vanessa, and Jane, and Sara, and Chet, and Mark."

"And I'm Roger."

"Hi, I'm Lola."

Everyone stared surprised at her, again. "Hi, Lola," everyone said again.

"Hi," Lola said again.

"Is *this* everyone," Roger asked again?

Bren looked around, and counted, and turned to Roger. "Yes. This is everyone."

Roger looked at everyone, sighed, and smiled at Bren. "Aaaall right, then," he said. "Let's go."

"Yaaaay," Calli cheered.

They all followed Roger down the residential street.

"So where we going?" Lola said.

Roger sighed again.

"An apartment party," Calli said. "At Roger's friend's."

"All right," Skip said. "That'd be, um."

"Less crowded and loud?" Mark said.

"Yeah," Skip said.

"We all think so too," Kris said, smirking at Bren, then sharing a look with Mark, and grins, intimate grins, emotion-stirring intimate grins. Kris looked away from him. She walked through the night with the group that was now even more populated, with Vanessa still filming them and a stranger leading them further north, down the wide sidewalk, up the quiet streetlight lit street with shiny parked cars, deeper into the Marina's residential neighborhood, ambling toward whatever was next, walking between Mark and Calli, with Mark's magnetism on her right and Calli's dependence on her left while passing the pretty four-story rectangular apartment buildings on both sides of peaceful Webster Street where people lived, single people, couples, and families. One day she'd might be in a family apartment up there, on a Saturday night, instead of barhopping down here, and fun nights like this wouldn't exist for her anymore. And if she was down here she'd be walking down the street with a family, and it might feel like this, between Mark and Calli, cozy but claustrophobic, and nowhere near as fun? But the coziness was really, really nice. Too nice?

DINGY-DING-DING.

"Ruby texted me," Vanessa said. "Hannah and Billy are flirting, Chloe and Nick are fighting, and Layla and Sarah are fondling."

"What am I doing?" Sara said.

"Not you, Sara. A different Sarah. Wow. I know seven Sara's."

"That could be a song," Calli said. "This year's had a lot of good, new songs," she said to Dan. "I like Darius Rucker's new song "Radio." I first heard it on the radio while milking the goats for ice cream. My favorite flavor is Bluebaaaaaaaaahrry. That's what we call it at my family's scoop shop. I like to dance while I scoop. I invented a dance move I call the 'Jump Up and Down.' I invented it when I had to pee real bad but the bride and groom were doing a loud prayer in the bathroom. That was the wedding where the bride's daddy brought a shotgun and stood right by the groom for some reason. My daddy's proud of his shotgun. He'd tell my boyfriends all about it. He probably tell you all about it. You've got a nice butt. Do you know that I'll never see my own butt in real life, just pictures and reflections. I've tried to turn my head and look but my head won't turn that far. My whole life I'll never get to see my butt. Isn't that strange?"

Dan looked at Calli, then looked at Kris, like "*this girl is strange?*"

Kris grinned.

"Skip," Mark said. "Did you just meet Lola at the bar?"

"Yeah," she said, smiling.

"*Yeeeeah*," Skip said, smiling.

"That's great," Mark said, smiling at them.

"Skip screwed me over but he's got better karma than *me* tonight," Chet griped.

NATHAN BAYLET

"Hang in there, Chet," Mark said, patting Chet on the back. "The night's not over yet. I'm sure you'll find someone. There's magic tonight."

Kris felt Mark's eyes turn to her. She totally felt their heat. But she totally didn't look at him. The magic between them might ensorsel her so much she'd end up in an un-barhopping family apartment. Her eyes escaped up to the sky. Patches of pink fog wifted inland overhead, like the city pulling a fluffy blanket over itself as if ready for bed while having to hear the ruckus of all these inebriated karaoke-adrenalinized partiers still up and their drunkenly laughing and loudly gabbing voices bouncing off the buildings, a wonderful partying ruckus, a wonderfully fun partying ruckus. And fast footsteps?

Fast footsteps got louder and louder behind them.

Kris spun around, ready to kick ass, and then saw Collin racing after them. *Damn, almost got rid of him.*

He raced up to Holly, then slowed, panted, and walked with her.

Bren looked at Roger. "*Now* we're all here."

Roger polite-smiled at Bren again. Then he asked Bren about some book.

Kris wondered what the hell the story was with Bren and Roger.

"Oh my gosh," Holly exclaimed to Collin. "I'm so sorry we left without you."

Collin shrugged, and pulled out his phone, and looked at it again as he walked.

262

Holly apologized to him for about half a block.

Kris feared that's what a long relationship turned people into, silent and apologetic. *Fuck that.* Kris walked her and Calli faster, away from Dan, and away from Mark.

They all crossed the two-lane street toward the distant bay's foghorns and swung right, walking east up the non-neon, definitely residential part of Chestnut Street toward the moonlight. Four-story, fancy apartments on the right stood illuminated by the towering baseball field lights in the huge, open park on the left, lit up bright green, beyond the one-story library that Bren of course talked about.

"I've checked out so many books from that library that they call me Brenda Bookworm. Do you go the library?"

"Only when I wanna read old suspense," Roger said.

"What old suspense?"

"Authors like Christie, Poe, Bram Stroker."

"Stoker."

"Stoker?"

"Stoker, not Stroker."

"Oh," Roger said.

Whoa. Were Bren and Roger hitting it off with book talk? Kris sped up, grabbed Bren's arm, and pulled her bestie back to Mark's side. "I need to talk to you Bren."

"About what?" Bren said, flailing to regain her balance.

"Tell Mark about how my exercise routines have totally given you a hot rockin' bod."

Bren rolled her eyes.

Mark looked confused.

"*Wait for us,*" Lola called out behind them.

The group stopped and looked back.

Lola, way behind them in her little high heels and little steps, clack-clack-clacked toward them, taking forever.

Skip slowly walked beside her, smiling.

Kris sighed.

"Right now, we're waiting for Lola to catch up to us," Vanessa narrated to her camera. "And the air outside now is so chilly that I wish I'd worn undies, because my hoo-hoo is turning blue-blue."

"Lordy lordy," Jane exhaled. "Van, do you really have to film everything we do tonight?"

"Yessss," Vanessa answered, with a hair flip. "Her little steps are so cute. I'm filming the cute."

"Lordy."

The cute finally caught up with them.

"Ready?" Roger asked, then lead the group again.

Bren walked with him.

"It *is* really chilly," Sara said as she walked and snuggled Jane's arm. "Why is San Francisco so cold?"

"Well, the sun's not out right now," Jane teased.

"I thought California would be warm too," Calli said. "When I'm cold I think about growing my hair long so I could use it as a scarf."

Sara chuckled.

Jane looked at her phone. "It's 10-degrees warmer in LA."

"You knuckleheads," Kris said. "Stop giving Bren reasons to move to LA."

"You don't want her to move to LA?"

"Of course not. She's been my roommate for seven years. And she needs to keep staying here so my life won't suck."

"Oh. We didn't know," Jane said. "Sounds like you should stay here Bren."

"We shouldn't talk about this now," Bren said.

Kris pulled Bren back again beside Mark. "Hey, Mark," Kris said. "Did you know that Bren can suck a peanut through a straw?"

Bren scowled at Kris and walked back up to Roger's side. "San Francisco nights are cold in the summer because it has a Coastal Mediterranean climate," Bren said. "Surrounded by cold water flowing down from Alaska, which attracts fog and wind that becomes cold when blowing over cold water, which blows through the city."

Kris pulled Bren back to Mark again. "Mark, when it comes to blowing, Bren really knows stuff."

MARK'S POINT OF VIEW

Mark wondered why Kris kept telling him about Bren's blowing and sucking abilities.

"*Wait for us*," Lola called out behind them again.

One by one the group all stopped again and looked back again.

Lola, way behind them in her little high heels and little steps, clack-clack-clacked toward them, taking forever.

Skip slowly walked beside her, smiling.

Mark appreciated Kris's ankle boots all over again.

DINGY-DING-DING.

"Chantal texted me," Vanessa said. "Abby and Oscar are hanging out, Issac and Leo are making out, and Ezra and Ellis are moving out."

Lola and Skip caught up to them.

"Ready?" Roger asked again, then lead the group again.

"Sorry, everyone," Lola said. "I guess I wore the wrong shoes tonight."

"Your shoes are awesome, baby doll," Skip said to her, smiling wide. "Don't apologize for looking sexy."

"Ooooh, you're a sweetie," Lola said smiling too and rubbing Skip's chest.

Skip smiled wider, then looked at everyone. "I'm a sweetie."

Mark grinned.

Chet rolled his eyes.

"Skip's come a long way," Sara whispered.

"We've created a monster," Jane said.

"Have you read *Frankenstein*," Bren asked Roger.

"Yeah, *Frankenstein's* cool," Roger said. "I like those gothic novels. *Turn off the Screw, Sleepy Hollow, Dr. Jackle.*"

"Jekyll."

"Jekyll?"

"Jekyll, not Jackle."

"Oh," Roger said.

Kris pulled Bren back with Mark again. "Mark, did you know that Bren reads erotic novels?"

Bren scowled at Kris.

Mark wondered why Kris kept pulling Bren back to him. Was she trying to match-make Bren with him? Did Kris not like him? He thought she did. But maybe she was just being nice. Maybe her mentioning him going home with her was just a joke. *Dang.* So maybe she and he wouldn't one day play baseball with their three kids as a family on the diamonds in the park over there.

"This whole area was once underwater," Skip said.

Chet *didn't* say something lewd like "and in that apartment I was under Wanda."

Mark wondered why.

Mark smiled at the bright silvery lights shining over the open field, like a green calm among the concrete buildings. So many fun baseball games with friends here. "This is a famous park," Mark said. "Marilyn Monroe and Joe DiMaggio walked across it just hours before they got married."

"Where'd they get married?" Sara asked.

"San Francisco City Hall."

"So formal," Sara said. "They should have gotten married on this big, pretty green park. I wanna get married in a pretty park."

Jane looked uncomfortable.

"This is the park where I streaked naked," Kris said.

"This is the park where I vomited three vodkas," Chet said.

"What a fun tour," Calli said. "Holly, do you have fun memories of this park?"

"I do. But I can't say."

"This is the park where Holly first smoked pot when we were in high school, and walked into a tree," Vanessa said, laughing.

Holly polite-smiled.

"*Don't pick on Holly*," Kris hollered.

"Oh my gaaaaawsh. I'm not picking on her. It was funny."

"Say something nice about Holly for once," Kris demanded.

"I say nice things."

"It's fine, Kris," Holly said, sweetly.

"I wanna hear you say something nice to Holly."

Vanessa looked at Holly, sighed, and thought.

Mark's heart did cartwheels for Kris again. Kris standing up for her friend was so great, she tolerated no malarkey. She was amazing. He hoped that at this party he and Kris would finally stop walking and sit down, without Bren, and get talking again. Maybe there was a chance she still liked him. Maybe.

"I was impressed by Holly's singing voice," Vanessa complimented. "There are you happy, Kris?"

"I'm happi*er*."

"Holly's singing was amazing," Calli cheered.

"It was."

"Holly kicked ass up there."

"Really great."

"So great."

Holly polite-smiled. "You all are very sweet, thank you. It wasn't that great."

"Are you kidding? Your voice is incredible."

"Awesome good."

"Phenomenal."

"No no. It was just silly fun," Holly said. "Whose apartment are we going to?" she asked Roger.

"She's changing the subject!" Calli shouted.

Kris O-faced at Calli, then laughed.

"We're going to Anton's," Roger answered Holly.

"Oh," Holly said. "I know Anton."

"He's dating Debbie," Vanessa said.

"Mama always told me to smile so my teeth can see the world," Calli said.

Dan raised an eyebrow.

Kris pulled Bren back again beside Mark. "Hey, Mark," Kris said. "Did you know that Bren does kegels?"

Bren scowled.

Mark worried. "How much farther to the apartment party?"

Roger pointed to the buildings up ahead and left in front of the park. "Right over there."

They all crossed the two-lane street and swung left, walking north up the residential part of Laguna Street toward the foggy bay in the distance. On the right, four-story fancy apartment buildings stood lit up by the bright park on the left, and their group was just an exciting, short walk away from him being able to sit and talk with Kris again, he hoped.

Bren & Roger talked books again.

Kris pulled Bren back to Mark again.

Bren scowled again.

Mark worried again.

"*Wait for us,*" Lola called out behind them again.

The group stopped again.

Mark watched Skip reach down and swoop Lola up into his arms.

Lola laughed. "My hero."

Skip carried her a few feet, then his arms collapsed.

Lola squealed, then stood on the sidewalk again.

"I need to get that boy needs some biceps," Kris said.

"I've got some," Chet said, raced back, swooped up Lola into his arms, and carried her away from Skip's open-mouthed face.

Lola laughed. "My *new* hero."

Skip frowned.

Chet smiled.

Mark shook his head.

They all regrouped.

"Ready?" Roger asked again, then lead the group again.

Kris handed Skip her business card. "In ninety-days I'll get you strong enough to carry *two* girls."

Skip nodded. "Thanks."

Mark liked her even more.

DINGY-DING-DING.

"Shane texted me," Vanessa said. "Camille kissed Blair, Tallulah banged Blaine, and Emma proposed to Blake."

"I wanna see more San Francisco parks," Sara said. "Jane, let's look at parks tomorrow."

"Uh, let's focus on tonight."

"Technically this is tomorrow," Bren told them looking at her watch. "It's now June 23."

"Hey, did we sing '22' on June 22?" Calli asked.

"Yep," Bren answered. "Just before midnight."

"That's a cool co-winkie-dink."

"It's not No-Panty Day anymore," Kris announced. "You bare-assers can put your panties back on."

"I'll wait 'til we're inside to re-panty," Vanessa said.

"I will too," Sara said.

"I will too," Chet said.

"What?" Lola laughed.

"I'm just kidding," Chet said, still carrying Lola.

Skip cringed, then pointed up, and changed the subject. "It's also the night of the supermoon."

"The what?" Calli asked.

"A supermoon is a full moon when it's closest to Earth, so it looks really big," Skip explained. "Just look behind us."

They all stopped, turned, and looked up at the supermoon, and the full moon *was* really big, SUPER BIG.

"Wow, that's a big ass moon," Kris said.

"I'm sorry we keep stopping," Bren said to Roger.

"It's all right," he said. "We're here."

Everyone turned back around, and looked up at the four-story tall apartment building.

Calli looked up, and her eyes flew wide, and her hands stretched behind her, and her arms flailed as she fell backwards into Kris's arms, and then slid down Kris to the sidewalk.

Oh whoa, Mark thought. What was wrong with Calli?

KRIS'S POINT OF VIEW

Oh whoa, Kris thought. What was wrong with Calli?

Calli clung to Kris's leg.

Kris knelt down and put her hands on Calli's shoulders, studying her face. "Sweetie, what's wrong?"

Calli just stared at Kris.

"Bren, bring me your inhaler."

"Is Calli asthmatic?"

"Are you asthmatic?"

"I'm a Leo," Calli said.

"What's wrong?"

Calli pointed up to the top floor.

"Oh," Holly said. "Remember? She said she's afraid of heights."

"Is that it?"

Calli nodded.

"Oh, sweetie," Kris said. "Even just four stories?"

Calli nodded.

Kris rubbed Calli's shoulders.

Calli turned away from everyone hovering around her and buried her head in Kris's neck, unusually hiding from everyone's eyes.

Kris felt this intense need to protect this wilted flower of a girl. "Everyone, give her some space."

Everyone kind of backed off.

Kris held Calli, and holding her became the most important thing in the world right then, and so was getting her to be happy again. "Why are you so afraid of heights?" Kris said.

Calli slowly brought her face out of Kris's neck and back into to view. "Well," she said. "When I was just an eight-year-old-Calli, I got to be in the school play. I don't much remember the plot, but one kid chopped a cherry tree, one kid wore a tall hat and a beard. And I got to be an eagle, for the grand finale. So at the end of the play, I came out on stage, opened up my wings in front of everyone, and everybody cheered. It felt soooo good to have the whole town smiling at me. I loved being on stage. And that summer, after the school play one day, I wanted to feel that great feeling again of everyone smiling at me, and I thought the higher I am the BIGGER smiles I'll get. So at the July family picnic I put on my eagle wings, and in front of all the family eating tatters and barbeque, I climbed on top of Bubble's doghouse. We called our dog Bubbles, 'cause she liked to bite bubbles."

"Right."

"And Bubbles came out of her doghouse and looked up at me like 'what are you doing on my doghouse?' And I said 'I'm gonna *fly*, Bubbles.' And Bubbles looked at me like 'really?' And I said 'yeah.' And I spread my wings and shouted to everybody 'look at me, I'm gonna fly.' And they shouted 'noooo,' but that was after I jumped. It was a short flight. One second Bubbles was below me, then she was above me, licking my face. And my arm really, really hurt. And I had to wear a cast 'cause I broke my funny bone. And since then when I see buildings I just see big doghouses, and I think 'we're not supposed to be up there,' that's for real eagles. That's why I don't get in planes, go up buildings, or wear high heels. Up high was fun, but falling really hurt. I won't do that again, I'm not an eagle."

Kris felt so many emotions she didn't know what to do with them all, but she did know one thing. She put her hand on Calli's shoulder. "Sweetie, you're *totally* an eagle, 'cause –" Kris saw Vanessa filming them.

"Holy pile of dicks," Mark heard Kris shout at Vanessa. "Stop filming us. This is a personal moment. Don't you have *any* boundaries?"

"I was gonna talk to Calli after she was feeling better, and have her talk about her phobia of heights because other people might have the same issue, and we could help people by showing them that they're not alone with their heights-struggle. So you see, I'm coming from a good place."

"My fist's gonna come at your face," Kris said.

Bren slid between Kris and Vanessa.

"I could be a phobia for people?" Calli asked.

"No," Kris said to her. "You just be you, off-camera."

Jane stepped in front of her sister. "Kris is right. You gotta chill. I want you to put your camera away," Jane said. "You're always filming everything. Your crazy is driving me crazy, and now you're driving them crazy."

"It's fun."

"I want my sister back!" Jane yelled.

Vanessa startled.

Jane stared. "I want us to spend fun time together like we used to without you having to 'film the moment.' Do you get it? You're losing me."

"We *do* have fun," Vanessa said. "Even more fun since you moved up here."

"It's not fun for *me*."

"People are expecting fantastic content from me," Vanessa said. "So I have to film all the time incase something fantastic happens."

Jane rolled her eyes. "If you film something fantastic, you'll put your camera away for the rest of the night."

Vanessa scoffed. "It'd have to be something *really* fantastic."

"All right," Jane said, then took a big breath. "Film me."

Van raised her camera and filmed Jane.

Jane looked right at Vanessa's camera. I'm going to moon the supermoon.

Everyone watched Jane grab her skirt, pull it up, bend over, and moon and the supermoon.

Everyone O-faced, then broke into cheers and applause.

"Wow," Kris said. "She did no-panty night."

"How much did she have to drink?" Bren said.

"Now *that's* a supermoon," Chet said.

Jane redressed, laughed, and tossed up her arms like she had won the Tour de France, or the Booty de Marina.

Vanessa was all smiles.

"I wanna moon the supermoon!" Calli shouted, jumping up.

Nice to see Calli happy again.

"I'm in for a mooning," Chet said.

"So am I," Skip said.

"All right," Sara said.

"Ah, fuck it," Kris said, and joined their back-facing-the-moon-line forming on the sidewalk.

Mark laughed and joined the line too.

Bren didn't.

"Bren," Kris said. "Get your butt over here and join us."

"I might be regional manager. I can't be in a butt video."

"Madeline said we gotta live it up while we can," Kris reminded her. "For once in your life, before you leave me and break my heart, let loose, and let's make one last wild memory."

Bren fidgeted with her hands, pursed her lips, then clapped her hands together. "Oh, screw it," she said, then joined the line.

Kris smiled big!

Holly and Collin and Roger did not join the line, and Vanessa filmed.

Then the backs of Jane, Sara, Chet, Skip, Mark, Dan, Lola, Calli, Kris, and Bren all faced the brightest part of the sky, and grabbed their pants or skirts.

Kris counted. "3 ... 2 ... 1!"

And they all mooned the supermoon!

Mark laughed.

Cold air on bare butt. Face facing sidewalk. Feeling ridiculous, and awesome!

Hollers! Laughter! Cheers!

Lola spanked Chet's bare butt.

Mark wished he didn't know Chet liked being spanked.

Skip grimaced at Chet.

Mark wished Vanessa wasn't filming him really making an ass of himself.

Then everyone stood back up and they all redressed, laughed, and high fived.

Neighbors from the window down the street leaned out with their beers and applauded.

Everyone bowed and laughed back to them.

"Wow," Vanessa cheered. "That *was* fantastic!"

Everyone cheered and high fived.

"Don't crazy things happen under a full moon?" Calli asked.

"Crazy things happened," Kris answered high fiving Calli, and Bren, and Mark's hand. Her hand felt lovely and powerful, Mark thought.

Jane fixed her skirt and laughed to Vanessa. "Now put your camera away."

Vanessa tilted her head. "Um, I really can't show something that graphic on my online platform. But, good try."

"*Seriously?*" Jane said, then tossed up her hands. "I give up."

"We mooned for nothing?" Calli said.

"It meant something to me," Chet said.

Sara cleared her throat. "Um, what if you film me proposing to Jane?" she said. "Wouldn't that be fantastic?"

Everyone O-faced, then cheered.

Kris's point of view

"That *would* be fantastic," Vanessa cheered.

Jane didn't cheer. She looked frozen, like a deer in the headlights. "Sara, what are you saying? You know I'm not ready for that."

"*Still?*"

"Yeah."

"Well, I'm starting to think you're never gonna be ready for it."

"Well, I'm not ready to talk about it now."

"*I'm* ready to talk about it," Sara said. "I got us an apartment."

"You what?"

"I rented us an apartment, to live together, so we can move out of Vanessa's place and live together, finally."

"You got us an apartment?"

"Yeah. I wanted to surprise you. So, surprise."

"I am surprised."

"You're moving out?" Vanessa said.

"Um," Jane said.

Sara folded her arms and stared at Jane. "We've been dating for two years. It's time for us to live together."

"You're moving out?" Vanessa exclaimed.

"*I* am," Sara said. "I don't know if Jane is. It's crowded with three of us living there. And loud, especially when you and Jane argue. I need quiet and calm, and I need you, Jane, living with me, in our own place, finally. Will you at least live with me?"

Jane still stood frozen, staring over at Sara, her hands clutching her sides, and not saying a thing.

Everyone's eyes darted back and forth between them, like an invisible tennis match.

Then Sara's shoulders deflated. "I think your silence just gave me your answer."

Jane stepped forward. "I'm just still not ready. I don't know why. I'm just not. Yet. Don't give up on me. Just not yet."

"Whatever," Sara said, and pulled out her phone.

"What are you doing?"

"Taxicab."

"You're leaving?"

"I'm going to my apartment," Sara said. "Thanks for a fun time tonight, everyone. It was great meeting you all. And I'm sorry you had to see this."

279

Jane sighed and walked around.

Skip went over and talked to Sara.

Kris put her arm around Calli.

"You really can't just go up four stories?" Kris asked her.

Calli shook her head and grabbed onto Kris again, with such an intense hug. "If I try to go way up there I'll totally freak out." Calli clung to Kris's leg.

"Wow," Kris said. "I didn't know your fear of heights was so intense?"

"It's not just the tall building," Calli said, wiping her sniffling her nose with her sleeve. "It's also that if I don't go up the tall building with you you'll leave me down here, or take me to that Hazel lady's house, and then I can't be part of your fun group anymore, my new, you know, *family*."

Ooooooooh wow. Kris felt everything in life kinda just fall away with Calli's words, and suddenly nothing else mattered, nothing except hanging on tight to her new friend, her new *family?* And making her feel happy. She grabbed Calli's shoulders and looked in Calli's wet eyes. "I was trying to tell you a minute ago, sweetie, you're *totally* an eagle, 'cause you snatched my heart."

Calli looked at Kris, sniffling. "I did?"

Kris smiled at Calli, BIG! "You did."

Calli smiled BIG!

Kris hugged her again. "So now you can't leave me, or else I'll hurt. All right?"

Calli hugged Kris tighter. "All right."

This felt *amazing*.

"Does that mean you're not gonna send me to that lady with the house to wash dishes in the bathtub?"

Kris hugged Calli tighter. "Sweetie, you're not going anywhere. You're not going to Hazel's. And you're not running off tonight with this guy you picked up. Sorry dude."

Dan frowned.

Calli and her rocked back and forth in their hug.

Kris came out of their hug and looked at her. "Calli, you're coming home with me and Bren. And if Bren moves out then you're moving in. And if Bren stays then you and Bren can share a room."

"What?" Bren said.

"Or we'll figure something out."

"*Really?*" Calli shouted, her teeth totally seeing the world as her face smiled a smile so huge it almost exploded Kris's heart with joy!

"Yes really," Kris said.

Calli threw her arms around Kris and hugged, hugged, hugged her soooo hard!

This feeling, *wow*, this feeling of making Calli happy felt so damn good. It felt like everything, everything she needed in life. It, *holy wow*, this feeling felt better than any party ever, and that was saying something.

Calli flew out of their hug and looked at Kris. "But you have to go up to the party."

"What?"

"You have to go up to the party up there, or else I feel totally guilty from keeping you from it."

"No. You're more important than a party," Kris said, kinda
stunned at what she had just said. "I'm taking you back to my
and Bren's place now."

"Noooo," Calli insisted. "You have to go up. I don't wanna
ruin anybody's night with my phobias. Bren should still go
up with her new friend Roger and you and Bren should spend
more time together if this is your and Bren's last Saturday night
together. I don't wanna feel guilty that I messed that up."

Kris scoffed. "I'm not gonna leave you down here?"

"I'll go with Sara," Calli said.

Sara perked up. "Yeah. That's cool. Calli can hang with me,
and hear me gripe about Jane's cold feet."

"I'm cold too," Calli said. "So I'll go with Sara and you guys
all go up to the apartment party, and we'll hang out later."

Kris hesitated. "Really?"

"Yeah."

Kris looked at Bren. And felt a lot of the feelings she felt
with Calli. And it probably would be good to squeeze as much
out of their last Saturday night as they could until they got
that fart sound. Kris looked at Sara.

"It's a great idea," Sara said. "We'll do a dance video game.
And my apartment's on the first floor."

"I love a first floor," Calli cheered.

Kris thought about it. Sara seemed sane, and really nice.
Kris chuckled to herself, when they were on upper Laguna

282

Street she wanted to send Calli away, now on lower Laguna she never wanted Calli to leave her. This night really *was* crazy balls. But, she didn't want Calli to feel bad, and letting her hang with Sara would get Calli away from Vanessa's stupid camera. Kris looked back at Calli. "All right," she said. "I'm going up, but just for a bit. Then I'm coming to get you and we're going home."

Calli smiled and teared up again. "*Home.*"

Kris's feelings fling-flanged all over the place again. She hugged Calli once more real quick, then her hands gave Calli over to Sara's.

Taxicab arrived.

So did some tears in Kris's eyes.

"Bye, Dan. It was nice meeting you," Calli said.

Sara flung her arm around Calli and they headed towards the car, as Sara glanced back at Jane, and Calli glanced back at Kris and waved goodbye, and away they went, into the night.

And watching Calli go away fucking tore Kris's heart apart. Wow, she thought, so this is why people get in families, they end up with people they just can't live without, and it changes everything. Kris felt *changed*. Really *changed*. *That little bugger.*

"So, ready?" Roger asked again, then lead the group again.

MARK'S POINT OF VIEW

Mark, after seeing one of the most moving scenes he'd ever seen in his life, saw Kris and Jane standing alone on the sidewalk watching their loved ones zoom away.

Jane turned and walked towards the building.

Kris followed, and eyed Mark with an unreadable look as she passed him.

Then Mark saw Dan and Lola still standing on the sidewalk.

"I got ditched," Dan said to Lola. "You going up?"

"No. I'm over Skip and Chet ditched me."

"You wanna go get a burger?"

"Sure. You wanna carry me?"

"Sure."

Mark watched Dan swoop Lola up into his arms and carry her laughing down the sidewalk, under the crazy, full supermoon, smirked, then followed Kris to the apartment building's entrance, wondering what more crazy stuff the supermoon had in store for this crazy night.

Chapter 10

KRIS WIPED her watering eyes.

Vanessa danced passed everyone to the building's front door. "Everyone lighten the F up. It's Saturday night. Wooooooooo!"

"Actually, it's Sunday morning," Bren said.

"It's Sunday morning! Wooooooooo!"

Kris wanted to kick Van in her off-switch.

Bren stepped between Kris and Vanessa. "Hmm. It's not 'day' so 'Sunday morning' should really be 'sun-morning,'" Bren joked.

Kris exhaled big.

"But there's no sun and no morning," Chet said. "So what would right now be called?"

Bren grinned. "I don't know."

"Everything in life should be relabeled," Skip joked.

"I'll head up that committee and start by relabeling this glass door 'anal muffin,'" Chet joked. "Quick, Roger, open this anal muffin."

Roger rolled his eyes and pushed a button by the building's front door.

Party laughter crackled through the intercom.

"Yeah?"

285

"It's Roger."

"It's about time."

Party "whoops!"

The anal muffin *buzzzzed* open.

Roger held the door open for Bren. Then her menagerie of inebriated friends all followed her in. He sighed.

Kris glanced back at the empty sidewalk where Calli had been as the glass door clanked shut, and the group drunkenly staggered as quiet as a mosh pit into the echoey marble lobby. She felt heartache and longing, and made a decision. "I'm going up to the party 'cause Calli wanted me to," Kris made clear, joining the group. "We're staying for just a minute and then we're all going to Sara's place."

"We are?" Jane said.

"See, Bren? I can plan things."

"Well done. As long as it doesn't involve me parking things."

Roger pressed the elevator button

"We're all waiting for the elevator," Vanessa narrated to her camera.

Jane pushed Vanessa's camera away. "Give it a rest."

Kris stood in front of everyone. "We'll tell Calli the party was lame and we left and then she won't feel like crap that we didn't go 'cause of her. We left 'cause it sucked ass-balls."

"What are ass-balls?" Chet said.

"Where's Lola?" Vanessa asked.

"Chet stole her," Skip said.

"I let her go," Chet said.

"She went with Dan," Mark said.

"Where's Dan?" Bren said.

"He went with Lola," Mark said. "For burgers."

"Bizarre how things end up," Jane said.

Kris agreed while watching Mark's eyes on her. She tingled, needing his eyes on Bren.

Ding.

The elevator opened.

Kris rushed in.

Bren followed.

Roger followed Bren.

But Kris stepped in front of Roger.

"Can Sara's apartment fit everyone?" Vanessa asked.

"I don't think this elevator can," Bren said.

"Anybody bring lube?" Kris joked.

Mark looked at Chet.

Chet shrugged. "I don't have any."

They gave it a dry try by *squeeeezing* ten bodies in tight together in the tiny metal box, coed and cozy. Determined with her other plan, Kris squished Bren beside Mark. Mark squished beside Chet, Chet beside Skip, Skip beside Collin, Collin beside Holly, Holly, beside Jane, and Jane ended up beside Vanessa. Roger grimaced as he squeezed in last, not near Bren, as all their drunken voices became almost unidentifiable.

Chet = "I feel very close to you all."

Jane = "Any closer and we'll become one person."

Kris = "One uncomfortable person."

Roger sighed.

Vanessa = "Let's keep things FUN!" Vanessa's fast fingers pushed aaaall the floor buttons.

"Aaaaah," everyone protested.

Vanessa laughed.

Kris = "You fucking b –"

The doors closed.

Rrrrrrrr, the elevator struggled to ... lift ... them ... all ... up.

Roger faced the doors, shaking his head.

Mark = "Oh, jeez. I think we over-stuffed this thing."

Chet = "That's what I said to your mom."

Mark = "In your filthy dreams."

Skip = "Do girls ever say 'that's what I said to your dad?'"

Bren = "It doesn't really work that way."

Kris = "That's what I said to your dad."

Bren = "Hmm, it does work."

Chet = "That's what I said to your mom."

Bren = "You're such a perv."

Chet = "That's what I said to your housekeeper."

Bren = "You said that to my Roomba?"

Chet = "One of you is wearing way too much perfume."

Jane = "I think it's all five perfumes mixed together."

Mark = "And colognes."

Bren = "And hairspray."

Kris = "And alcohol breath."

Jane = "And all of our walking-around-B.O."

Bren = "We should bottle this blended scent and call it *'Elevator.'*"

Chet = "Everything a perfume can be. Literally *everything.*"

Jane = "You should be in advertising?"

Chet = "I am."

Kris = "I don't wear perfume. I already got body and laundry soap goin' on."

Mark = "And green apple hair." Mark grinned. "It's nice."

Kris = "Thanks."

Vanessa = "What's an 'anal muffin?'"

Ding.

FLOOR 2.

Doors opened.

Pause.

Really long pause.

Kris = "Vanessa, I hate you so hard."

Vanessa = "This is funny."

Kris = "Me hurling you off the top of this building will be funny."

Bren = "If we ever get to the top."

Doors still open.

Really, really long pause.

Kris = "Mother f –"

Doors ... closed ...

Mark's point of view

Rrrrrrr, the elevator struggled to ... lift ... them ... all ... up.

Skip = "What would be funny is if the elevator broke down, and we were all stuck in here together."

Bren = "Don't even."

Jane = "What if we were all trapped in here for days?"

Kris = "We'd have to eat each other."

Chet = "That's hot."

Jane = "Who would we eat first?"

Kris = "Mark's the most meaty."

Mark = "Thank you."

Bren = "I bet Holly would taste the best."

Holly = "Me?"

Bren = "Because you're so sweet."

Holly = "Aaaawe. *You're* so sweet."

Chet = "If you two start making out my big erection will squish us all together like a raft in a phone booth."

Vanessa = "What's a phone booth?"

Chet = "Elevators are rectangles."

Bren = "What?"

Chet = "We're literally inside the box."

Jane = "I need another drink."

Chet = "There's booze up here, right?"

Bren = "If it's not drank already."

Jane = "If there's no booze, I'm leaving. Down the stairs."

Bren = "Is it time for pancakes?"

Kris = "I don't know yet."

Chet = "I could go for a grilled cheese."

Jane = "I could go for a burger."

Stacy = *Grrrrrrrowl.*

Vanessa = "Whose stomach growled?"

Kris = "Quiet, Stacy!"

Ding.

FLOOR 3.

Really, really long pause.

Bren = "This is taking forever."

Kris = "Fuck this, I'm taking the stairs –"

Doors ... closed ...

Vanessa = "It's just one more floor."

Kris = "Until your doom."

Rrrrrrrr, the elevator struggled to ... lift ... them ... all ... up.

Skip = "I could go for pizza."

Bren = "I could go for *Green Eggs and Ham.*"

Chet = "I could – oh my *God.*"

Kris = "Who fucking farted!"

Gasps and laugher.

Vanessa = "Oh my God."

Bren = "I'm never buying *this* perfume."

Jane = "*This* is an anal muffin."

Kris = "See what you did!"

Vanessa = "I didn't toot."

Kris = "You trapped us with the toot by pushing all the buttons."

Holly = "Please don't fight."

Chet = "We're all gonna die!"

Mark = "Everyone be nice. Let's not embarrass the person who farted. No one is above this. In our lives we've all let loose some stinkers."

Vanessa = "I haven't."

Jane = "Oooh yes you have."

Mark = "It's just a natural human function. Let's just be nice to the farter and see the comedy in this situation and wait for the doors to open. We're not gonna die."

The elevator STOPPED!

Silence.

Stinky silence.

Mark = "Alright, *now* we might die."

PANIC!

Kris = "What the fuck!"

Holly = "What happened?"

Bren = "Is the elevator broke?"

Chet = "We're trapped!"

Bren = "Push another button."

Holly = "Don't eat me first."

Jane = "Don't eat me second."

Chet = "Don't fart again!"

Jane = "I didn't."

Skip = "Is this the last air I'll ever breath?"

Bren = "Call for help."

Jane = "I'll call Sara."

Kris = "No, don't upset Calli."

Skip = "I'm gonna text my mom."

Chet = "Tell her I say 'hi.'"

Jane = "Call the police."

Bren = "We'll be dead before they get here."

Kris = "I'm not ready to die."

Chet = "Not like THIS!"

Skip = "I stole a candy bar once."

Bren = "Oh lordy. You're confessing things before you die?"

Jane = "I stole my mom's perfume."

Chet = "I nap in the bathroom at work."

Mark = "I flush with my foot."

Bren = "I move my food to your side of the fridge when I'm mad at you."

Kris = "I'm not really allergic to cats."

Jane = "I hated your hair short."

Holly = "I want to quit my job and scuba."

Kris = "We saw a guy at your party eat one of your fish."

Bren = "She dared him to."

Jane = "I use my big teddy bear to drive in the carpool lane."

Kris = "I like to roll around on your soft carpet naked."

Jane = "I had sex in your bedroom."

Kris = "I had sex in your car."

Chet = "I own a cock ring."

Skip = "I sold the Moon to a movie studio!"

Kris's point of view

Mark = "I shaved my balls."

Chet = "*Holy shit, dude.*"

Holly = "Is this what it was like on the Titanic?"

Bren = "A band needs to be playing."

Jane = "I've got iTunes."

Bren = "Dial up 'Nearer, My God, To Thee.'"

Chet = "Dial up 'Love In An Elevator.'"

Jane = "Don't get an erection!"

Chet = "Holly could sing for us."

Mark = "If it falls we'll jump up before it hits."

Bren = "Actually, the G-forces would prevent you jumping."

Vanessa = "Why do you always correct people?"

Kris = "You shut up. She's my friend. My wonderful over-correcting friend, and I'll kick your –"

Holly = "Please don't fight."

Bren = "I'm over-correcting?"

Kris = "Yeah, but in a fun way. You keep my life full of over-correcting fun facts. I love them. I need them. I need *you*, to not move away."

Bren = "I feel so guilty and confused."

Vanessa = "Jane, you can't move either."

Jane = "I'm confused too. Sara only took Calli home to make me jealous."

Vanessa = "Is it?"

Jane grimaced.

Jane = "*Yes!*"

Kris = "I gotta pee."

Chet = "Don't do it here."

Kris = "I may have to."

Holly = "There's no reason to fight. Let's just all just keep calm and think this through."

Kris = "I think we should fight."

Skip = "I think we should scream for help."

Chet = "I think we should group hug."

Jane = "Why did we come here?"

Kris = "Roger, this is your fault."

Roger = "I've never had this problem before."

Chet = "That's what your dad said."

Roger = "What?"

Kris = "Open the doors!"

Mark = "I'll try to open them."

Skip = "With what?"

Vanessa = "Use your big foot."

Skip = "Put your back into it."

Kris = "Put your balls into it."

Chet = "Shaved balls."

Kris = "Do they stick to your leg?"

Mark = "They do."

Kris = "So you're all smooth down there?"

Mark = "Sort of."

Kris = "Sort of?"

Mark = "I have an ingrown hair."

Kris = "An ingrown hair?"

Mark = "Down there."

Kris = "Down there?"

Skip = "What's an ingrown hair?"

Mark = "It's a big red bump."

Skip = "You have a big red bump on your balls?"

Chet = "I can't believe you're telling them."

Mark = "I'm tired of hiding. Kris has inspired me to be bold."

Kris = "I have?"

Jane = "Inspire him to open the doors."

Bren = "Pry 'em open."

Mark = "I can't get my fingers in the crease."

Chet = "That's what I said to your mom."

Kris = "Lay off his mom."

Chet = "I'd love to."

Bren = "How are you two guys friends?"

Mark = "He's funny. I've needed funny in my life lately."

Kris = "Why? Are you sad? Are you not over your ex?"

Mark = "I am now."

Kris = "Why now?"

Mark = "Because I met *you*."

All charcters = "Oooooooo."

Holly = "Oh my gosh. That's the sweetest thing I've ever heard. Kris he likes you."

Chet = "Playaaaa."

Mark = "It's not a line. I'm telling truth. Kris, I really like you."

Kris = "I – I know you do."

Jane = "Sara says romantic things like that to me all the time. I don't say enough romantic stuff to her. She's right, I don't appreciate her enough. But I do appreciate her; I just don't say it enough. It's hard for me. She wants to marry me so badly. I love her, but I'm scared."

Kris = "Maybe you're just not ready, Jane. Maybe you meet the perfect person but you're not ready for their perfectness yet 'cause if you give in to their perfectness you know that this perfect person for you will be that last person you'll ever date and your single days will be over forever, your youth over forever, and maybe that's a LOT to deal with and maybe you just need some time to – to – to –"

Mark = "Date other people some more?"

Kris = "Maybe. I don't know. I don't. This is too much! I can't stay in here anymore! I need OUT!"

Bren = "Calm down, it's alright, you're with friends, we love you. I love you."

Kris = "I love you too, Bren. You can't move! I need you here! I'm too scared to like Mark!"

Mark = "What?"

Jane = "I love Sara."

Chet = "You're a good roommate, Mark."

Mark = "Thanks, man. You're a good friend."

Vanessa = "I love you, sis."

Jane = "I love and hate you, Van."

Vanessa = "I'll take it."

Skip = "I liked Lola. Why'd you steal her from me?"

Chet = "I didn't steal her."

Skip = "You picked her up and ran away with her. That's the definition of stealing."

Chet = "I was being funny."

Skip = "You were getting back at me."

Chet = "I was not. Maybe a little."

Skip = "I said I was sorry."

Vanessa = "Kris, if you like Mark, then why don't you tell him you like him?"

Kris = "*We just met.*"

Mark = "Everyone chill. I like Kris. But she doesn't have to like me."

Kris = "I ... I ..."

Jane = "No more talk of likes or loves."

Kris = "But what about you, Collin? Aren't you gonna say you love Holly?"

Collin = "   "

Holly = "He doesn't have to. He doesn't like public displays of –"

Kris = "Collin, you snobby mother fucker, tell Holly you love her."

Collin = "   "

Kris = "Tell Holly you love her!"

Holly = "Please stop fighting. Let's change the subject."

Kris = "We're *not* changing the subject!"

Holly = "*I'M* THE ONE WHO FARTED!"

Everyone looked at Holly.

Skip raised eyebrows.

Click.

The elevator rose up again.

EVERYONE CHEERED!

Holly hid in her hands!

Vanessa = "I am so sorry, everyone. I accidentally flipped the emergency switch and made the elevator stop."

Everyone's eyes sssssssslid over and burned at Vanessa.

Kris = "That's it. I'm throwing you off the fucking roof."

Mark squeezed between Kris and Van.

Vanessa = "It was an accident."

Kris = "Bullshit."

Bren = "Yeah, right."

Vanessa = "It was."

Jane = "It wasn't funny."

Skip = "It was a little funny."

Vanessa = "I didn't flip it on purpose, I swear."

Jane = "Give it a rest, Van."

Vanessa = "I didn't flip the switch on purpose!"

Ding.

FLOOR 4.

They all ejaculated out of the elevator!!!!

Eager for fresh air!

Glad to be ALIVE!

Bren used her inhaler.

Kris no longer felt curious to experience an orgy.

Jane walked away.

Vanessa followed Jane.

Skip wiped his sweaty forehead.

Chet whistled "Love In An Elevator."

Collin walked, looking at his phone.

Bren and Kris put arms around Holly.

Roger walked beside Bren, shaking his head, and leading them all fast from the large fourth floor lobby, down the green carpeted hall, toward all the music entering the apartment's hall, turned right and squeezed down the main hall tight with party people, and zooming right, into the bright, modern kitchen, with a view of a nice large living room with lots of lights, plush couches, and fancy paintings that could hardly be seen 'cause of so many twenty-something people standing, drinking, making-out, and Roger went straight to the keg, poured, and drank. "Bren, you wanna talk about books?" he asked her.

"Oh, in a minute," Bren said. "I need to cheer up Holly."

MARK'S POINT OF VIEW

Glad to live outside the box, Mark and the other survivors hung around the crowded and loud party, smelling booze, perfume, and pot.

Some got drinks.

Within seconds Vanessa had poured orange juice into a cocktail glass and then held her signature drink in her hand, that she never drank, as she joined the party.

Mark watched all his post-elevator-stressed friends each go their own way.

"Skip," Chet said to him in the living room. "I took Lola away from you 'cause she was no good for you."

"She was great for me."

"In the bar I heard her tell you that she doesn't like space movies, and that's your whole world," Chet said. "You can do better. I was looking out for you."

Skip tilted his head. "Why were you looking out for me?"

Chet shrugged, then fist bumped Skip's shoulder. "'Cause you need a wingman."

Skip looked at Chet, then grinned.

"Hey, man. I'm sorry I called you skinny tonight. I under-estimated you."

"Thanks, man."

Vanessa filmed the party.

Jane grabbed Vanessa's camera.

"Hey."

Jane turned it off. "I need to talk to you, unrecorded. Sara hanging out with Calli is driving me crazy. I gotta text her."

"I need to talk to *you*," Vanessa said. "I didn't flip the eleva-tor switch on purpose."

"Don't worry about it."

"I *am* worried about it. I didn't flip it on purpose. No one believes me."

"Of course they don't. It's something you would do just to get it on camera."

"Do you believe me?"

"No."

Vanessa paused. "Am I really losing you?"

Jane half-shrugged. "Kinda."

Vanessa took a big breath.

With Chet on his wing, Skip approached a group of girls, as he leaned to one side. "Hey there," Skip smoothed. "I'm Skip, and this is Chet. Do any of you beautiful ladies like to travel?"

Mark smirked.

Collin looked at his phone.

Bren hugged Holly by the tall plant.

And Mark saw Kris zip away from him and disappear down the hall, replaying in his mind the shocking stuff she said in the elevator, that meeting the perfect person for her might be the end of her single days and youth and not a good thing. *Wow.* But was she talking about him or someone else? Either way, disheartening stuff to hear. She made it really clear that she was not ready for a relationship. *Dang.* So now what, he worried? Should he wait around? Should he leave and give her space? Forever?

Bee beep.

Mark heard is phone *bee beep*, and looked, and saw a text from Jill: "Nice karaoke u did tonite. Saw you there. Wanna meet up?" Super surprised, Mark stared at Jill's text, at her *bext?*

KRIS'S POINT OF VIEW

Kris stormed around to find the bathroom and found a long line. And waited. And waited. And waited. "Hey, toilet hog, pinch it off and get out, there's people in line out here!"

People stared.

"I gotta pee!" Kris said as she did Calli's Jump Up and Down dance move.

Someone offered Kris a plastic cup.

"Oh I'll do it. I really will," Kris said, feeling a hand grab her arm and yank her out of line. "What the fuck?" She saw Bren pulling her out of line and down the hall. Kris huffed, annoyed that Bren kept pulling her out of pickles and not letting her fight and not letting her pee!

Roger appeared. "Hey, Bren. You finally got time for *me?*"

"Sorry, I gotta help Kris first."

How was Bren helping her, Kris wondered?

They zoomed past Roger's frown.

Kris let Bren haul her back out to the hall, past all the other apartment doors and back to the elevator.

"I'm not getting back in *there* again."

"We're taking the stairs."

"To the street?"

"To the roof," Bren said as she grabbed the side of a large floor-to-ceiling painting and swung it open to reveal a staircase going up.

Kris's mouth popped open. "What the hell?"

"Holly and I went to a party here last year when you were camping with smells-like-salmon guy, and she showed me this. There's a secret passage."

"Holy secret passage."

They hurried through the opening and Kris watched Bren close the painting behind them then lead them up the secret stairs, out a door, and onto the roof, to the secret roof garden.

Holy scrotum bags. Kris stared in awe.

Supermoonlight illuminated a big beautiful garden of flowers spread all over the rooftop. High above the street lights. High above the green baseball fields below. Stars and thin fog above them, sprinkles of city lights everywhere around them, like standing in a garden floating through the cosmos. Splendorous. Quiet. Calming.

And a perfect place to pee!

Kris raced around beside the wooden shack housing the stairs, out of sight, quickly pulled up her leather skirt and her undies aside, crouched and, in the dark, in the dirt, among the flowers, watered them in the moonlight. *Aaaaaaaaaaaawe.*

Life kinda paused.

"Bren."

"What?"

"Come here."

"Why?"

"Come here."

"Why?"

"Come over here."

Bren clacked over the hardwood floored rooftop and around the wooden shed. "What?"

Kris looked up at the sky as she squatted. Whiffs of fog past like ... fog, below all the scattered twinkles as she tinkled under a disco ball moon. "Look at all the pretty. I told you it be magical to pee among the stars and –" Kris fell over backwards. "Oh shit!" She clenched and flailed. "Help me!" She heard Bren run through the flower bed and felt her hands grab her arms from behind and try to right her back, but laughing so hard she couldn't get a grip and slipped and slid as Kris laughed, and clenched and flailed some more, until finally Bren got her back up and unclenched, but laughing so hard she wobbled as she peed on petunias, laughing and wobbling and peeing and held up by Bren's helpful hands under the stars.

And she finished.

And she stayed crouched, in Bren's clutch as they both laughed and laughed among the flowers until they calmed, and stayed there in the quiet of the night, their last fun night together? This was the climax moment to seven years as roomies and friends? *Yeah, this seemed about right. Ridiculous, but also heartachey.* Kris savored the feel of her friends hands on her shoulders, being there for her, getting her out of another pickle. But, now, maybe those hands needed to fly away, and Kris would need to get herself back up right on her own the next time she fell over while peeing in a flower bed.

Kris inhaled a big breath of cool air, let it change her, then exhaled it out as she slowly stood up, letting Bren's wonderful hands slip away, and feeling heartache like watching Calli walk away, but ... enduring it.

She stood all the way up, all on her own, just like she'd done all those years before Bren, and would survive again, somehow, and she slowly turned around and faced her fantastic, still-chuckling friend, and even though it hurt like hell, she decided to be happy for the time they did share together in this magical town of parties and passion and pancakes, but without these now damp undies. Kris peeled them off, pulled down her skirt, then left the flowers. "Now *I'm* celebrating 'No Panty Day' too."

"Technically, that was yesterday."

"Whatever." She clacked across the wood rooftop to the building's edge, hearing Bren's clack-clacks behind her and join her, as Kris felt free: free of pee, of panties, and wanted to feel free of all stress as she *FLUNG* her undies like a green Frisbee off the roof, into the night, watching their spinning greenness sale away, like releasing everything to chance, feeling freer, stronger, more adultish, and watching them fling toward the lit up green park, but fall doooooooown and land just before the park, on the sidewalk, in front of a couple holding hands.

"Aaaah!" they screamed.

Kris ducked down. And so did Bren. And they laughed again together and wobbled against each other, like it was just another dumb Saturday night. "You might be right," Kris said. "Peeing among the stars might be a bad idea."

Bren chuckled.

Kris smiled. "Maybe I'll tape up colorful Christmas lights around the bathroom mirror instead a disco ball. That'd be safer."

"Since when do you do anything safe?"

"Well, if you're not going to be here to save me when I get into pickles, I might have to do things differently." Kris smirked, her heart feeling squeezed.

Bren looked up at the night sky.

Kris stood back up and looked out over the bright green park and all the little Marina buildings beyond it, all the places they partied, laughed, argued, then laughed again, for seven lucky years. Really lucky.

"You were right," Bren said. "If we just get a seatbelt for the toilet, I think we can get a disco ball."

"No. I'm over it. I'm going with Christmas lights."

"No," Bren said. "We gotta do the disco ball."

"What about the shower? There's no seatbelt for the shower."

"You don't need one for the shower?"

"The spinning stars might get me dizzy and I'll fall into Shelly the Shower Curtain and onto the floor."

"We'll get thicker bathroom rugs."

"Six inch thick?"

"We could always close our eyes in the shower."

"If you close your eyes there's no point in a disco ball at all."

"There could be a safety bar in front of Shelly to prevent falling. We could call it Sophie the Safety Bar."

"Sophie's the Sofa."

"Sally."

"Sally's the Salad Bowl."

"We'll figure it out."

"No. It's a silly idea and – wait, what'da you mean '*we?*'"

Bren exhaled, then grinned. "What if I don't go to LA?"

"What? Seriously?"

Bren nodded "What if I don't?"

Kris's heart pound-pound-pounded like a puppy jump-jump-jumping! "*Holy hallelujah-gasm!*"

Bren smiled.

Kris threw her arms around her bestie! And hug-hug-hugged her! Rocking her back-and-forth, elation bursting serotonin all through her, as she smiled – then oxytocin, as she calmed – then fresh bay oxygen, as she slowly sobered up, back to reality. Then she gently came out of their hug and held onto Bren's hands, looked at her sweet friend, and felt something new: grateful. "You have to go to LA," Kris found herself saying.

Bren did a double take. "What? Seriously?"

"You do," Kris said again. "You have to go to LA."

"What are you talking about? You freaked out all the bathroom girls shouting how heartbroken you were that I was going to LA. Now you *want* me to go?"

"I don't *want* you to go," Kris said. "But you *have* to go."

Bren looked stupefied, then relieved, then sad. "I don't *have* to go."

"You *do* have to go. It's what's next. You earned it. And, I should have told you when you told me, congratulations!

Fuckin'-A. You made regional manager! That's amazing. You're so damn impressive. And you inspire me. And I don't want to stand in the way of what's next for you."

"For real?" Bren asked, with raised eyebrows.

Oh, wow, this both felt right and heartbreaking. "Yeah," Kris said. "It's like what Calli said to me, I don't want to feel bad that I got in the way your fun. So, you gotta go."

"But what about *you?*" Bren asked.

Kris fought back the tears her heart was trying to squeeze out of her. "We'll figure it out," she said with a muscled up smile.

Bren smiled back, a shaking smile.

Kris stood up tall. "We'll talk through the videophone thing. I'll fly down. You'll fly up. And I've got Holly. And now I've got Calli. And I've got –" Suddenly someone tall appeared in the little shack's doorway, and stepped into the moonlight, and *Holy too-fucking-much,* it was Bigfoot.

MARK'S POINT OF VIEW

He saw Bren look at Kris, then him, then grin.

"I have a confession," Bren said. "I'm not really into Roger."

"You're not?" Kris said.

Bren shook her head. "When I met him I had fun talking to him about books, and I wanted to talk to him more, but the bar was crowded and loud," she said.

"It wasn't that crowded and loud," Kris said.

309

"Anyway," Bren said. "As we were walking here I realized that Roger's not as into books as I am."

"Yeah," Kris said. "He thought Danielle Steel invented steel."

Bren nodded. "Yes. So unfortunately he's not a perfect match for me. But the other reason I agreed to come here with all my friends is that I knew about this building and its quiet, romantic rooftop, and I thought that this would be the perfect place for the two of you to talk stuff out. While you were peeing, I texted Mark to come up here."

"Are you serious?" Kris said. "You planned this?"

"How do you think I got my promotion? I'm good at planning and managing stuff."

"You little funster."

Bren smiled proudly at each of them. "Now, I'm going to go down to the apartment party and politely let Roger realize that he and I are not a good match, while you two park up here and have some alone time together, because you *are* a good match."

Mark felt a zing of energy, now knowing that Kris and he were gonna have another chance to talk. *Yes. Awesome.* But also feeling nervous. He watched Bren hug Kris, tightly, for like seven-Mississippis, like there was more drama going on between them than he knew about. Then they de-hugged and Bren's hands turned her friend's shoulders until Kris faced him with her fantastic face. Then Bren winked at Kris, walked away, smiling at both of them, then disappeared through the doorway, and down the stairs, and suddenly he was on this quiet, romantic rooftop together, with the awesomest woman in the world.

Chapter 11

HOLY HUNK on a rooftop.

Now it was just her and him, surrounded by night and stuff, the first time they were truly alone with each other, and it was wild, wildly silent. Neither of them saying anything. Not knowing *what* the hell to say after their admission in the elevator that they like each other. Staring at Mark staring at her. Sexy Mark. Wonderful Mark. About twelve feet between them, twelve of her not as big feet. She could leap into his arms with just two big steps if she let herself.

She did *not* let herself. She stayed still, in the chilly air, bare arms hanging at her sides, heart thumping between them, thumping at the handsome man, on this romantic roof. She'd come along way from that lonely sidewalk ten years ago, all the way up here, to this night, to standing with a guy she might never want to leave.

His eyes on her were too intense! She looked up into the night, for relief, for help, for a damn UFO to fly down and get her the hell out of here! But no help, just night, but now she saw a few little stars, little specks of pretty, making all the darkness not so dark. And a big, bright supermoon. The sky

311

didn't look as dark and hopeless as it had after seeing David with Lisa. Now it looked happier, and ... romantic. *Damn, that wasn't gonna help.*

She looked back down and saw Mark, looking hot as hell, with romance in his eyes. *Damn,* he wasn't helping either. Neither was her now-flowing feelings from Bren, Holly, and Calli cracking open her emotions tonight. Neither were all these beautiful flowers around them, and the picturesque rooftop, and the glittering city, and the stunning Golden Gate Bridge out there lit up red like the color of love. What the F? Everything was getting more and more romantic, like the climax of one of Bren's books. *Whoa,* was this *her* climax? Was this her life's cheesy rom-com finale that she always scoffed at, but secretly hoped would happen one day? Was this *it?* Was it finally here and happening now? She wasn't ready for this, not yet, not now. She breathed fast. Her heart beat fast. Everything was moving too fast!

Grrrrrrrrowl.

"Not now, Stacy."

Mark broke into laughter.

Kris gently touched her stomach and found herself speaking much nicer than usual. Kris looked up at him laughing, laughing at her. She felt the funny, but also confused, and miffed. "You think I'm nutty?"

"No ... no ..." he said between chuckles, straightening up tall, and looking at her with his romantic eyes again. "You're not nutty," he said to her. "You're awesome."

Tingles. Good and bad ones. "I'm awesome 'cause I talk to my stomach?"

He nodded. "And all the other fun stuff about you. You totally brightened up this night."

She grinned back at him, then sighed. "You brightened my night too. And confused the hell out of it."

He nodded. "I heard you say that you don't want a relationship right now."

"Oh, you heard that?"

"Well, you yelled it, in an elevator, right next to me."

"Yeah, that sounds like something I'd do."

"Should I back off?" he asked.

"Hell no! I mean, um, I don't know. It's been a strange night."

"I don't mean to pressure you."

"Do you wanna back off?"

"Heck no," he said.

She smirked, then exhaled, and kept staring at him while gripping her skirt, as if it had the answer of whether she could let herself fall for this great guy or not. Kris sighed again, and walked around, then turned around and faced the roof railing and the beautiful baseball fields. "I'm so confused."

"I'm not," he said. "Before I came up here to the roof, I got a bext from my ex, and I didn't feel *anything* romantic for her anymore."

Kris raised an eyebrow. "*Why* are you tell me this?"

"'Cause I want you to know what's going on with me. I like you. You're awesome. I like to be clear about things. Though

313

I fear my being clear might make you wanna zoom away from me again."

"I might," she said humorously, then pointed to the side of the building where she stood. "This wildness between me and you is literally pushing me to the edge."

He chuckled, then stepped back to give her some space, then smirked.

"What?" she said, rolling her eyes.

He tilted his head. "I don't understand why you don't like a glass near the edge of a table, yet you like rock climbing where you're actually hanging over the edge."

She shrugged her shoulders. "I don't know. When I rock climb I'm in control. Someone else's glass could fall, and though I like the crash, it's the awfulness of not being able to prevent it."

"*Aaaawe*," he said. "You realize we just met. There's no pressure here."

"Yeah, there is," she said. "I know what this is. I can feel it. This is *it*. Me & you, this is peanut butter and jelly meeting each other. This is movies meeting popcorn, thunder meeting lightning, Christmas meeting vibrators."

"Um, what?"

"They're the perfect stocking stuffers."

Mark smirked. "All right."

"They *are*. Whoever came up with Christmas stockings hanging had to be thinking: 'I hope Santa figures out what I want for Christmas. I know, I'll leave him a hint with a perfectly-shaped container for it.'"

"I'm sure that's how it happened."

"So every year I give my friends what they *really* want from Santa."

"A *vvvvvvvery* Merry Christmas?"

She smiled. "Exactly."

"And not very silent nights."

"Good one."

"Thanks."

MARK'S POINT OF VIEW

Mark grinned. "I usually give out gift cards."

"That's not as cheery."

"They're for associates. For close friends I throw a Christmas party every year at my apartment, and I bake my grandma's big upside down cake. But it's served upside down, so technically it's a downside up cake. Grandma had a sense of humor," he said.

"You make it with cricket powder?"

He grinned. "No, some people don't like that for some reason. So I go with apples."

"Apples?"

"Yeah. They stick to the pan more than oranges or pears, but I started using this new kind of butter; it comes in a squeeze bottle and –"

"What?!" Kris exclaimed.

"I use butter."

"Butter in a squeeze bottle?"

"Yeah."

"Squeeze bottle butter?"

"Yeah."

"The squeeze bottle butter in the yellow bottle with the cone top?"

"Yeah," he said. "And it's got the confused-looking cow on the side, like: 'Why am I on the side of a bottle?'"

"Yeah," she exclaimed. "I use that butter too."

"Really?"

"Yeah."

"It's great, huh?"

"So great."

"I love the squeeze bottle butter."

"It's the best."

"Better than tub butter."

"*Soooo* much better than tub butter. I try to tell people the squeeze bottle butter's better but they don't believe me."

"So do I. I can't believe they don't believe the squeeze bottle butter's better."

"Do you really like squeeze bottle butter or are you just buttering me up?"

"Come to my apartment right now," he said. "And you'll see I've got squeeze bottle butter."

"If I go to your apartment right now I'd jump your bones and bang ya."

He smiled. "Would you use squeeze bottle butter on me?"

Kris O-faced. "I never thought of using it with sex. Have you?"

"Not until now."

"Wow, squeeze bottle butter might make sex better."

"Maybe *that's* why that cow looks confused she doesn't understand why we're not using her butter for sex."

Kris laughed. "Fucking dammit!" she shouted.

"What?"

"*This*. Talking stupid stuff with you. It's fun."

"Great."

"It's really great. That's the problem. I know what this is. This fun between us is what Bren is always blathering to me about in all the romance books she reads. This is the two starcrossed lovers of the story really hitting it off so well that it's the beginning of their glorious love relationship that lasts forever and happily ever after. I've never felt that kind of fun before, until tonight, with *you*. I'm feeling it. Are you feeling it?"

"I'm absolutely feeling it."

"Yeah. *That's* what this is."

"Excellent."

"It would be excellent if I was ready for it. I like my single, party life."

He put his hands in his jeans pockets. "What if the starcrossed or supermoon-crossed, lovers' relationship was even *funner* than the single party life?"

Kris scoffed. "Yeah right."

Mark grinned. "Baseball games together, camping together, barbecues together, reality show watching together, hanging out and talking stupid stuff together. How could you and me not be better than partying and hookups?"

She paused, staring at him, her mind whirring behind her beautiful eyes.

Mark looked at her eyes full of caring and nervousness and fell for her.

She stared at him for a silent, suspenseful ten seconds, like a million things were spinning around behind her beautiful eyes. But then, just one thing, as she straightened up tall, locked her electric stare on him and inhaled a big breath of moonlit air into herself. "We're gonna go slooooow," she said.

He felt *tingles of excitement.* Suddenly there was hope, that she and he could be on the road to romance at whatever pace she wanted venture it. "Slow?"

She gently nodded at him. "Yep. Slow. We'll go slow."

Yes, he thought, but stayed calm.

"You'll restraaaain yourself from asking me to move in and jump into a relationship with you right away, and I'll mellowly enjooooy my control of deciding to have fun now and not freak out worrying about happily ever after," she slowly explained. "We'll go sloooow."

He felt his lips curl up into a big smile. "What a wonderful negotiation."

She smiled big and beautiful back. "A wonderful compromise."

Yes it was, he thought, as a million ideas of what they could do at a steady pace spun around in his mind. And then just one thing, one wonderful thing, as he straightened up tall, gently focused on her electric stare, and inhaled a big breath of moonlit air into himself. "I know what we could do slow," he said.

KRIS'S POINT OF VIEW

His kiss-a-licious lips grinned, as his arm stretched out, and, once again, he offered her his big, beautiful hand.

Oh wow.

More than a hand, an invitation to something, maybe something as fun as their talk walking to Silver Cloud, as feely as his silly singing to her, or maybe another heartbreak. But, *damn,* she wouldn't know if she didn't find out, and she could always leave.

His hand still offered.

She ... she ... she decided to take his hand.

Wow.

She inhaled, slowly walking away from the edge towards him.

He grinned more, patient and so damn handsome.

She exhaled, slowly laying her hand on his palm.

He totally smiled, slowly lifting her hand in the air.

Tingles from the touch of his skin.

He slowly inhaled like he felt *tingles* too.

She stepped closer to his tall, reMarkableness.

He stepped closer to her thump, thump, thumping heart.

She slowly let him rest her hand on his shoulder.

He slowly let her hand go and slid his gently to her back.

She slowly felt the gloriousness of his massive shoulder muscles and the paradise of his big hand cupping her left shoulder blade, lots more *tingles* and *holy damn, holy damn, holy damn!* She breeeeeathed. She could do this. She could stay in control and not lose herself in this *wonderfulness*, not lose her singleness or endup with a heartful of hurt again. She could leave him at any time. She had control. *And wow, this was hella fun.*

He slowly offered her his other hand.

She slowly *grabbed* that big thing, even more *tingles*.

Now, somehow, they were in a couple's dance position, her left hand on his shoulder, his right hand on her shoulder blade, and their other hands melted together warmly in the cool air near their other shoulders, and their eyes looking at each other, with the Moon reflecting in them. *Oh wow.*

Saturday night sounds around them, but much softer up here, closer to the stars: distant party chatter, distant foghorns from ships doing mating calls, and wisps of their breathing so close to each other now, in this *oh-my-God-actually-touching-each-other* dance stance, where anything could happen, where her and this mountain-of-a-man might make even more magic or F everything up.

He held her confidently. "How you doing?"

She took a big breath, still feeling pretty damn in control. "I'm good."

He grinned. "Do you know how to do the Box Step?"

She smirked. "I think I'm about to."

He nodded, and kept being a solid frame for her to enjoy holding onto, and then began moving, slowly. His foot stepping forward and his body guiding hers very nicely. "We glide as you step back," he said calmly, "and then slide to your left, then glide with me forward, then slide to your right, then we glide back home." *They did it, they danced, gliding and sliding, slowly, and very enjoyably.*

She was tingling all over.

"You wanna go around with me again?"

"*Oh hell yeah,*" she heard herself blurt out. *Stay in control,* she reminded herself, as she let him lead her around again, slowly, to first base, second base, third base, and go all the way with her, back to home plate. *Ooooh wow.*

She took control and stepped back, pulling him forward, then left, then sexy stepped towards him as he stepped back, then gliding right back home again, and then again, and again, over and over, never getting redundant, their moves always growing funner, as he added a sway, a really fun sway, and she added a groove, and he grooved with it too, and they were dancing, holy heart flutters, they were *dancing.*

<hr>

MARK'S POINT OF VIEW

He got lost in her beautiful eyes and accidentally stepped on her foot. And she stomped on his foot right back. Yes, he thought, excellent.

They were dancing so great.

Moving so well together.

He liked her taking charge, then letting him show her moves too.

And he liked the funky flair she added to their revelry.

He liked the excitement in her eyes.

He liked holding her close.

She moved great.

They moved great together.

Each of them definitely different, but successfully around.

Her carefree, him more careful.

But she tried to do the steps, and he tried to feel her groove.

She loosened him up; he helped hone her zeal.

And they slowly moved around the bases again ... and again ... and again, enjoying being with her, and holding her felt awesome, and moving with her felt even more awesome, just moving in a square, but their togetherness amped up each time around, feeling closer each time, more comfortable each time, feeling awesomer each time.

Moving in the pattern, yet in their own styles within it: her hesitation, his eagerness, her energeticness, his calm, all sort of happening and happening more and less, less and more, as they each kind of adjusted a little further and further each time they stepped around, like a jagged rock being weathered over time until smooth. Each slow time around their dancing felt smoother and smoother until they slid and glided like they'd been dancing together for years, within minutes.

Amazing. Being with her felt so easy. Talking was easy. Now dancing was easy. They just naturally fell into a synergy, *their* synergy, their *rhythm. Wow.* They had a rhythm, a rhythm all their own. It was slow, yet spirited. Tender, yet intense. Steady, yet *sultry.*

Oh yeah. They could do a relationship. He could feel it. A great relationship. They could figure things out together pretty quickly, they could cooperate, coordinate, collaborate, and other kinds of ate without argument, just adjustment, until they were a really great match. *Jeeze Louise.* Their simple, synergetic Box Step was the best relationship he'd ever felt. The best negotiation ever.

And it kept getting better.

Soon they were swaying further and further beyond the borders, not thinking, just doing, just moving, just enjoying, like Zen or something, silently agreeing through moves that moved them outside the box, outside the building, around the roof, making up their own dance.

They did an arm swing thing with aerobic leg lifts.

They did a bizarre Foxtrot spin with breakdancing flails.

She spun away and twerked while he did The Robot.

Then they reunited for some Boogie Woogie feet shuffles, whirling into weird clogging, then somehow they two-stepped into a Hokey Pokey, and it felt silly and great. He'd never im-prov-danced like this before. He showed her what he knew, and his Foxy, Waltzy moves got bumped to the next level; she added wild moves he'd never thought of, like jumping up and down and disco arm thrusts to the sky, and she even cupped his junk at one point, much nicer than her crotch-smack in the bar. And this was a blast!

She laughed and tossed her head behind her as he held her hands and she arched back and aroooound through the night, trusting his grip, then flinging her body back to him, until they were face to face again, and Tango arm stretches and struts, into twirls and then into swoony dips, and she spun and fell back to him and he caught her fall and rose her back up, and they grooved right back into more dance position adventures. Heck, they even ended up in the lift-her-up-and-hold *Dirty Dancing* move, with her sprawled like a flying superhero up there and laughing out "*woooo!*"

It was *on.*

Without words, without music, without argument, without confusion, just instinct, and play, yeah, play: silly, sultry play.

Was this the kind of wild magic that his neighbors Vicki and Charles had? It sure felt as magical as that kind of magic. Would Kris and him have tumbling take-home boxes too?

And she looked as happy as he felt.

KRIS'S POINT OF VIEW

He looked as happy as she felt, and she felt amazing!

And surprisingly carefree.

Doing a different kinda "swinging" than she imagined earlier, but way funner.

She had no idea what wild would happen next, and not knowing was fun, making it up together was fun, swaying and twirling and dipping and rockin'.

Segue-ing from one wild, made-up dance move to another.

Her hand even flew up and messed up his hair.

He laughed.

She smiled, and then they were back into a moving embrace, attraction on-the-go, arms out-stretched, "Dancing Cheek-To-Cheek." *Hey, a song about cheeks, the face ones.* She loved cheek-to-cheeking with him!

Mark twirled her, dipped her, and didn't drop her. *Impressive.*

No longer cold in the crisp night air.

Steamy hot. Dripping sweat.

Loving this wild workout.

And they danced.

Taking turns leading, as they danced, together, surrendering, then controlling, surrendering, controlling, back and forth, like breathing together, as a team, a twosome, a dynamic duo, without worry of losing control forever, just sharing control, trusting, knowing, enjoying the thrilling chemistry of being a couple, a couple of *kick ass* dancers!

Finding their own rhythm, together, all over their wooden rooftop dance floor.

Fused into one, four-legged dancing party.

Definitely melting with him. But wilding *with* him felt far more funner than being alone. Funner than being single. And he was such a good one to melt with.

They definitely, definitely *clicked.*

Clicked awesome!

Clicked hot!

If this wildness was what a relationship with him would be like, she was waaaay into it!

Mark was fun! Maybe with Mark the party-life didn't have to end. Maybe it could continue, as a different party, partying together, a party as a team.

Not feeling fear anymore, just feeling fun, *their* fun, soooo much *fun!*

And their fun rhythm moved them close, then apart, then back together, and over here, and over there, rockin', and swaying, to a twirl, to a deep, delicious dip, and soooo erotically slow back up into his strong, gentle arms, for a sexy sway, with a sultry stare, then starry-eyed stare, then a sweet, simple, and super sincere stare, as they slowed, and slowed, and slowed to a sway, together, a soft, slow, *fun* sway, just the two of them, on the rooftop, above the world, up in Heaven, surrounded by city lights and flowers and stars and the Moon and a beautiful, bright green baseball field below, and everything felt wonderful, and he felt wonderful, and she felt wonderful being with him in all of this wonderful, and *woooow,* their wonderful was a wonderful more wonderful than drunk dancing with some random dude and pulling him home for a half-hour of *whoo hoo.* Slow dancing with Mark was way more *wonderful.* And their dancing could go all night, all week, all month, all year. And they kept *clicking.* And reMarkable Mark was slowly becoming another someone she didn't want to live without, a really, really wonderful someone. A boyfriend? *Ooooh holy wow.* Everything kinda changed, but a really, really *fun* change.

Knowing she could leave him, she didn't wanna leave him. And she wanted *more* of this change. She wanted to feel how much *funner* their wonderfulness could be. And he was moving way *too* slow. And she totally took control, by deciding to let loose.

Mark's point of view

He really, really didn't want an asteroid to fall right now. He wanted to spend lots and lots of time with Kris. Eyeing each other again, but in an intimate embrace, close, eye-to-eye, lips just inches apart, looking at each other, grooving together, holding hands, holding bodies, staring, suggesting, teasing, then smiling, feeling her sweet breath tickle his face, feeling her heart banging against his. He felt her relaxed in his arms, so comfortable, her breathing slowly calming, yet excitement still dancing in her eyes, and wheels turning in their too, as if she was deciding something, like deciding if she wanted to do more than dance, as she stared, and smiled, yet hesitated. His eyes asked her: "What's goin' on?"

She smiled smilier, as if saying: "You know what's goin' on."

He had a pretty good guess, as his heart now did backflips, and he watched her slowly breeeeathe in a big breath, and stare at him with deepness in her eyes, as if this amazing moment was an even bigger deal for her, and she slowly breathed out.

"10 ... 9 ... 8 ..." she exhaled, then breathed in deeply again.

He felt a zing of excitement. *She was counting down to something, something even better than butter.*

"7 ... 6 ... 5 ... 4 ..."

He watched her leaning in to his face, so slow, so close, so amazingly, as her tongue lightly licked her lips. His smile prepared for them.

"3 ... 2 ... 1 ..."

The door burst open!

They turned.

"Kris!" Holly hollered, her face filled with a smile!

They stared.

"Oh my gosh," Holly exclaimed, stopping and staring. "I'm so sorry. I didn't mean to interrupt you. I'm so, so sorry." She spun around and ran back into the shed, shutting the door behind her, and clacking down the stairs.

Kris and Mark looked at each other.

Mark grinned.

Kris smiled, and stared, as she clapped her hands playfully to his cheeks, clearly feeling the elation and frustration he felt too, and knowing they had to press pause on their better than butter. "Something's wrong," she said. "Holly's never this happy."

KRIS'S POINT OF VIEW

Kris un-embraced and grabbed his hand, taking control, and taking him off their romantic roof, through the doorway, down the stairs, out from behind the painting, and grabbing Holly's shoulder in the hall in front of the elevators!

Holly spun around.

"What's wrong?" Kris said.

"I didn't mean to interrupt you."

"Tell me what's wrong," Kris said again.

Mark swung the big painting closed behind them.

Holly held up her phone.

Kris looked at it, and scrolled through it, and smiled.

And Holly smiled.

"Look at all the positive comments," Holly exclaimed. Then Holly played the video of her singing karaoke that someone had filmed with their phone, and posted online, and people all over the world were praising her in the comments section. "So many kind compliments of my voice and performance and I'm just, just overwhelmed with happiness!" Holly burst into tears.

Kris's face scrunched like she was about to cry too, for her friend, and grabbed Holly into a tight hug. It was as if this was the first time Holly had gotten complimented for something about herself from strangers, not a party she put on, but just for her being *her*, and that she finally believed their positivity of her.

Wow, what a wild night. So much had happened. What wild thing would happen next?

Before she could even imagine, she heard shouting.

MARK'S POINT OF VIEW

Mark heard shouting, from the party in the apartment down the hall.

Kris's head shot up. "That's Bren," she said. "Who's yelling at my other friend?" Kris grabbed both Holly's hand and Mark's and hauled them down the hall with her, and through the doorway.

"*Ooof*," Mark said as he clunked the doorframe.

But she pulled them through, and down the apartment hall, and through the crowd, and past the kitchen, and into the crowded living room, and stopped, and they all saw Bren sitting on the sofa with a new guy and all the party people watching Roger drunkenly yelling at Bren.

"What the hell are you doing?" Roger slurred his words at Bren. "I invited ya here, I put up with all your friends, I've been waiting for you to give *me* your attention and now you're gettin' cozy on the couch with some *other* guy? What the hell?!"

Bren stood up and her passive palms asked him to calm down. "Peter and I are just talking."

"You're supposed to be cozy with *ME!* You've been dodging me all night. You *tease.* All the hassle of bringing you and all

330

your annoying friends here – hell, I should have never invited you. *You're a floozy!*"

Kris's face turned to rage!

She *zoomed!*

Across the room!

Over the couch!

Through the air!

Right toward Roger!

BAM!

Before her hands could grab the jerk Kris's body flew sideways and down to the floor from Bren's tackle!

Bren held Kris down!

Mark rushed around and stood protectively between the tussling besties and drunk-raging Roger.

"I'll pull his ass over his head!" Kris yelled.

Jane and Holly ran over to help Bren calm down Kris as she struggled.

Chet ran over to help Mark. But no need since Roger was clearly intimated by Mark's muscled super-size and totally thinking twice about fighting Bigfoot.

Kris slipped away from Bren and friends and was back up to wreck Roger!

But Kris saw Vanessa rushing towards Mark! She looked like she'd clobber Roger *and* Vanessa!

But Vanessa put up her palm. "Stop Kris! You can't hit Roger or you'll get a second assault charge," Vanessa said, *without* a camera. "I'll do this for you."

Kris looked stunned!

Vanessa threw her orange cocktail at Roger's face!

Kris's surprised face smiled.

Roger's wet face looked dumb-shocked!

Vanessa cheered!

Mark stood calmly in front of Roger.

But now Roger looked pissed!

Mark saw Kris clench her fists and –

"Kris!" Calli shouted.

Everyone turned!

All eyes on Calli!

"See? I *AM* an eagle!"

Her friends' jaws dropped!

Calli came back. She was up here. In spite of her fear.

Calli stood, panting and shaking after facing four frightening floors, and smiling at everyone's attention on her. Smiling and smiling.

Then Sara whispered to Calli.

"Oh yeah," Calli said. "The cops are coming up!"

EVERYONE SCATTERED!

People running, chairs tipping, drinks spilling, pot flying!

Mark didn't know where Roger went but saw Bren grab Kris's arm and pull her out of there!

Kris grabbed Calli's arm!

Calli grabbed Holly!

Holly grabbed Vanessa!

Vanessa grabbed Jane!

Jane grabbed Sara!

Sara grabbed air – as the Marina Girl Express left the station and zipped down the hall with Mark and Chet and Peter caboose-ing right behind them!

Skip stood in the doorway, looking bewildered.

Mark saw cops at the doorway behind him and saw Bren re-route their train further down the hall!

Mark saw Skip see his friends all trying to get away, and decided to help them escape, by making some personal history on the fourth floor of this vintage Marina apartment building built in 1927 as Skip stuck his fingers down his throat and vomited all over the place, blocking the doorway so the cops couldn't enter! Giving his dudes a secret thumbs-up as they waved thank you and followed their friends down the hall, out a window and down the fire escape! Into the darkness! Into a courtyard! Into a backyard! Into an alley! Into the streets! And into the night!

Chapter 12

NOW IT WAS TIME for pancakes!

Kris's way-more-than-usual *energy* and long strides rocketed her ahead of the chatty, laughing group and led them through the night, with Mark keeping up with her and holding hands awesomely tight with him, and with her arm wrapped tightly around sweet Calli, feeling like a family, and *enjoying the feeling,* as they laughed up apartment-building-packed Octavia Street, then down headlight-lit Lombard, past lots more charming four-story buildings, past Silver Cloud, passed Fillmore, toward the big red, white, and blue candy-looking neon of Kris's favorite late night diner, and into it's bright, warm prettiness, full of 1950s-style metal chairs with plush upholstery being squished by the butts of lots of other hungry late-night, laughing revelers scarfing omelets, and burgers, and big chicken pot pies.

But Kris knew exactly what she wanted off the menu as she led the group through the spacious, packed place, and she pushed two tables together as her party-of-eleven surrounded them and plopped their butts into chairs after a wild, wild Marina night.

"That was *fun*," Calli cheered.

"And other adjectives," Bren said.

"I really like San Francisco now," Jane said.

"It's getting better all the time," Sara said.

"Calli," Kris said across the table to her. "Thanks for telling us the cops were coming up."

Calli smiled. "You were so nice to help me tonight. I'm so happy I could help you back."

Kris held Calli's hand for a bit. "You're such a sweety."

"You still have a temper," Bren said to Kris. "But I see that you did make some good changes tonight." Bren pointed to Kris holding hands with Mark and smiled wide.

Kris smiled huge. "I did. "And you got this new guy ..."

"Peter," Peter said.

"Is Peter a reader?"

Bren nodded. "Peter's a reader. A real reader."

"*Finally.*"

"What a great night," Jane said.

"Not the night I expected," Mark said.

"Aren't you glad I bugged you to go out?" Chet said.

"I really am. Thanks, man." Mark smiled and rubbed Kris's back.

She giddy-smiled back at him.

"Oh wow," Calli said pointing at Kris and Mark's hand holding. "Are you two lovers now?"

"Not yet," Kris said. "But we're in serious like."

"We're *likers*," Mark said.

"I just knew you two would end up together, like destiny."

"Thanks for bringing Mark to me."

Bren smiled at her.

"I'm so sorry I interrupted you."

"It's all right, Hol," Kris said. "I was happy to hear that your singing went viral."

"And Vanessa did something without filming it," Jane said.

"She did?" Calli said.

"And she got Roger back and kept me out of jail," Kris said.

"You were in jail?" Calli said.

"I've got a record for pummeling my friends' cheating boyfriends," Kris said.

"Good to know," Chet said.

Kris turned to Mark. "I'm a lawbreaker. Is that a deal breaker?"

Mark smirked. "It's a surprising turn-on."

Kris smirked. "Mmmmm." Kris wanted to get him home and squeeze her butter aaaall over him.

"So you no longer hate me?" Vanessa asked.

Kris tilted her head. "Are you gonna stop flirting with Mark?"

Vanessa smirked, and nodded. "I've given up Mark. I met a new guy I like."

"Who?" Calli said.

BOMP-CHICKA-BAH-WAH

Mark saw Chet look at his phone. "Did you get a bext?"

"No," Chet said. "Just telling a friend where we are."

"Calli," Holly said. "What made you come back and face your fear of heights?"

"Well," Calli said. "Me and Sara went to her cute apartment with no furniture to sit on and Sara showed me her box of lint she wants to make art out of and she said she'd order us a hub of grub and then we'd play the dance game on her TV, dancing to NSYNC's "Bye Bye Bye." But I said "this doesn't feel right," that me and Sara shouldn't have said bye, bye, bye to our friends, that I should have tried to go up to the apartment 'cause Kris is so fearless and she would have gone up to the top floor even if she was afraid, and I wanted to be like Kris, and Sara said she shouldn't have let Jane upset her and should have worked stuff out, so I told Sara we both needed to go back and go up to the party. So Kris wouldn't think less of me."

"Sweetie, I didn't think less of you. But I do think more of you that you faced your fear." Kris smiled. "See, you *are* an eagle."

Calli smiled BIG!

Kris smiled at Mark. "And I'm thinking more of me for facing my fears tonight too."

Mark smiled at Kris.

"I'm sorry I hurt your heart," Jane said to Sara.

Sara squeezed Jane's arm. "We're good now." Sara smiled big then looked at everyone. "Jane's moving in with me."

Jane smiled. "I am. I'm facing my fears too."

Everyone cheered.

"So you're moving out?" Vanessa said.

"I am," Jane said. "Sorry."

"I'll miss you, but don't worry. I'm thinking that I have a new boyfriend. Maybe he'll be hanging out at my place a lot."

"Boyfriend?" Jane said.

"Wow," Calli said. "You're with Mark, Bren's with Peter, Jane's living with Sara, and Vanessa's got a boyfriend. Things happen fast in San Francisco."

Jane looked at Vanessa. "Who's your maybe-boyfriend?"

The waitress walked over. "Well, hello there."

"*Mary*," Kris, Bren, and Holly cheered.

"Pancakes?"

"Hell yeah," Kris said.

"Ah, better luck next time," Mary said.

"No no," Kris said. "These are celebration pancakes. We had a great night."

"Oh, wonderful."

Vanessa held up the menu. "Do you have egg-white omelets?"

Kris grabbed the menu. "You're eatin' pancakes."

"I guess I'm eating pancakes."

"It's tradition."

"Kris doesn't like change," Bren said.

"I'm getting better," Kris said, hugging Mark's arm, and smiling at Calli, Bren, and even Vanessa.

"So," Mary said, grinning. "Eleven plates of pancakes."

"Twelve," a voice said.

"Skip!" everyone cheered.

Skip pulled up a chair and squeezed in between Vanessa and Calli.

Mary took drink orders.

Mark smiled at Skip. "What happened?"

Skip wiped his sweaty forehead off with a napkin. "I got the heck outta there."

"How?"

"A police dude took me out to the hall. But he had to go back in to help arrest Roger, because Roger was mooning the cops."

"That copycat," Jane said.

"The police dude's radio said Roger was drunk and running around, and then he tried to hide under a lampshade."

"Boy, I sure can pick 'em," Bren said.

"I didn't know that side of him at all," Holly said. "Maybe I don't *really* know everyone."

"The cop left me alone, and I couldn't go down the stairs with the police parked out front. But I was leaning against this painting that popped open and I found a secret passage to the roof."

"Nice," Kris said.

"I jumped to the next building and went down the fire escape. Then I texted Chet and he said that you were all here."

"Did Roger mention Kris or anyone," Bren asked.

"Roger was drunk off his ass. He didn't even know his own name."

"None of you hit him," Mark counseled. "Legally you're fine."

Bren looked at Kris. "Another pickle averted."

Kris exhaled.

Mark smiled at Kris. "It was awesome to see you in action."

Kris canoodled with him. "Not too much energy for ya?"

"I love your energy."

"I love that you love my energy."

"I love that you love that I love your energy."

Bren rolled her eyes. "Oh lordy, what have I done putting you two together?"

"But," Kris said to him. "I might wanna dial down my energy a little so I'm not dating you from a jail cell."

Mark smirked.

"I could teach you to yoga," Chet said.

Bren nodded. "Please teach Kris to yoga."

"Why did the cops come?" Jane asked.

"Loud music, smell of pot," Skip said. "And I guess some lady screamed when someone threw green panties off the roof."

Bren looked at Kris.

Kris grinned. "Oh my goodness. Who could've done that?"

"It's a mystery," Bren agreed.

They smiled at each other.

"I love SF," Calli said. "New friends, mooning, panty-flinging, and everyone falling in love."

"Including me," Vanessa said.

Everyone looked at her.

"With who?" Jane asked again.

Vanessa snuggled next to Skip.

"Skip?" they all exclaimed.

Vanessa nodded.

Skip gaped. "You like *me?*"

"Yeah. You're my new boyfriend."

"I am?"

"Yep. I *loved* the way you sacrificed yourself to help us all escape out of the building. That was *hot*."

Skip smiled. "Hotter than Mark wrestling a bear?"

"Ooooooooh yeah."

Kris looked at Mark. "You wrestled a bear?"

"It was a bush. It was dark."

Skip looked at Chet.

Chet smiled, then fist bumped Skip's shoulder. "Huh. I guess a guy doesn't need to be muscled to get the hottest girl in the Marina."

Skip smiled. "You're cool with me and Vanessa, bro?"

Chet nodded. "Yeah, I'm cool. I like a new girl."

"You do?" Mark said. "Who?"

Chet grinned. "Your mom."

Mark frowned, then smirked, then smiled at Vanessa canoodling with Skip. "Things are working out. Weirdly. But they're working out."

Kris nodded.

"How come you're not filming this fantastic moment?" Jane asked.

Vanessa shrugged. "I think I've filmed enough for one night."

Jane ran over and hugged her!

Vanessa smiled.

"*Finally*," Jane exclaimed.

Mary brought drink orders.

So many friends hugging lovingly, Kris thought, except Collin and Holly. Her adrenaline still bubbling, she aimed in his direction. "*Collin*," Kris hollered at him.

MARK'S POINT OF VIEW

Collin looked up from his phone.

"Kris –" Holly said.

"Sorry Hol, I can't tolerate his disrespect to you anymore." Kris stared hard at him. "You're so damn snooty to us and unappreciative of Holly. She's so great, but while dating you she isn't the vibrant, happy person that I know she really is. And tonight you've been extra rude, looking at your phone all night instead of paying attention to Holly and how extraordinary tonight was for her and –"

"*Kris*," Holly blurted, actually raising her voice. "Collin and I broke up."

Kris paused, with her mouth open. "*What?*"

"Everything's fine," Holly said firmly. "Collin and I broke up, yesterday."

Collin went back to looking at his phone.

Kris's mouthed closed as her eyebrows flew. "What the F are you talking about? Why didn't you tell me?"

"I couldn't say."

"Screw that stupid 'can't say' stuff. *Say!*"

Holly exhaled. "I didn't want to tell anyone yet that Collin and I broke up because I didn't want to steal attention away from your and Bren's special anniversary, nor bring any sadness to tonight."

Kris sat back. "Sadness? I would have been *thrilled* you finally dumped Collin." Kris looked at Collin. "Sorry, man. I just think she'd be happier with someone else."

Collin smirked.

Holly grinned. "I didn't know you'd be thrilled. So I asked Collin to pretend that we were still together for tonight. It wasn't a stretch. His and my relationship has been one of appearances for a while, mostly for our hoity-toity parents. So one more night of show was just routine for us."

"*Holy hella yeah.*" Kris cheered. "Good for you, Hol. You finally stood up for yourself."

"Actually, your grandma broke us up."

Kris's mouth fell open again. "My grandma?"

"When your grandparents brought back my car, they hung out with Collin and I for a bit. She tooootally saw right through us, and insisted we end our 'for show' relationship. She's a pistol."

"Sweet Grammy?" Kris said.

"Wow," Bren said. "Maybe that's where you get your gumption."

Kris's world felt rocked.

Holly turned to Collin. "You can go now, babe. Thank you."

Collin showed his phone screen to Holly.

"Oh yeah, she'd be perfect for you."

Collin smiled. Then he stood up, nodded goodbye to everyone, and kissed Holly shockingly sweet on her forehead.

Holly shared a smile with him.

Then he walked across the floor and out the door.

Everyone sat, looking stunned.

"Your Gramms was right," Holly said. "I did need to stop worrying so much what other people think and do some stuff for me. Then Calli told me I should let loose, and I did, and I felt so much *fun*."

Calli smiled BIG.

"And even though it was scary," Holly continued. "It reminded me how I haven't felt *fun* in a long while, and how much I want a relationship that makes me feel as *fun* as singing on that stage tonight."

From across the table, Chet cleared his throat. "*I'm* really *fun*."

Holly turned to him, along with everyone else.

Chet seemed unusually shy. "And, uh, your heart-rockin' singing reminded *me* how I haven't felt 'I-want-her-as-my-girlfriend' feelings in a long while, and how much I might want a relationship too, with you."

Mark's mouth dropped open. "It's a miracle. A mind-blowing miracle."

"I'm not your singer ex-girlfriend," Holly reminded him.

Chet grinned. "I know. You're you. You're awesome."

Holly grinned.

Kris smiled.

"And," Chet said. "If you wanna shock your hoity-toity parents, wouldn't a not-rich person be great for that?"

Holly's lips slowly spread a wide smile. "Absolutely."

Chet smiled.

"Do you really like to travel?"

Chet chuckled. "The only place I've really traveled to is San Francisco."

Holly leaned over the table towards him. "Would you like to travel to the Bahamas with me?"

Chet leaned towards her. "*Hell yeah.*"

Holly smiled. "Why don't you travel over here first?"

Chet didn't have to be asked twice. He zipped around the table and into Collin's chair beside Holly and they made googily eyes at each other.

They smiled.

Mark smiled.

Kris smiled! "Yes!" she cheered. "Finally a decent boyfriend for Holly." Kris glared at Chet. "I'm hoping."

Chet nodded at Kris wildly.

Mark felt so happy for Chet.

"I can't believe you're not filming this important moment," Kris said.

"Do you want me to film this?" Vanessa asked.

"If Holly and Chet work out they might want video of this moment. And you've got video of the night me and Mark met. I think I want that."

"But she's also got video of everyone admitting embarrassingly personal stuff in the elevator freak out," Bren said.

"There was an elevator freak out?" Calli said

"And Mark saying he shaved his balls." Chet said

"You shaved your balls?" Calli said.

"And got an ingrown hair." Mark said

"You've got an ingrown hair down there?" Calli said.

"And video of me scared about living with Sara," Jane said.

"We don't need to see that video," Sara said.

"I should delete the elevator video," Vanessa said.

"Wait!" Kris said

"What?" Vanessa said

"But that's when Mark first said that he really liked me," Kris said.

"And that's when I realized I wanted to live with Sara," Jane said.

"But that's when Holly admitted she farted," Bren said.

"You farted?" Calli said.

"Oh my gosh. Too much video of me tonight," Holly said.

"Just think of it as your ass singing," Calli said.

"Holly," Mark said. "I found out that my ex-girlfriend is the person who posted the video online of you karaoke-ing."

"Jill posted me singing?"

"Yeah."

"There's a video of you singing?" Calli said.

"Of all of us singing," Kris said.

"Should I delete the videos or not?" Vanessa said.

"No," Kris said.

"Yes," Bren said.

"Some," Jane said.

"Why don't you give some videos to some people and you all promise not to post them online," Kris said.

"Nice compromise," Mark said.

"Thanks," Kris said.

"But what if someone *does* post the videos?" Bren said.

"Then I'll kick their ass, within the legal limits of the law," Kris said.

Mary brought more juices and sodas and coffees.

"Calli," Kris said. "I'm sorry we couldn't find someone for you tonight."

"Oh I don't know," Bren said, as she pulled a stack of business cards out of her purse. "There were a lot of bar peeps interested in Calli. She's got a few to choose from."

"Wow," Calli exclaimed. "Look at all my new boyfriends."

"Look at all of the screening and chaperoning we're gonna do," Kris said.

KRIS'S POINT OF VIEW

DINGY-DINGY

Kris saw Holly look at her phone, raise her eyebrows, then hand her phone to Bren.

Bren's eyebrows flew up. Then she spun to Peter. "*You have a girlfriend??*"

347

Peter paused, then swallowed his cola. "Uuuum. Yeah."

Kris clenched her fists, ready to kick this douche bags ass for fooling Bren. Kris gripped Mark's thighs, tight. "10 ... 9 ... 8 ... 7 ..."

Then Kris saw a heart-bursting miracle as Bren slowly stood up, stared Peter down, and pointed her unshaking finger toward the door. *Holy-butt-smacks! Bren literally stood up for herself. Finally!*

Peter skeedaddled across the floor and out the door.

And Bren looked ten-feet tall!

Kris jumped up and hugged her. "I'm soooo damn proud of you!"

Bren patted Kris's back. "Well, you don't put up with any crap and you got a good one, so I've decided that I'm gonna not put up with any crap if I'm gonna stay here in SF."

Kris flew out of their hug. "*What??*"

Bren smiled at her. "I'm *not* leaving. I'm not leaving you, or any of my amazing friends. I'm waaaay too happy here to leave."

Kris's eyes started to water. "Really?"

Bren nodded. "I've lived with you for seven freaking years because I absolutely love you to pieces, and I know that when I think back on this rare, special time in my life it's not my job I'm going to miss, it's *you*. I realized that this wild night. You've changed everything."

Kris's heart zoomed around the galaxy and back! "But –"

"You're not holding me back," Bren said to her. "*I'm* holding me back."

Kris smiled, then hugged her again, soooo damn tight!!

They sat back down, still hugging.

Everyone applauded.

Kris didn't feel the need to name things anymore like she did when she was alone in SF ten years ago, to feel like she was surrounded by friends. Now she really was surrounded by real friends.

"Are me and Bren gonna share her bedroom?" Calli said smiling.

Bren came out of their hug and looked at Kris.

"Sure," Kris said smiling.

Bren tilted her head. "But if Calli stays in *your* bedroom then maybe you'll keep it clean."

"Or," Kris said. "Calli could stay in *your* bedroom and clean my bedroom."

"Or," Bren said. "Calli could stay in *your* bedroom and clean your bedroom."

"Or," Holly spoke up. "Calli could stay in my spare bedroom since I don't have a roommate."

"Wow," Calli said. "People fighting over me instead of ignoring me. This is cool."

Kris felt heart-squeezey about giving up Calli, but having her live with Holly did make the most sense.

"Calli," Holly said. "Would you like to share my apartment with me."

"The apartment with all the parties?

Holly grinned. "Yes."

"And me and you will hang out all the time letting loose, and have fun talks?"

Holly smiled. "Yes."

"I'd *love* that!"

"But it's on the third floor of the building," Holly explained. "Are you all right with that?"

Calli nodded wildly. "I feel like I can do *anything* now."

Kris's heart *really* squeezed.

Then Calli looked at Kris and Bren. "Is me living with Holly cool? Then you guys won't get mad at each other fighting over me."

Kris and Bren grinned.

"Yeah, Calli, that'll be fine," Kris said, even though her heart ached to be apart from Calli now. Holly looked so excited to live with Calli, and it would be great to see Holly a lot less lonely. Wow, Kris thought, her emotions had fling-flanged so much she felt like she'd grown a whole year in one night.

"Yay!" Calli shouted. "I went from the hard sidewalk to the top of the Marina."

Kris smiled. "The eagle has landed."

Calli smiled BIG again!

"But Holly," Kris said. "Don't spoil her. She's gotta still earn her being here, and now I can't live without seeing Calli all the time too. So send her over to me and Bren's place to clean my room once a week."

Calli raised her eyebrows.

Kris smiled. "Yeah, this is going to work out great."

"I wonder if Barry is closing up the bar right about now," Bren said.

MARK'S POINT OF VIEW

Mark smiled at Chet and Holly canoodling. No more Bonnie-banging or bexts from other women. Chet was now a relationship guy. He hoped Chet and Holly had stuff in common. He hoped Holly was in a spanking. He wondered what interesting stuff Kris was into. "So," Mark said. "Tomorrow night is the premier of a new reality show called *Naked and Afraid*. I could cook us a barbecue dinner and we could watch it together. What do you think?"

Kris grinned. "Are you asking me out on a date?"

"I'm asking you *in* on a date."

"Would *we* be naked?"

"Maybe," he said, grinning. "But not afraid."

"Not at all," she agreed.

He smiled.

"And I'm so unafraid that I would even risk also going to the game with you tomorrow to see the Giants beat the Dodgers," she said. "I could eat my drippy falafel and you could eat your eggplant."

Mark smiled again. "I am so unafraid that I might even eat a drippy falafel too."

Kris smiled.

"Oh," Holly said to Kris. "Your Gramms wanted to surprise you, but I think I should say that she was gonna demand that your parents and brother fly out here and visit you, to see what a wonderful job you've done with your life."

Kris's mouth dropped open *again*.

Mark felt how important this news was for her as she *gripped* his hand tight.

Holly pulled out her camera and took a selfie with everyone all together. "I'll make prints of this for you all to put on your refrigerators."

"Or hanging mobiles," Kris said.

"Next Saturday you're all invited to a party on my rooftop," Holly said.

"Yay," everyone cheered.

"And Vanessa, you are definitely invited."

Vanessa smiled. "Thank you. I will definitely be there, with a little less filming." Vanessa pulled the memory card out of her camera. "Here," Vanessa said to Kris. "You take the memory card first and download the videos you wanna keep."

SUDDENLY, SHAKING!

DRINKS SHAKING!

TABLES SHAKING!

LIGHTS SWINGING!

FACES FEARING!

THEN ... no shaking.

"*Holy rock and roll!*" Kris exclaimed.

"Did I just loose my earthquake virginity?" Calli asked.

Kris smirked. "You did. How was it?"

Calli smiled. "*Fuuuun!*"

"Bummer," Vanessa said with a sigh. "The one time I don't film something fantastic happens. I should have filmed the quake."

Jane nodded. "Yeah, *that* would have been fantastic."

Kris held Mark's hand.

Mark held her close.

"An earthquake," Kris said. "How appropriate. Everything in my life got shaken up tonight, why not an earthquake to top it all off."

"Did it get shaken up in a really good way? Mark asked her.

She looked around at all their friends, and smiled. "It did."

Mark smiled too, agreeing.

"Oh no!" Vanessa exclaimed. "My memory card fell in my hot coffee!"

"Holy tickle-tackle," Kris said.

Vanessa quickly tried spooning her memory card out of her hot coffee, with several attempts, and finally success, then loaded the steaming, wet card into her camera. "Oh no," she said. "It totally doesn't work anymore. All of tonight's videos are lost, *forever!*" Vanessa's mouth hung wide open.

Some people sighed. Some smiled.

"Well," Sara said. "At least we all have our memories of a great night."

"And a reminder that things can change really fast," Kris said, looking around at all her new and improved friendships, and at her new boyfriend.

Mary brought everyone pancakes!

Grrrrrrrowl.

Kris gently patted her stomach.

Mark grinned.

Kris held up her fork full of pancakes. "Earthquakes and asteroids can happen anytime," she said. "Here's to living it up while we can."

They all held up their forks full of pancakes and toasted to each other, then ate.

He noticed that Kris did not clink her fork on her teeth, and smiled. He noticed that he had gained lots of friends tonight and that he'd never see this fun restaurant the same again; now this rectangular building had important personal history.

"I can't wait to get you home tonight and really be energetic," Kris said to him. "I've decided that we're not using handcuffs. I want your hands free to roam."

Mark's eyebrows raised. The night was definitely not over yet.

"You do know that you're coming home with me tonight, right?" Kris said, eating with one hand and rubbing his back with her other.

He grinned, eager to smell her green apple hair all night and make her cricket pancakes in the morning. "I should let you know," Mark said to her. "I've never gone home with a woman the same night that I met her."

"Really?"

"Yeah."

She grinned. "I'll show you how it's done."

He smiled. "What about my in-grown hair?"

She winked at him. "We'll figure it out."

Mark's heart did even more cartwheels, as he moved Chet's glass away from the edge of the table for Kris.

She smiled and squeezed his thigh.

And life felt like a homerun as they leaned their syrupy smiles towards each other, and finally, without interruption, kissed their first kiss, the sweetest, most delicious kiss ever.

Everyone cheered.

Kris and Mark smiled stupid, making googly eyes at each other.

"And I thought it was just gonna be another fun Saturday night," Kris said, throwing her arms tightly around him, and smiling big at his big smile. Then leaning her face beside his, cheek-to-cheek, she whispered into his ear. "But tonight I got passion *AND* pancakes."

Bren's rom-com coming soon!

Check for updates on my social media stuff:

www.nathanbaylet.com

Twitter: twitter.com/NathanBaylet

Instagram: instagram.com/nathanbaylet

Pinterest: pinterest.com/paperbeach22

my YouTube vlogs coming soon!

audiobook available at Audible.com

Thanks for reading!

Made in the USA
Las Vegas, NV
18 December 2023